ALSO BY YAN GE

Strange Beasts of China

ELSEWHERE

Stories

YAN GE

SCRIBNER

New York London Toronto Sydney New Delhi

Scribner
An Imprint of Simon & Schuster, Inc.
1230 Avenue of the Americas
New York, NY 10020

First Scribner hardcover edition July 2023

SCRIBNER and design are registered trademarks of The Gale Group, Inc., used under license by Simon & Schuster, Inc., the publisher of this work.

For information about special discounts for bulk purchases, please contact Simon & Schuster Special Sales at 1-866-506-1949 or business@simonandschuster.com.

The Simon & Schuster Speakers Bureau can bring authors to your live event. For more information or to book an event, contact the Simon & Schuster Speakers Bureau at 1-866-248-3049 or visit our website at www.simonspeakers.com.

Interior design by Davina Mock-Maniscalco

Manufactured in the United States of America

10 9 8 7 6 5 4 3 2 1

Library of Congress Cataloging-in-Publication Data has been applied for.

ISBN 978-1-9821-9848-0
ISBN 978-1-9821-9850-3 (ebook)

To my mother, 楊世蓉.

流水今日，明月前身。

——司空圖《二十四詩品 洗練》

And flowing water is right now, the bright moon, its former self.

—Ssu-K'ung T'u,
Washed and Refined,
The Twenty Four Categories of Poetry

CONTENTS

THE LITTLE HOUSE

Outside the Little House, Old Stone was talking about geese.

"Their intestines. That's the best part," he said. "The best goose intestines come from White Family Town; do you know why?"

"No idea," I said.

"The women there have strong and slender fingers. The perfect kind of fingers for plunging into the goose's asshole and yanking out the entrails while it's still alive. They do it with precision and determination. They do this in a flash to preserve its tenderness."

"I'm a vegetarian."

He shook his head. "Why?"

I thought about how to reply.

"That's no good," he said. "Plus, I don't think I've seen you eating since you came here."

"I don't feel hungry," I said.

He turned around to the table next to us and shouted, "Small Bamboo! Can you talk some sense into this girl?"

Small Bamboo had fallen asleep in his chair. It was almost 3 a.m.

"Anyway," he said, turning back to me, "guess which part of the cow the yellow throat comes from?"

"Its throat?"

"Ha!" He reached for his beer and took a long pull. "I've asked more than a hundred people this question. Nobody's got it right. It comes from the cow's coronary artery. And it has to be the right one. Because the right one's thinner than the left one, so it gets cooked very quickly in the hot pot. Do you know how many seconds it takes to cook the yellow throat?"

"Uh-uh."

"Eight seconds. Lots of people overcook it. That's why you should never throw a piece of yellow throat into the pot. Hold it with chopsticks and dip it into the soup. Count to eight and take it out. Only this way will it be crispy and chewy."

"I need to go to bed now," I said.

"Sure. You go." He took another mouthful from his beer bottle.

"Aren't you going to sleep?"

"Ah no, no, I'm fine. When you are old you don't need to sleep. I'll just get another beer."

He stood up and walked into the Little House. The light was still on. Sister Du was curled up on a booth seat, snoring. I watched through the window as Old Stone went behind the bar, grabbed a Tsingtao, and returned.

"I'll ask her to put it on my tab in the morning." He slumped back into his chair.

"I'm going now. Good night." I stood up and walked back into the tent I shared with Vertical.

———

Small Bamboo had brought me to the Little House three days earlier. When he bumped into me, I was sitting on a bench outside my apartment compound, reading a book.

"Hey, Pigeon," he said, coming swiftly across the street towards me. "What are you doing here?"

"Just reading," I said, waving my book at him. "To kill some time."

He tilted his head and read: "*The Plague*. I didn't know you kids still read Camus."

"Some of us do."

"Where are you staying these days?" he asked.

"I'm camping in the courtyard, with my neighbors." I pointed back over my head.

"That's no fun," Small Bamboo said. "Why don't you come with me to the Little House? We're all staying there in the square: Old Stone, Young Li, Six Times, Vertical, Chilly, and lots of other poets."

"But I don't write poems," I said.

He grinned. "It doesn't matter. Just come with me."

We walked to the Little House. The buses hadn't been running since the twelfth and there were no taxis. Small Bamboo had smoked three cigarettes by the time he finally remembered to offer me one. I told him I didn't smoke.

"You're sensible. Cigarettes kill you." He nodded, taking out another one and lighting it up.

We went across the Second Ring Road and turned into Ping'an Square.

"Wow," I said.

The sunken square was brimming with tents, of various sizes and spectacular styles, their colors spanning the full visible spectrum. Small Bamboo pointed at the building at the far end of the square and told me the Little House was on that corner. We descended into the square and wove our way through it. The tents were clustered closely together and cast shadows over one another. People sat outside, eating, chatting, bartering. Vendors elbowed past with their baskets, selling food, magazines, T-shirts, and cosmetics. Kids chased one another, laughing. We steered through, Small Bamboo nodding at acquaintances and friends. Ahead of us, I saw a gigantic scarlet tent. It looked like a castle.

"That's Young Li's," Small Bamboo said. "One big living room and three bedrooms for him, his wife, and two kids. There's even a kitchen inside. God knows where that prawn got it from!"

It was a warm late May afternoon. The air was stale and humid. We walked from the sunken square up the steps and arrived at a run-down pub. Above, three big white characters hung, which read: *The Little House*. A dot in the first character was missing. A large group of men and women—the poets—sat outside, drinking beer. Small Bamboo introduced me: "This is Pigeon."

"Pigeon!" they called out together, like a choir singing.

"I've heard about you," one of them, a man in his forties, said. "You're the kid who writes fiction."

A middle-aged woman in a red floral dress looked me up and down. "You seem like a smart kid," she said. "You should write poems."

"Ignore these old drunks," Small Bamboo said apologetically. "You go sit with Vertical." He pointed me to a table on the side, at which a young woman and two men in their twenties sat. They waved at me gleefully.

Later I realized they were all in varying degrees of drunkenness. Some had been drinking since Monday; some had started on the evening of the twelfth. Sister Du, the owner of the Little House and Small Bamboo's cousin, had driven her mini-truck to the wholesale market outside the city three times to restock beer. The supermarkets nearby had nothing left.

"And all of these rats here, they don't even bother to pay," Sister Du said. "'Put it on the tab' they say—but nobody ever opened a tab!"

"I'll have tea, please," I said, taking out my wallet.

"Ah, come'n take a beer," she said, and opened a Tsingtao for me. "I'll put it on the tab."

I took the bottle, walked outside, and sat down at the table with Vertical, her boyfriend Chilly, and Six Times. A woman with a basket approached, wondering if any of us would be interested in purchasing her goods. She lifted up the lid, revealing the little turtles inside. They were luminous, as white as pearls.

We were admiring the turtles when the alarm rang out in the sky.

"Always this time of day," the woman said. She covered her basket and trotted away.

That night I washed my face for the first time since the twelfth and slept in Vertical's tent. There was moaning coming, off and on, from different directions. Someone sang until the small hours. Eventually, I slept like a dead person and did not dream of anything.

———

It was 2008. My father had been dead for six years. My grand-father had died in 2000 after having a stroke outside a convenience store. My first aunt, she'd lost her life in 1998 due to a hemorrhoid removal operation. My uncle had broken his neck in the summer of 1990, when going for a dive in the river with his friends.

"Both of my parents died in 1989," Small Bamboo said, "my mother at the beginning of the year because of diabetes; my father at the end of year, in prison."

"My girlfriend has been dead for ten years now," Old Stone said. "She struggled with anorexia for years and killed herself in the winter of 1998."

"You prawns!" Young Li puffed out a mouthful of smoke. "Can we talk about something else? Haven't we had enough of dead people?"

"Shall we have a game of mahjong?" Old Stone suggested.

After they left the table, I took out my book and began to read. The TV was on in the next room, and Sister Du and the waitresses were watching the news, weeping.

Six Times wandered over and sat down beside me. "What are you reading?"

I showed him the cover.

"Camus," he said. "Interesting. Do you like him?"

"He's all right," I said.

"You should read Márquez," he said. "*Love in the Time of Cholera* is a better choice."

I put down the book and looked at him. "What are you getting at?"

He smiled shyly. "Vertical and Chilly are having sex in my tent. Shall we go to Vertical's tent and have sex as well?"

I thought about his proposal for a while. "Okay," I said.

We walked into Vertical's tent and removed our clothes. He touched me for a short while before entering. We hugged and moved towards and away from each other repeatedly. I felt cold the whole time because I was lying on the ground. He cried when he came.

Afterwards, we sat outside the tent, sharing a cigarette.

"Four days ago I was a nonsmoker," I said.

"Five days ago I had no idea there'd be an earthquake," he said. "What were you doing?"

"I was giving my cat a bath," I said. "And you?"

"I was trying to fix my laptop," he said. "How's your cat?"

"She ran away wet. Hope she's dry now. How's your laptop?"

"Dead," he said.

"I heard earlier on TV," I said, "that the number of casualties is now sixty-two thousand, three hundred and fifty-seven."

He took the cigarette and smoked. "You have a good memory."

The alarm rang sharply across the city again.

Sister Du rushed out of the Little House and shouted: "Another one is coming! The news just said there's a big aftershock tonight! Magnitude seven point eight to eight. The government is telling us to seek shelter."

"Relax, cousin," Small Bamboo said, half-turning from the mahjong table. "We are already in a shelter."

That night, nobody could sleep. We went into Young Li's tent and sat down in the living room. It was surreally spacious, furnished with a pair of ivory four-seater leather sofas, one white armchair, and a cream chaise longue. There was even a bookshelf.

Small Bamboo sat down in the armchair. "Bloody hell," he said, slapping his thigh. "This is a palace." Young Li and Six Times walked in, carrying a square table. They put it down and flipped up four curved extensions. An enormous round table emerged.

We all stared at it. "Bloody hell," Small Bamboo said.

"Old Stone asked me to get a big table for dinner," Young Li said.

"If this is the table we're sitting at, I'll need a telescope to see the dishes," said Chilly.

"When the aftershock comes, we can hide underneath it," Six Times said, knocking the tabletop.

While Old Stone was busy cooking in the kitchen with Calm—Young Li's wife—and Sister Du helping out, we talked about him. Apparently, after his girlfriend died, Old Stone immersed himself in the study of how to make the perfect twice-cooked pork. From there, taking it dish by dish, he had become a chef and a reputable food critic. He'd published three books: *Love and Lust in Sichuan Cuisine*, *The Pepper Corn Empire*, and *The Night We Ate Armadillos*. The last one was a collection of poems.

"I actually have the books here." Young Li stood up and searched on the bookshelf. "Here." He took a book out, leaned on the bookshelf, and started to read: "'When language becomes corrupt, we need to talk about fish. Are fish happy? someone asked, a long time ago. You have no idea because you're not a fish. If a tomato knows a fish well . . .'"

"Is this the poetry book?" I asked.

"No, it's his cookbook," Young Li said, and pushed it back.

Everybody laughed. I laughed with them. We drank beer.

Calm came out from the kitchen, wearing a purple apron on top of the red floral dress. She dropped a stack of bowls and chopsticks on the table and said: "The food is coming."

We pushed over the sofas and each grabbed a bowl and chopsticks. As we took our seats, Sister Du carried out the starters on a tray and put them down one by one: chicken feet with pickled chilies, fried fish skin with coriander, marinated pig's tails and thousand-year eggs with green pepper.

The poets cheered and dived in.

"What can Pigeon have? She's vegetarian," Vertical said.

Young Li examined the dishes. "Fish skin? There's no meat in it."

"It's fine. I'm not really hungry," I said, and drank my beer.

The starters were gone within minutes and Sister Du delivered more dishes: hot, steaming, and aromatic. Old Stone's signature twice-cooked pork was served, followed by braised pork belly, stewed pig feet with fermented black bean, sautéed pig kidney and liver, and braised pig knuckles with bamboo shoots.

"Where does he get all this stuff?" Chilly marveled, jabbing a knuckle with his chopsticks.

"Old Stone has connections," Young Li mumbled between chewing. "Do you know who his father is?"

Chilly shook his head. "No, should I?"

Young Li spat out a bone and disclosed a name that I had learned in my Local History class at elementary school.

"Seriously?" Chilly said.

"Yep." Small Bamboo nodded. "This prawn could have been sitting in an office in the central government now if he hadn't got the wrong girlfriend and joined the protest with her at the wrong time."

"Our generation is just fucked," Young Li said.

"We're fucked too," Chilly said competitively.

They continued arguing while the second round of food was brought out. This time: sliced beef in chili oil, stewed beef brisket in casserole, spiced calf ribs with Sichuan peppercorn, and beef offal soup.

The room was filled with hot steam. I sneezed.

"Can I get you anything?" Vertical said. "Poor Pigeon, you must be starving."

"I'm fine," I insisted.

She looked around the table. "How about the soup? I can get you some soup without offal," she said.

"Uh, okay," I said.

She ladled me a bowl of offal-free soup. I stared at it and drank. The soup flew into my mouth and diffused into my guts, like a long, soft exhalation. It made me think of when my grandfather carried me on his back to the cattle market to see the cows. They smelled like manure and peat. Their eyes were the eyes of Buddha. They looked at me.

"Can I have another one?" I said. "With offal, please."

We were all devouring like wretched beasts. It began to rain outside. The rain fell, drumming the roof with an urgent rhythm while more food was served. We had a round of poultry: chicken, duck, goose, quail, and ostrich; and then six types of fish: rudd, sea bass, mandarin, silver jin, golden chang, and fugu; afterwards some rare delicacies whose names I learned from the others: boar, abalone, soft-shelled turtle, muntjac, and armadillo.

"Bloody hell," Small Bamboo said, his chopsticks gnashing. The rain fell in torrents.

A group of beautiful women walked out from the kitchen, wearing shiny silk dresses embroidered with pearls. Their hair was embellished with small crowns and colorful feathers, their lips glossily red. Together, they held a huge brass pot, in which a dense and hearty chili stew bubbled, exuding a brawny fragrance of meat, chili pepper, and Chinese five-spice mixture. It was head stew, and had been extremely well cooked so the heads cracked, mushed and melted together—some eyes were missing, some noses crooked, lots of tongues stuck out. They were the heads of men and women.

My stomach turned sharply. I bent and threw up under the table.

The Night We Ate Armadillos
By: Old Stone

About five in the afternoon Small Bamboo asked me
to have dinner with him and his friend Boss Huang.
Huang has got some rare delicacies, he told me.
In a private dining room Huang locked
the door and served us a huge pot of braised
armadillos.
Dig in, said Huang, it's a first-class national protected animal
so we are all committing crimes together.
Speaking of criminals, said Small Bamboo,
the armadillos were Chairman Mao's favorite
when he was a guerrilla

in the Jinggang Mountains
back in the old days

The day after the dinner party, a real crisis set in. It had rained so much the previous night that the water had swept through the wreckage, where hundreds of thousands of bodies were still buried, and into the reservoir.

"Now we'll have to drink skin-flavored water," Chilly said.

"Ew," Vertical said.

We were sitting outside the Little House. Old Stone had advised us earlier to relax and not to worry about the water. There were at least eight or nine cartons of beer stocked in the Little House, so we should be well hydrated for another couple of days. "Trust me, before we finish the beer somebody will sort the water out," he concluded, and went to join Small Bamboo, Young Li, and Calm for a game of mahjong.

The rest of us sat, drinking beer and smoking cigarettes. In the center of the square, a man stood on a table, looking down at the crowd while shouting: "One last ticket to Beijing! The train leaves at ten tonight! Any higher offers?" In the opposite direction, a young nurse held a megaphone, calling: "Volunteers needed! Volunteers needed! The bus leaves at eight a.m. tomorrow at the community medical center!" A group of teenagers chased a boy out of a convenience shop a few doors down. "Give us the milk, you cocksucker!" A woman walked by in front of us, weeping, holding a small child in her arms.

"It's like watching a movie," Six Times said.

"I feel troubled that I'm not really sad," said Chilly.

"I'm not very sad either," Vertical said. "And you? Pigeon."

"I've been thinking," I said slowly. "All of this is great material. But I don't think I'll ever write about the earthquake."

"I'll never write about it either," Six Times said.

"And what do we say when many years later people ask us about the big earthquake in 2008?" Vertical said.

"We can talk about the aggressive beer drinking," Chilly suggested.

"And the sounds of intercourse at night," Six Times said.

"And the banquet Old Stone cooked for us," I added.

Vertical turned to me and smiled. "Is everything all right, Pigeon?"

A woman screamed in the square. A tent fell. Some young men shouted loudly.

"What do you mean?" I said.

"You've mentioned that dinner a number of times already," Vertical said. "And you're reading Old Stone's poetry book."

"Young Li lent me the book," I said. "But I find it difficult to understand."

"Poetry is not for understanding," Chilly said.

Six Times downed his beer. "Think about it this way," he said, "when you write a story, you're essentially creating a dish. You want people to see the meat and the veg and even to smell the fragrances. But they can't actually eat it. They can only imagine the taste of the food by interpreting the image of it."

I thought of yesterday's dinner again. They all seemed to have forgotten what happened.

"But none of these matter to us," Six Times continued. "When poets come into the room we simply chomp on the fictional dish you've created. We eat up the food and shit it out later. And the shit is poetry."

Chilly laughed and clapped. Vertical and I laughed as well.

That night, I stayed in Six Times's tent and we made love like primitives. There were no condoms, so he came on my belly. Later, to help me clean up, he poured some beer on my belly and wiped it off with his socks. I told him I would prefer to have dried sperm on my belly than cold beer and the filth from his socks. He said he was sorry.

Afterwards we slept. A series of magnitude 4 to 5 aftershocks struck, rocking us into deeper sleep. In my dreams I had a conversation about the earthquake. I remembered it clearly even after waking up. My deceased father sat in front of me, his face stained by a thick tawny paste, his nose crooked. And he asked me: "How do you know this is all real and happening? How can you be sure you haven't already died in the earthquake and are just living in the afterlife?"

I told Old Stone about my dream and he laughed for quite a while. "That is a very Zhuangzian dream," he said.

"You could say that about every dream," I said.

"Have you ever eaten butterflies?" he said. "I haven't had butterflies per se but once in Kunming I had caterpillars. They were nicely deep-fried, lightly seasoned with chili powder and cumin, and tasted like crispy air."

We sat outside the Little House, facing the square. Nearly one third of the tents had disappeared, leaving discolored spots on the ground, like the surface of the moon. Young Li's red tent remained standing.

"How much longer do you think we can last without water?" I asked.

"Not long," Old Stone said. "But we might surprise ourselves— this morning, a search team dug out a man who'd been buried for more than seventy-two hours, still alive."

"That's something," I said.

"So I suppose the real question is—another Zhuangzian one— do you actually want to live or not?" He continued: "With my girl- friend, I realized she had given up when she lost her appetite. First she said she wasn't hungry and then she just hated food, couldn't stand looking at it, smelling it, or even hearing about it. One day we got up, I said, 'What do you want to have for breakfast?' and she screamed as if someone had stabbed her with a knife. That was when I knew she'd made up her mind."

I was about to say something when the others came back in Sister Du's mini-truck, carrying cardboard boxes and bags of bot- tled water, instant noodles, and other stuff. Small Bamboo sat down by us, unscrewed the lid from a bottle of water, and gulped down half of it. "Motherfucker!" he said. "I'll never drink beer again."

"Where did you get these?" Old Stone asked.

"The community medical center," Small Bamboo said. "Sis- ter Du heard a new batch of volunteers arrived from Xi'an, so we called over."

"You prawns," Old Stone said. "These are for the victims of the earthquake."

Young Li sat down and started taking cartons of cigarettes out of his box. "We are the victims," he said. "We're all enduring."

A man walked by. Young Li whistled and threw him a bottle of water and a carton of cigarettes. The man caught them swiftly and went away.

Later, Chilly, Vertical, Six Times, and I sat by the flower bed, eating tins of braised pork and sweet chili fish.

"These are not very good," Chilly said, exerting himself to swallow.

"Xi'an people don't know how to cook. They live only on noodles," Six Times said.

"Taste fine to me," I said.

Six Times turned around. "Since when are you eating meat?"

"I think Pigeon has a crush on Old Stone," Vertical said.

They all looked at me and I said: "What?"

"You're reading his book all the time. You put it right beside our pillow," Six Times said.

"Because I'm trying to understand poetry," I said. "Plus, I finished Camus."

"Can I have Camus? I've always wanted to read *The Plague*," Chilly said.

We then talked about *The Plague* and *The Myth of Sisyphus*, drinking beer and smoking cigarettes. Not far from us, Old Stone, Small Bamboo, Young Li, and Calm were playing mahjong on a square table. Calm wore a green cardigan on top of the red floral dress. She hurrahed, pushed down her tiles, and clapped. The three men handed over their money. The others were watching TV inside the Little House. The volume was loud, announcing that the government was installing a new water filtration system in the reservoir. ". . . We are fighting minutes and snatching seconds," it said.

For the first time in many years, I felt a tingling of content-ment. I ate meat and drank water. I had a bed to sleep in. Before long, I would go to my bed and have a dream about butterflies, and, just like Zhuangzi, I would not be able to tell if it was me who dreamed about the butterflies or a butterfly who dreamed about me.

SHOOTING AN ELEPHANT

When Shanshan woke up, Declan had already left the house. It took her a while to remember where she was. Ireland. Quietly she pronounced the word, her tongue curling back, brushing across her upper palate with a soft tingling. "Ireland."

The country was still new to her and the horse chestnut trees in Phoenix Park were rustling freshly as Shanshan walked beneath. Around her, the wild fields extended, the wind combing through the tall and lush grass. Shanshan had never seen a place so green and immense. It made her breathe deeply.

Shanshan had been coming to the park regularly since moving with Declan into a terraced cottage off North Circular Road. At the viewing, she hadn't particularly liked the cottage because it smelled of mold, but Declan had told the agent right away they'd take it. "It couldn't be more convenient," both he and the agent had agreed. The house was five minutes' walk to the Special Criminal Court, where Declan had started his new job as a court reporter.

Declan had promised her that this job would allow him plenty of holiday and spare time, so he could repaint the house, show her around the city, and even, when the weather permitted, drive her to the sea. However, a big case had come in as soon as Declan had started, and he had been stationed at the court ever since.

The case involved someone called "Slab" Murphy. The name sounded odd to Shanshan, so she asked why the man was named Slab. "I have no idea," Declan said, typing on his laptop. "Maybe he has a flat forehead?"

A couple of days after this conversation, when Shanshan was getting milk from Londis by the quay, she glimpsed a headline on the newsstand: "Tight Security Outside Court as Case Against Ex-IRA Commander 'Slab' Murphy Gets Under Way." Then she saw underneath the headline a picture of an old Irishman with a weathered face and red cheeks. The man wore a khaki-colored flat cap, so there was no way for Shanshan to know the shape of his forehead.

Shanshan brought the milk to the cashier before remembering the thing Declan had asked her to get. She took out her phone and opened Notes.

"Can I also get this, please?" She raised her phone to the cashier so he could see the words on the screen.

"Blu Tack," the cashier read out. "Sure." He walked away and soon returned with a slim, square packet.

"What do you need this for?" he asked, scanning the packet.

"I don't know," Shanshan said. "My husband asked me to get it."

The cashier smiled. "My little brother used to love Blu Tack," he said. "It was his favorite thing and he played with it all the time."

He popped the packet beside the milk. "Four sixty-five, please."

While Shanshan searched for the change in her wallet, the

cashier said: "It's been five years since he died. My little brother. He had autism."

Shanshan looked up at the cashier. He was a tall man with a full, dark beard, his hair a neat crew cut. "I'm sorry to hear that," she said, giving him the money.

"Thanks." He punched open the cash machine and handed her the receipt. His forearm was covered in tattoos. "Have a good day."

Shanshan had been learning to enjoy her days since moving to Dublin. In this foreign city, her anonymity soothed her, although she was struck that, here, anyone could turn to her at any moment and start a conversation about practically anything.

One day, in Phoenix Park, she complimented an old couple on their adorable beagle, and they told her in turn about their son who had lived in Shanghai for seven years and had just proposed to his Chinese girlfriend.

Another rainy day at IMMA, when she and a young man happened to stop, at the same time, in front of a painting of the Ox Mountains, she learned about the time he got totally pissed in Sligo and fell into the river.

In the cafeteria of the Chester Beatty, as she was queuing beside the salad bar, a woman behind her asked where would be a good place to get authentic tofu. The woman was pleased that, since she had begun a vegetarian diet, her eczema had cleared up like a miracle.

At dinner, Declan said: "Did you enjoy the Chester Beatty? Did you see their ukiyo-e collection?"

The radio hummed in the background. Some country music was playing.

Shanshan nodded, chewing the chicken. "There were also Ming dynasty snuff bottles."

"An oriental paradise." Declan reached out for the butter. "Back in college, it was one of my favorite places to go."

"I took their brochure for the winter exhibitions and talks," Shanshan said. "I'll definitely visit again."

The music stopped. A soft-spoken man began to speak. A man of constant sorrow, Shanshan heard the voice saying.

"Sorry you're doing everything by yourself," Declan said, mashing a potato with his fork. "I wish I could go with you, but this case is just crazy. They are going through the ledgers and checkbooks the guards found at Slab Murphy's farm, and it's taking forever."

"I didn't know he had a farm." Shanshan cut the broccoli.

"Sure he does. It's what all this fuss is about. Some tax he didn't pay for extra herds of cattle." Declan poured some gravy on the potatoes. "Mam wants to know if we're going back for the October bank holiday."

"I thought we are painting the house that weekend, to get rid of the mold," Shanshan said, glancing across the table at her husband.

"That's right," Declan said. "Then I'll tell her we'll be back for Christmas."

"I can't believe we're already talking about Christmas," Shanshan said, letting out a big yawn. The radio host's voice was hypnotizing.

Declan reached over and squeezed her hand. "Go lie down," he said. "I'll sort out the dishes. Remember you still need plenty of rest."

Shanshan did not tell Declan that, in fact, she had not thought of the mold for a while. The odor had either disappeared or had subsided into the ordinary along with the other mundane aspects of her life. She kept it hidden from her husband that the real reason she didn't want to go back to Longford was that she could not bear the attentive and measured inquiries from Declan's parents, their incessant wondering whether she had got better.

Shanshan thought she was doing well, as much as circumstances allowed. She had been dutifully taking iron supplements every day, plus three red dates. She had told the translation agencies that she would not take on any new jobs until perhaps next year. She had moved to a new country where the sky was azure and the air revitalizing and clear. She had been coaching herself not to look back.

At Londis, after she paid for an Innocent smoothie, the cashier said: "Can I ask you something if you don't mind?"

"Sure." Shanshan screwed open the bottle and took a sip. The icy drink ran down her throat.

"Do you speak Chinese?" he said.

Shanshan told herself not to frown. She thought of the homeless guy on Seán Heuston Bridge who'd always shout "Ni hao" to her whenever she passed by. "Let's say I do."

The cashier grinned and rolled up his short sleeve to show her a fist-sized tattoo stretching on his upper left arm. "Can you check this for me? I told the artist I wanted the word for 'home,' does it look right to you?"

Shanshan then recognized the black curlicues, 冢.

"Oh no." She gasped slightly.

Behind her, a man queued with a full basket. "Just one second," the cashier said to the man before asking Shanshan: "Is it not right?" He checked his biceps.

"Uh," Shanshan said. "This is not the character for 'home.' It means 'grave.'"

"You're kidding me."

Shanshan glanced at the uncomplaining customer. "It should be easy to get it fixed," she said to the cashier quickly. "You just need to move the dot in the middle to the top of the character and then it's 'home.' Do you want me to write it down for you?"

The cashier thought about it for a few seconds. "Ah, never mind," he said, "I'll keep it as it is. 'Grave' is grand." He rolled down his sleeve and waved to the man to come over.

Later that day, Shanshan returned home after a long walk in town and slumped on the sofa in exhaustion. She stared at the slanted white ceiling and the apex farthest away from her and fell asleep.

Then she had a dream, in which she was still a girl, about nine or ten. She was in a residential area with nobody around. The sun beamed above the potholed asphalt road. As she walked on the road, she felt the sharp heat grilling her soles. All the houses seemed abandoned, the roofs covered by moss and the paint on the walls peeling off. She noticed this smell coming from somewhere. The stink of moldy food and dead animals. She walked for a long time and thought she was lost. The street signs were in a language she couldn't understand. Eventually she saw someone approaching in the distance. She ran towards them and recognized it as a thin Burmese woman, carrying a basket on top of her head. The woman looked at her, and in English she asked: "Are you okay, little girl? Do you need help?"

The girl in her dream looked up, her face covered in tears. She cried to the Burmese woman in Chinese: "Wo zhao bu dao wo mama le."

Shanshan woke up with a shiver, her mouth dry and bitter and her feet cold as ice. Mawlamyine, she thought. Outside the window, it had gone completely dark. The clock on the wall said five past six. There would be another hour or two before Declan finished work and came home. She walked to the kitchen to prepare dinner and turned on the radio.

The days were getting shorter and much wetter. The rain had been lashing down for days and, even when the bank holiday weekend began, showed no sign of stopping.

"I don't think we can paint the house," Declan said, sipping his coffee. "In this weather, the paint would never dry."

Shanshan looked out the kitchen window. The geranium drooped, drowning in its flowerpot on the windowsill. "I don't understand," she said. "A week ago, it was so glorious and sunny."

"Welcome to the Irish winter," Declan said. "Be prepared. I heard this one is going to be stormy."

The radio was tuned to RTÉ News. A woman spoke in a shrill voice. Let's talk about now. The latest numbers show we have an unprecedented 4,080 homeless people in Dublin.

"What are we going to do, then?" Shanshan sliced her egg. The yolk seeped out like pus from an old boil.

"Rich people go to Spain to their holiday homes. The rest of us start heavy drinking."

"I mean for this weekend."

"I have some work I need to get on with," Declan said, spreading a good layer of jam on his toast. "An editor in London approached me, asking if I would write a full-page feature on 'Slab' Murphy."

"Will your boss be okay with it?" Shanshan asked. Declan worked for a news agency that sold court reports to different news channels.

"He won't be back from Valencia until February," Declan said. "Plus, it might not happen. The editor is only running the story if Slab is convicted, which will not be clear until maybe mid-November at the earliest."

It was a man speaking on the radio now. Enough of this, Mary, he said.

"So you don't need to start working on it right away, no?" Shanshan said. "Maybe we could go to IKEA instead."

"Why? Haven't you been there like, seven, eight times already?"

"Because there is stuff we need to get that can only be brought back by car." Shanshan downed her coffee. It had turned lukewarm, which had brought out a staleness.

"Like what?" Declan looked around.

"Like a new mattress. This one from the landlord is too old. I can't sleep, having all the springs prodding my back. And a bookshelf for the five boxes of books collecting dust in the study. A rug for the sitting room, so I could cover that stupid stain which is proving to be impossible to remove . . ." Shanshan stood up and stuck her coffee in the microwave. "I'm really trying, Declan, to make this place home. So can you please work with me?"

"All right, all right," Declan said, throwing his hands up in the air. "I'll work with you, lady."

Shanshan didn't reveal to Declan that the reason she loved going to IKEA was because it reminded her of China. Every time she walked into the bulky structure, beneath the thick yellow letters against their blue background, got on one of the identical escalators, and entered the display area with its familiar decorations and furniture, Shanshan would be convinced, unfailingly, that just outside this place was not Dublin but her hometown, the highway to the airport cutting through the rapeseed flower field and the tall and dense eucalyptus trees murmuring on the horizon.

In IKEA, kids flooded the floor, running, hopping, and sometimes crying. Shanshan found Irish children unbearably adorable, their crystal-like eyes large and colorful, their hair curly and fluffy, making her think of unicorns. She watched three kids looking around a showroom, giggling with excitement. *A smart studio apartment on Bachelor's Walk*, the display board read. Two older girls and a younger boy, probably siblings. The sisters went to the kitchen, turning on the unplugged oven while the brother relaxed on the sofa, watching a pretend program on the cupboard TV.

Shanshan felt a hotness surge to her eyes. She walked away in a hurry and found Declan standing beside a pile of cushions, chatting with two young women. One of them was blond, the other a brunette with a ponytail.

Declan saw Shanshan walking towards them and waved at her. "Here you are! This is my colleague Maeve"—he pointed at the blonde—"and her housemate Laura."

"Hello." Shanshan smiled at them, looking up. They were both taller than her.

"You must be Shanshan," Maeve said. "I've heard so much about you."

"Really?" Shanshan continued to smile.

"And your name is beautiful," Maeve said. She wore a marshmallow-blue jumper, which matched the color of her eyes, and a thin golden necklace.

"What does it mean?" Laura asked.

"It means the color coral, or moving very slowly."

The two women laughed. "Isn't Chinese a great language?" Maeve said.

After they said goodbye and carried on shopping, Declan gently held Shanshan's shoulder. "I never knew your name also means 'moving slowly.'"

Shanshan turned away from him to fetch an attractive woven basket from the display shelf. She was disappointed when she saw that inside was a smaller one with ugly patterns and the two baskets were stapled together by a plastic ring. "I've never heard about your co-workers," she said, returning the set to its display.

As Shanshan had wished, the couple bought a mattress, a bookshelf, a rug, a coffee table, a bathroom shelf, and many small items that neither of them had planned to possess. However, after a rainy yet productive bank holiday weekend, when the furniture was put together, the boxes emptied, the shelves filled, and a cotton-rich sheet tightly secured on their new mattress, Shanshan once again woke up in the middle of the night, eyes wide open, staring into the dark where green and purple dots flickered.

She pushed herself up. Declan's low, deep snoring continued. She went to the sitting room and turned on the floor lamp. Beside the fireplace, the bookshelf had been assembled and screwed to the wall. All five boxes of books had been put away, neatly fitting next to one another like rows of soldiers.

Shanshan slid her finger along the spines and read the titles one by one. She stopped at *Burmese Days*. Declan owned a full collection of George Orwell and had always, no matter where he had gone, moved around with them. Without thinking, she drew out the book.

It was pitch-dark outside. Even the streetlights were off. Through the bedroom door came the sound of Declan's breath, like the slow waves of the sea. Shanshan held the book in her hand. On the cover was a sepia photograph of a well-dressed Burmese woman sitting in an ornate wooden chair, leaning forward. Her eyes were slender and dark, staring back at Shanshan.

As if captivated, Shanshan walked to the sofa, curled up on it, and opened the book.

She was woken by Declan in the early morning. "Why were you sleeping on the sofa?" he said.

Shanshan moaned and shifted to her side. Before she could think of a good answer, Declan frowned violently.

He hauled the book out from underneath her arm. "Why are you reading *this*?"

She knew what he meant but she had no answer. Instead she said: "I thought he was your favorite writer." The Burmese woman looked down at Shanshan from the cover, a sarcastic expression on her face.

"It doesn't matter." Declan shoved the book back on the top shelf of the bookcase. "You should focus on getting better."

"I am getting better." Shanshan sat up.

Declan shook his head. "Stop kidding yourself." He went into the kitchen and put on the kettle.

Shanshan tried to stand up but Declan's assertion had pinned her to the seat.

"Would you just go to the bed and lie down?" he shouted from the kitchen. The kettle was boiling with an earth-splitting noise.

Shanshan stayed in the bedroom until Declan had left the house. In the afternoon, having finished a deep clean of the kitchen, she decided to go out for a stroll. She put on her winter coat, wrapped her scarf around her neck, and walked down Infirmary Road. All the London plane trees had lost their leaves, their branches bare in the air.

The Special Criminal Court was at the bottom of the road. Shanshan stopped opposite a bunch of schoolboys standing in two lines, waiting at the traffic light. One of the boys glanced at her. She smiled involuntarily. He turned around, said something to his friends. They all laughed.

When, after the traffic light changed, they passed her in the middle of road, Shanshan heard them murmuring. "Is she Chinese, or Japanese?" "I think she's Chinese." "I'd say Japanese."

She walked quickly along the quay, and, before she knew it, drifted into Londis. The cashier was loading sandwiches by the fridge. He smiled at her. "It's freezing now, isn't it?"

"Yes, very windy," Shanshan said.

He lined up the sandwiches and adjusted the price tag. "You should wear a hat."

"Excuse me?"

"Believe me. Hats are important for weather like this. Or you'll get a migraine."

"I might not be here for too long," she said, fetching an Innocent smoothie.

"Well, nobody knows the future." He picked up the empty basket.

"That's right."

"Wear a hat. Keep yourself warm." He tapped her shoulder before walking away.

When Declan got home, the house was suffused with the scent of roasted chicken. He walked into the kitchen and saw Shanshan was chopping a Chinese cabbage.

"Just one more stir-fry, and then the dinner is ready," she said, her cheeks gleaming red.

Declan's throat tightened. He poured himself a glass of water and settled beside the dining table. "They found some good evidence from the ledgers today."

"What?" Shanshan half-turned from the chopping broad.

"The 'Slab' Murphy case," Declan said, gulping down half of the water.

"Great. Does it mean he'll be convicted now?"

"It'll probably take some time. But I've told the *Guardian* editor I'll start writing the piece now."

The timer in the kitchen rang. Shanshan put down the knife and turned to pull open the oven. The hot air rose and engulfed her face. She stepped back. "Would you check if the chicken and spuds are done?"

"Sure." Declan stoop up, put on the glove, and carefully took out the roasting tray. The chicken was coated in a golden sheen, and so were the potatoes. "They're perfect," he said.

When they sat down to eat, Declan finally told his wife what he'd been struggling to say. "I'm sorry."

"Why are you apologizing?" Shanshan looked up from her plate.

Declan swallowed. "For this morning," he said. "I was being harsh. But I really don't think you should read George Orwell. You need to move on from Mawlamyine, for your own good."

"Funny you mentioned it, I was just thinking about Mawlamyine today," Shanshan said. She looked at him with a deadly serenity on her face, which unsettled Declan.

"Maybe we should go away for a while," he blurted out. "You know the *Guardian* piece. They're paying me a thousand pounds once the article is out. So, perhaps, after I get the fee, we can go somewhere nice for Christmas. To take a break from the horrendous winter and everything going on. We can go to Spain, Portugal, or even Greece. Is there anywhere you'd prefer?"

She took in what he said. "This is mad, Declan." She smiled dreamily. "I've been literally thinking all day about this."

"This?"

"Exactly." Shanshan nodded, putting down the cutlery. "It has been on my mind for a long while now, Mawlamyine. I was trying to figure out what has gone wrong between us and I thought of Mawlamyine. You see, I have tried to move on, to get better. But I can't. And I realized the reason I cannot move on is because I don't have closure. We're not finished with Burma. We ran away, we just"—she shook her head, took a deep breath, and continued—"we just fled. And I've been trying to work it out today, so I walked and walked along the quay until I got to Capel Street. Then I thought the only way to resolve this is for us to go back."

"Back?" Declan said, his face turning sullen.

"I'm saying, the place I want to go for Christmas is Burma. I want to return to Mawlamyine, and then to Mandalay and Bagan as we had originally planned. We need to finish our honeymoon."

Looking back, it had been Declan's parents who had first advised them not to go to Burma. March 10, the pair had registered at the Provincial Marriage Registration Office. Later that day, Paul and Rita called them on Skype.

"Big congratulations from the whole family!" Rita waved her hand. "Us and Aoife and Cormac and Róisín and Sean. We're all delighted for you."

"Thanks, Mam and Dad, and everybody," Declan said.

"How are you going to celebrate?" Rita asked.

"We'll go out later, to meet a few friends at a restaurant," Declan said.

"That's lovely," Rita said. "A restaurant!"

The newlyweds held up their marriage certificates to the camera. Paul and Rita marveled at the striking red color of the covers. They asked Shanshan to explain the Chinese characters and praised how incredible the language was.

Paul asked: "Remind me, when are you going to Burma?"

"Saturday week," Declan replied. "We're flying to Yangon and then go from there to Mawlamyine. I'm so excited."

Paul paused for one good second and said: "Your mother and I were checking about Burma the other day. Do you know there is a war going on there? And we're wondering if it is the safest place to go at the moment."

"It's hardly a war," Declan said, glancing at Shanshan. "There has been some dispute in the north . . ."

Rita cut him off. "The group of rebels are armed, am I right? And what are they called?" She turned to her husband.

"Myanmar National Democratic Alliance Army," Paul said gravely.

"Anyway," Rita carried on. "These terrorists are fighting the government's army and bombing civilians. Only this year, more than one hundred people have been killed."

Shanshan's eyes widened. Before Declan had proposed the trip, she had only heard the name of the country in her secondary school geography class.

"The Chinese-Burmese border has always been a troubled area. But it's hundreds of miles away from where we are going. We'll be fine," Declan explained to his parents.

"Shanshan," Rita called, leaning forward. "Are you happy with this? Are you sure you want to spend your honeymoon this way?"

Shanshan was caught off guard. She searched for a plausible response. "I don't know."

Rita shook her head. "You don't want this. No girl wants to have her honeymoon in such a place. You should cancel the trip and book somewhere nice."

Shanshan wanted to look at Declan. Isn't it ironic, she thought, I never considered that Declan's mother could be so much like mine.

After the Skype call, Shanshan couldn't help worrying about their trip. To assure her, Declan took out the Lonely Planet *Myanmar*, circled the Kokang area on the map, and then their destinations: Yangon, Mawlamyine, Mandalay, and Bagan—all in the south. He even emailed the Chinese embassy in Mandalay and got a prompt reply that said: *We do not encourage citizens to travel to the northern region.*

"They're pretty much saying it's fine in the south," he said.

Shanshan felt they should cancel the trip, but Declan refused to give in. To make this point, he retold, fervently, the dream he had had since his sophomore year in Trinity, of visiting Burma, the country that had once nurtured the likes of Maurice Collins, H. E. Bates, Kipling, and the great George Orwell. He told Shanshan he'd be insane to give up the chance of this literary pilgrimage for some minor disruption far away. But Shanshan insisted, saying this was not how she'd like to spend her honeymoon. In turn he accused her of having an impressionable nature, which his manipulative mother used to take advantage of her. She became very agitated because he was right. After the fight, she left to stay with a girlfriend and turned off her phone.

Two days later Declan showed up at the door, with plums under his eyes and stubble covering half of his face. He said he was sorry, and he needed her to come back more than anything else. He surrendered and said they could go wherever she wanted. She looked at him, his long, melancholic, and sleep-deprived face, and said: "Fine, let's go to Burma."

———

Reinvigorated, the couple flew to Yangon and started their honeymoon. They visited pagodas and markets, sampled mango pickles, and tasted French-Burmese fusion cuisine. The city was blazingly hot and buzzing with motorcycles. The streets were dusty, covered by rubbish, banyan sap, and crow shit. "Why are there so many crows?" Shanshan frowned.

"They're just birds." Declan squeezed her shoulder.

"Crows are vicious birds, and ominous."

Declan chuckled. "Well, no need to dwell on the stereotype. Ted Hughes would have disagreed with you." He then held up three fingers and declared: "I promise you, my wife, our trip is going to be pleasant and blessed by good fortune."

"Good to know, husband." Shanshan laughed, dizzy in the heat.

Four days later, they took the train to Mawlamyine. The moment they entered the rusty, oil-green carriage, Declan scampered up and down the aisle like a child, nearly bumping his head on the ragged ceiling. "Look! This is exactly like a hundred years ago, when it was built by the British."

"Maybe that's the problem," Shanshan said as she stared at a rip in her seat, the tatty filling black as an infected eye. She got up and switched to a different seat.

There were only five people in the carriage, all foreigners. The train was ancient and poorly maintained, rattling slowly along the tracks. It would take sixteen hours for them to arrive at Mawlamyine. Outside, on the yellow fields, stood houses built from bare planks of wood.

There was no food service. Small mice ran up and down the aisle and jumped on passengers' seats looking for biscuit crumbs. Four or five hours after all the biscuits were finished, when Shanshan was getting light-headed and hungry, a Burmese woman emerged through the swinging door, carrying a basket on her head. Shanshan smelled food. She asked the woman what she had. "Chicken curry," she answered in English. They ordered two, and the vendor produced two leaf-wrapped heaps. "Can I have a fork, or chopsticks?" Shanshan asked.

"Eat with your hands." The woman gestured.

In the end, Declan finished two portions of chicken curry with his hands while Shanshan, along with two Swedish women across the aisle, watched him in awe. She didn't feel hungry anymore, a blunt pain sinking in her stomach.

They arrived in Mawlamyine near midnight and checked in at the hotel at 2 a.m. The next morning, Declan woke her at 8, asking her to join him for breakfast.

"I don't feel well." She turned towards the wall.

He touched her forehead. "You don't have a temperature. Some food would help you. You haven't had anything since yesterday morning."

"I don't feel like eating. Just thinking about the hotel breakfast makes me sick. I want to sleep." Shanshan closed her eyes. The pain in her stomach had cramped her whole lower abdomen.

"Okay," Declan said and left.

He returned with a bowl of rice porridge and chicken wanton soup sprinkled with scallions.

"Where did you get these?" She sat up, couldn't believe her eyes.

"I found a Chinese restaurant up an alley and I begged the cook to make some comfort food for my wife," he told her.

After she finished eating, they left the hotel and wandered along the strand into town. The dust rose as skinny Burmese people passed them on motorcycles. The sun was already up, bright and dull, high above the gray waters of the sea. Eventually shops appeared. Seafood wholesalers, ship repair and maintenance depots, ice cream and beer outlets. Vendors stood by the road in their shorts and sandals, crying their wares. Shanshan looked around. Contrary to the vibrant inhabitants, all the buildings were deteriorating, walls mottled and windows missing. A stench lingered. She held on to Declan's hand, which was warm and moist.

"There's a lassi shop," he said, fine sweat beads dripping along his face. "You want to try some?"

They had one glass each, with ice. Later, in a different shop, they drank chilled Myanmar beer. Another stop for pancakes with small fried fish in them. Then they sat down in an air-conditioned restaurant in the town center, and ordered octopus curry and iced coffee.

"After this we can walk down the road. Take a look at this old temple here. Then we'll get a taxi to go to the mountain where the Kyaikthanlan Pagoda is," Declan said, tracing the route on the map with his finger. "Afterwards we can just sit there and relax, waiting for the sunset."

"Sounds good to me," Shanshan said, checking herself in a small cosmetic mirror, dapping her sweaty forehead with a tissue.

"Do you feel all right? Still a bit sick?" he asked.

"No, I'm fine now." She put down her mirror and swigged the iced coffee. "It's just, I don't think I like Mawlamyine."

"No?"

"It looks so run-down. It's messy, garbage everywhere. The food is salty and the weather is too hot."

"Well, this is why we travel," Declan said with a slight laugh. "We seek discomfort, as if it is only through misery that our experiences can be etched in our memories."

She drank more iced coffee, feeling a sharp cooling sensation ripping through her abdomen.

Later, when they sat in a taxi, passing the slums, Shanshan was thrown back again to her childhood: the dilapidated houses, the garbage-heaped streets, the flies, mice, and stray dogs, the smell of sweat and excrement. She thought of her mother, of the years when the two of them lived in the compound before her mother remarried for the first time. When the taxi stopped at the traffic lights, a small gray house by the road caught her eye. Through the front window, she saw a tattered doll sitting on the windowsill. It looked just like the one her mother had given her on her tenth birthday. Her doll had had two glassy blue eyes that were supposed to shut when it was put to bed, lying horizontal. However, hers was a secondhand doll, and one of its eyes would always remain open, no matter how hard she had thumped its head.

She felt lighter when they finally arrived at the foot of the mountain and started to ascend. The thick foliage of ancient trees cast shadows on the stone steps. She heard the birds.

"The Kyaikthanlan is the highest pagoda in Mawlamyine. It was also visited by Kipling. Allegedly, his famous poem 'Mandalay' was written here," Declan announced from a few steps ahead of her.

Shanshan smiled. "Then we must see it."

It was just another golden pagoda, surrounded by walls painted with murals of Buddhist stories. They sat down beneath a wall, waiting for the sun to sink.

Declan unzipped his backpack and took out a book. It was old, and its jade-green cover read: *A Collection of Essays.* "This is something I've been rehearsing in my head since college," Declan said. "Now bear with me."

He opened the book at the dog-eared page, gave a weak cough, and began to read "Shooting an Elephant" by George Orwell. It was written nearly a hundred years ago, when Orwell had lived in Mawlamyine as a police officer.

When Declan finished, the sun had almost disappeared. The last thread of light traveled through the dusk, the trees, and the declining city underneath the hill, and finally perched on the golden railing in front of them.

"This is too beautiful," Shanshan said softly.

"It is." Declan sighed.

She stared at the darkening sky. There were still lots of things she could see.

In the taxi back to the hotel, they sat in silence. Shanshan found herself in a weird state of lucidity. She could hear her blood rushing through her vessels and her heart expanding, shrinking.

Long after Declan had fallen asleep, she was still awake. Her heart palpitated with a strange and itching anticipation. She got up, put on her robe, and went to the bathroom. Just as she sat on the toilet, an acute pain slit her lower abdomen. She nearly let out a scream.

Clutching the edge of the basin, Shanshan waited for it to pass. Had too many cold drinks today, she thought.

But the pain came again, sharper and deeper, gnawing her pelvis like a snake. She cried out. "Declan! Declan!"

Declan rushed in and found Shanshan collapsed on the bathroom floor, unconscious. He called the front desk. An ambulance came after twenty minutes.

They spent a long night at Mawlamyine General Hospital. When the light came into Shanshan's eyes, a middle-aged Burmese doctor was standing before her and he told her two pieces of news:

That she had been pregnant but was not anymore.

Shanshan woke up and realized that Declan was gone. Light peeked in through the blind of the bedroom window. It had been four months since they moved in, but still the house felt like a borrowed place. She heard a rubbish truck humming along the street, the bin being lifted by its mechanical arms and the waste thumped down, the thought of its smell stirring her stomach.

She pushed herself up from the bed and rushed into the shower. Meticulously, she applied shampoo, rubbing every inch of her scalp. Afterwards, with her sanitized self wrapped in a towel and a robe, she fished out a small disk from her toilet bag, shook a pill into her palm, and swallowed it with tap water.

She had kept it secret that she had been taking birth-control pills since her period returned. She could not explain this to Declan, or anyone at all, including herself. As the medicine was being absorbed by her body, the heaviness in her stomach dissipated. Shanshan walked into the kitchen and turned on the radio. After fetching an egg from the fridge, she cracked it in the bowl and, with a pair of chopsticks, blended the yolk and the white.

On the radio, a young man was speaking enthusiastically. As Christmas shoppers flooded the Jervis Centre and Grafton Street, Thomas Burke, the director of Retail Ireland, predicted a staggering increase in total sales of more than one million euros by end of December.

Shanshan poured the egg into the sizzling pan and stirred the golden liquid with the spatula. Do we need to buy presents for everybody? she thought. Even if we might not be in the country?

She didn't like the uncertainty of their travel plan, but Declan had insisted that they should not book any tickets until "Slab" Murphy was convicted and he was guaranteed to get the *Guardian* money.

"But shall we look into the tickets now?" Shanshan had said. "They might get expensive soon. We can use my credit card."

"Relax. It'll be my treat," Declan had told her.

Shanshan ate her breakfast. The man on the radio was now talking about the case. After last week's twist and turns, during which "Slab" Murphy's lawyer applied to dismiss the case and the judges had rejected the motion on Friday, it is expected that, in the next couple of days, the judges will deliver a verdict, before the court closes on the twentieth for the Christmas holidays. The gardaí had . . .

She turned it off. Chased by an inexplicable agitation, she pressed her palms together in front of her. "Please," she said quietly. "Please help us. Please help me."

After cleaning the bathroom and the kitchen, Shanshan went for a walk. A large gathering of people stood outside the Special Criminal Court at the bottom of Infirmary Road. Men and women in gray or black coats. Blocks of cameras. Big microphones with signs for RTÉ and the BBC. In the ferocious wind, they looked undisturbed and solemn, as if they were waiting outside a church.

Shanshan made a fast turn to the quay, where, above the gray water of the Liffey, seagulls were flapping in the wind like torn plastic bags. Then she heard: "Hey!"

It was the cashier, standing at the entrance of a passageway beside Londis, smoking. He wore a T-shirt.

"How about keeping yourself warm?" Shanshan walked towards him, smiling.

"Trust me, I'm sweating all the time," he said. "Where're you heading?"

"Nowhere," she said. "Can I have a cigarette, please?"

He raised his eyebrows slightly. "Sure."

He handed her a cigarette. She perched it between her lips. He leaned over and lit it. She inhaled.

"I've been thinking about your brother from time to time," she said.

"My brother?"

She puffed out a mouthful of smoke. "The one who had autism. You said he died five years ago."

"Ah, Oisin," he said. "Yes, it'll be six years next year."

"It'll be six years next year as well, since my mum died."

"I'm sorry to hear that."

Shanshan felt the smoke tingling the back of her nose. "It's funny, because from time to time I'd forget that she's gone, and then I remember again."

"I know that feeling," the cashier said.

———

Shanshan returned home around midday and was startled to hear a man talking in the study.

"Hello?" she called, gripping her keys.

"It's me," Declan said. "I'm on the phone." The study door was shut.

Realizing the unexpected man was her husband didn't ease Shanshan's nerves. She could hear her heart beating in her chest, so strongly that her rib cage ached. She sat on the sofa. Through the hollow door of the rented house, her husband's voice sounded, with an unfamiliar concentration and cordiality.

"Yes, it's Declan McVey, Paul McVey's son . . . Yes, right!" He laughed. "Grand, I'm grand. I'm back to Dublin now, since September. Yeah, still a journalist . . . My dad's very well, enjoying his retirement . . . I'm writing an article on the 'Slab' Murphy case for *The Guardian* and need to get a comment from northern Sinn Féin, so I thought maybe you'd give me something? . . . Of course, I understand, sure . . . Yup. No problem. Just one second, let me grab a pen . . . Now, zero two eight, nine seven, six six six three four one. Okay, thanks a million . . . Yeah. Take care yourself, Brendan. Bye."

There was a loud sigh and the study door opened. Declan popped out his head. "The press room in the court has gone mad. Can you get me a coffee and a sandwich? I haven't had lunch."

"Is everything okay?"

Declan grinned. "Did you not hear the news? 'Slab' has been convicted."

"Oh," Shanshan said. "That's great."

"I need to finish up the *Guardian* piece now, they want it by the end of the day," he said, and disappeared again behind the door.

She stared at the door for a while before remembering the task she'd been given. She hurried to the kitchen, put on the kettle, and searched the fridge for tomato, bacon, cheese, and lettuce. Declan had shown her, back when they lived in China, how to make a good sandwich. Rinse and dry the lettuce. Slice the tomato. Spread mayonnaise bountifully on both pieces of bread—"Always a bit more than you initially thought." Stack the ingredients in mirrored layers, with protein on both sides and veggies in the middle. "Think of thick skin and frail heart," Declan had said.

Shanshan pressed the sandwich, crushing the tomato slices in the middle. Some light red liquid seeped out and colored her fingers. She wiped it off quickly before placing the sandwich on a white plate.

The next day, Declan didn't get up until after nine. He had stayed up the night before to finish the story and had told his colleagues he'd come in late.

The couple ate breakfast together, during which Shanshan brought up the question that had been simmering in her guts since yesterday. "Shall we book the tickets today?"

"Yeah," Declan said. "We can do it tonight. After the party."

"What party?"

Declan glanced at her. "I thought I told you. All the reporters in the court are going out to have a drink this evening. You know, it is the last day of work."

"You never told me this."

"You're invited too."

"I don't want to go," Shanshan said, pushing the scrambled egg around her plate.

"Come on!" Declan said. "Don't you want to go out a bit? Put on a nice dress and makeup—it would be fun."

Shanshan couldn't remember the last time she'd worn makeup. Perhaps it had been the first day they arrived in Burma. In the extreme heat and humidity, she had been suffocated by her foundation mixed with sweat and dirt and had packed away her makeup the day after.

After Declan had gone to work, she found her cosmetic bag in the chest of drawers and saw the blusher was crumbled and the mascara completely dry. She took the Luas to Jervis and, under rows after rows of glistening lights, walked into Arnotts to the tune of "Jingle Bells."

The department store was packed and smelled of cinnamon. It took Shanshan a long while to find a window of opportunity to squeeze in front of a cosmetic counter. A short woman with dark hair and a warm smile greeted her. "Hello, love, what can I do for you?"

"I need a mascara and maybe a blusher," Shanshan said.

"No problem," the woman replied, and bounced her red and green fingernails along the tubes and packs on the counter, as if playing a piano. "Do you want the volumizing one or the lengthening one?"

"I don't know. I haven't done my makeup for ages. It's just, I need to go to my husband's workplace party this evening."

"That's a big thing!" The girl turned. "Oh, love, I am happy do a full makeup session for you, if you want."

Immediately, Shanshan wanted to say no but then she saw her face in the bright LED-lit mirror. "Sure," she said.

The woman dabbed foundation on Shanshan's cheeks, forehead, and chin, outlined her contours, and brought forward her eyes, brows, and nose. In the end, after she had brushed scarlet red on her lips, Shanshan looked at her reflection and was relieved that her face had been perfectly hidden.

She bought a mascara, a blusher, and a lipstick and paid with her credit card. The saleswoman packed the products in a shining silver bag and handed her a long receipt.

"I've printed out the tax return for you and stamped it," she said cheerfully. "You just need to fill up the rest and drop it at the refund point at the airport when you leave."

Shanshan wondered if there was anything else in her, other than being Chinese, that screamed to people here that she didn't belong. At the party in the Dice Bar, when she finally arrived at the front of the queue and was about to place her order, the bartender, a young, curly-haired man, looked at her and said: "Hey, I've been to China!"

"Enough is enough," Shanshan muttered.

"What?" the bartender shouted, leaning over. The music was blaring in the background.

"Can I get two pints of Guinness and a gin and tonic," she said.

She held the glasses in the tray and, step by step, made a way through the crowd to Declan and his co-worker Conor.

"Thank you, Shanshan!" Conor said, lifting a pint.

"Thanks, wife, you're a legend." Declan took his drink and kissed Shanshan quickly.

"Bu yong xie," Shanshan said, and downed her G&T.

The two men carried on talking. "I don't know much about Ballymount. It's on the Red Line, right?"

"Yeah, it's well connected. And much better value for money. But Fiona's still reluctant to put down the deposit. You know that shooting there earlier this year."

"That's hardly in Ballymount, I thought it was in Tallaght, no?"

"That's what I told her. But the lady's stubborn as a mule."

Shanshan examined the slice of lime in her glass and the slowly swinging ice cubes. Just when she was about to step away, she was nudged by a woman. "Sorry!" the woman cried. It was Maeve. She wore a sapphire V-neck dress and the same thin golden necklace.

"Oh my god, you look gorgeous," Maeve said to Shanshan, stabilizing herself. She turned to Declan: "Isn't she just gorgeous?"

"She is," Declan said tolerantly.

"Shanshan, this is Maeve," Conor introduced them. "Our junior reporter."

"We have met," Shanshan said.

"We have met each other, Conor," Maeve repeated. "And Shanshan told me what her name meant. And it was really funny— and what is it? Urgh, my brain's not working. Can you tell us again, Shanshan?"

Shanshan looked at Declan, who seemed embarrassed. "You should sit down, Maeve," he said.

Conor grabbed Maeve's arm. "Come with me. Let's find a seat for you." He ushered her away.

The couple was left alone. The music and chattering roared like tidal waves, ready to swallow them from behind. Shanshan faced Declan and put on a smile. "You don't want to go to Burma again, do you?"

"Please, Shanshan," Declan said, looking annoyed. "Let's be honest. Do you want to go?"

She glared at him. Knocking back her drink, she shoved the glass into Declan's hand and pushed through the mob to get her coat.

It was frosty outside. The street was marvelously lit. Multi-colored Christmas trees were glittering through windows of the apartment buildings. Shanshan enfolded herself in her black coat and walked back along the quay. Outside Londis, the cashier was smoking at the old spot, wearing a short-sleeved shirt. He waved at her. "Good evening!"

Shanshan tramped towards him and reached out her hand. "Cigarette, please."

He laughed. "Am I your dealer now?"

They stood together, smoking. Shanshan could feel the heat rising from his arm, brushing her frozen cheek. She thought of the tattoo underneath his sleeve.

"Are you going home for Christmas?" she said.

"The in-laws' in Waterford," he said. "My wife's an only child and I have six siblings. Every year we go back to her folks' house. Fair enough. Yourself? Any plans?"

"My husband and I are going away as well. We are going to Burma." She exhaled.

"Where is that? Is that in Asia?"

"Southeast Asia."

"Imagine." He took a drag.

They continued to smoke in silence. Two 67 buses passed, both quite empty.

"I'd better go now." The cashier put out the cigarette on the ground. "Have a good evening and a happy Christmas."

"You, too," she said.

The next morning, Declan apologized. "Sorry for the fuss with Maeve. She's going through a rough time. Plus, she was really pissed."

"I could see that," Shanshan said.

Declan coughed. "The editor just emailed. My article is out today. Shall we look into the tickets now?" He looked at her with his brown eyes, as if their brief exchange in the pub did not happen at all.

Shanshan felt a twitch in her chest. There was a hopelessness on Declan's face that reminded her of the time before their trip to Burma, when he'd shown up at her friend's place. "Okay," she said. "Let's have a look."

They started checking the flights to Yangon. On Skyscanner, all the dates were marked red.

"It's probably too late to book anything now," Shanshan sighed.

"It's not too late," said Declan. "We'll find something, I promise you."

"But do you see the price?" Shanshan shook her head. "The cheapest ticket here is nine hundred and eight euros per person— and it takes three transfers and forty-nine hours."

"I'll find something." Declan took the laptop from her.

"Never mind," Shanshan said. "We don't have to go. It's not practical anyway."

"We'll go," he insisted.

She watched him type and search, sensing the familiar smell of his body intensified by perspiration. Every time when she was about to give up, he persisted. They were like two comets chasing each other in circles, sometimes getting closer, yet always light-years apart.

They sat for two hours and found out the cheapest option was to go to Hong Kong first, wait there for thirteen hours, and fly to Yangon the second day. It would cost 1,268 euros for the two of them. Then the hotels—Declan was on the laptop, scrolling, clicking, reading out numbers while Shanshan took notes, doing the sums.

The number kept getting bigger. Shanshan bent her sore neck and saw it had gone dark again outside. "Shall we take a break? I need to eat before making any decisions," she said.

Declan agreed. They were starving after the intense labor and he suggested they go to Mulligan's. They walked. It was quiet and dark on North Circular Road. Shanshan held Declan's hand.

"I know it'll be strange to go to Burma again. And it's a lot of money," she said.

Declan sighed. His exhalation turned white in the air and vanished like a ghost. "But you still want to go."

They turned into Aughrim Street and walked past a church. She said: "I'm sorry that it hasn't been great between us."

"You don't need to apologize," Declan said, looking ahead.

"And I'm sorry for the miscarriage. I can't understand how I did not notice that I was pregnant," she said in a small voice. "Sometimes I feel maybe it's because I don't want to have children. I don't want to be a mother."

He listened and thought for a few seconds. "You'll get there, Shanshan. Be patient. Give your body time to heal."

From the distance, they could hear music playing. They turned onto Manor Street and arrived at Mulligan's. They ate mussels and chips, drank beer, and went back home around six.

The cottage felt cold and empty. Across the sofa lay the laptop, notebooks, and pens. Shanshan asked: "Shall we book it now?"

"Sure." Declan hung up his coat and strode to the sofa.

The phone rang from Declan's coat pocket. Shanshan handed it to him. On the screen it said: "Home."

"Howya," Declan answered, and stepped into the kitchen. She could hear his voice coming. "Jesus . . . Sure, of course . . . Are you okay? . . . Okay, okay . . . Sure I will. No bother . . . Do you need anything? . . . No worries, we can get a taxi from the train station . . . See you."

He came back. "It was Dad," he said. "Mam fell from the stairs and they think she broke her hip, possibly some internal bleeding. And Dad, he's been in bed for a week now because his back got worse. Aoife's in Germany with her boyfriend. The others are too far away. They need me there."

"My goodness. Poor Rita."

"We'd better go soon. She is having an operation. Someone has to be there," Declan said.

They packed quickly and left Dublin by train at ten past eight. Declan looked out the window for a while before saying: "I'm sorry. But I don't think we will go to Burma this time."

"Of course. You don't need to say this," she said.

"We can go during the Easter holiday. We'll book the flights early and we can stay in nice hotels."

"That'd be good."

He soon fell asleep, crouching on the seat, head resting on her shoulder.

The train was full. It was already the twenty-first. People were going back to Mullingar, to Longford, to Ballymote, to Sligo, to the rain and snow.

They arrived at Longford at ten and went straight to the hospital.

Rita had hip replacement surgery the next day at noon. Afterwards, Shanshan and Declan met her in the ward. When they walked in Rita was lying flat on the bed with a pillow between her legs.

"It's been twenty-six years since I had an epidural, and that was for Sean," she said. "It all passed in a blink."

"How do you feel?" Declan asked.

"Great. I'm in no pain now, soon I'll be flying," she said. "Shanshan, can you come over? I haven't seen you for ages."

Shanshan had been standing at the foot of the bed. She walked over and looked down at Rita. Her mother-in-law's face was swollen and bruised liked a molded boule bread, stitches on her forehead.

"Ah, poor girl, no need be upset," Rita said, "I'm fine. I'll be fine."

"I know," Shanshan said, wiping her eyes.

"This is what happens when you get old. Look at Paul and me. One with a broken back, the other with a broken hip, both on the bed." She tittered and started to cough.

"Mam, please," Declan said. "You need to be still."

"I need some water," she said.

Shanshan went to get the water. She filled half the glass and put in a straw. Carefully she lowered the glass to Rita's cheek and maneuvered the straw into her mouth.

Rita drank. "Thank you, Shanshan," she said. "And congratulations on the *Guardian* story, Declan."

"Ah, that's nothing. It was only because of the case. The English wanted to know about 'Slab' Murphy, and I was there to tell," he said.

They chatted away. Shanshan stood under the fluorescent light, beside the chalk-white bed, feeling she was removed from the room. She pinned her nails in her palms to stop herself from trembling. She couldn't help but see her own mother's face, a swollen, ugly, and ridiculous face, covered by cuts and bruises. The body had been laid on a bare steel tray. A policewoman had asked her: "Can you confirm the victim's identification?"

When the visiting hour was over, the couple said goodbye to Rita, walked back to the house, and bought some groceries on the way. Shanshan cooked bacon and brussels sprouts, heated up two tins of refried beans, and made a green salad with feta cheese.

"The best dinner I've had in ages," Paul exclaimed after eating everything.

"Say it in front of Mam," Declan said.

The father and son drank wine and talked late into the night. The next day, the siblings began to return: Róisín flew back from London, and Sean arrived before midnight, taking the last bus from Dublin Airport. On the early morning of the twenty-fourth, Aoife got home and gave Shanshan a long squeeze. When Cormac and his wife, Silvia, came back and released their five-year-old and eight-year-old, the three-story house seemed too small to contain all the screams and laughter.

After dinner, they sat in the living room. *Coronation Street* was on TV. Róisín carried out board games. "Ah, I'd love to play *this*." Sean pulled out one box, reading the cover. "'Discovering Éire: A Strategic Game of Traveling Around Ireland.'"

"Sure," Declan said, sliding down the sofa to sit on the carpet.

"I'm in," Aoife said. She scooted over towards Declan and waved to Shanshan. "Come sit by me, Shanshan, I'll show you how to play."

"I'm a bit tired," Shanshan said. "I might just go to the next room and watch TV."

Declan took a look at her. "All right. Get a blanket. The heating in that room is not great."

She went into the second living room and turned on the light. It seemed that earlier on, the two little boys had had some fun in here. Books, magazines, and newspapers were scattered all over the floor. She started picking them up, putting books back to the shelves and newspapers underneath the coffee table. Halfway through, a familiar face surfaced, wearing a khaki flat cap.

She shivered, as if being bitten by the image, and nearly dropped the paper.

"The 'Untouchable' IRA Godfather Brought Down by Tax Law." It was Declan's piece in *The Guardian*. His parents must have bought the paper on the day it came out.

Shanshan sat down on the sofa and began to read: *Thomas "Slab" Murphy's farm straddles County Louth and County Armagh on the Irish border. It was there he amassed a multimillion-euro fortune through cross-border smuggling and ruled the IRA for more than forty years. Once considered a "good Republican" by Sinn Féin, he was charged on September 21 in the Special Criminal Court in Dublin with tax evasion, being accused of failing to make any returns to revenue . . .*

An irrecoverable cold was filling out Shanshan's body. She put down the paper and pulled the blanket over herself with quivering fingers, but it didn't help. Through the wall, she heard laughter, intermittently. At a certain point, someone screamed and then they were all clapping and chanting: "Declan! Declan! Declan!" She thought of getting up and joining them for the game but she couldn't move. She looked at the black TV screen, the dark and hollow fireplace.

She sat there for so long it felt as if Christmas was over and all the people had left the house.

Rita came home on St. Stephen's Day. There was a lot of resting and physio to do but she was on the mend. Róisín returned to London on the same day. Two days later, Cormac and Silvia packed up eight suitcases and flew back to Madrid with the kids. Declan, Shanshan, and Sean left on the thirty-first. They spent New Year's Day together in Dublin before Sean headed to Scotland, joining his friends for a stag party. In another week's time he'd recommence his teaching job in Abu Dhabi.

The court opened on January 10. This time, the case was of Donal Billings, a sixty-six-year-old man who had called the gardaí, stating he had planted a bomb on a Dublin-to-Longford bus ahead of a state visit by the Queen. He could face eight to ten years in jail.

In February, Shanshan read in the newspaper that the court

had jailed "Slab" Murphy for eighteen months. At the end of the month, the couple found out she was pregnant again.

They dropped their plan to visit Burma during the Easter break and finally painted the house. Shanshan would go to Phoenix Park for most of her walks, or sometimes she'd head to Rotunda in the city center for checkups or antenatal classes. As the days got brighter and the London plane trees began to sprout, Shanshan had taken on a few translation jobs and decided to read George Orwell. Starting with Declan's favorite, *1984*, then *Animal Farm* and *Down and Out in Paris and London*. She had grown fond of the author and was confident that one day she would be able to read *Burmese Days* and perhaps even discuss the novel with her husband. Although she would try to avoid, if possible, *A Collection of Essays*, especially "Shooting an Elephant."

Every time, just a glimpse of the jade-green spine on the bookshelves was enough to make her freeze, feeling in the pit of her stomach and remembering the moment, two days after being admitted to Mawlamyine General Hospital, when she had opened her mouth for the first time, and asked Declan if he could read this story to her.

In a low and slightly hoarse voice, he had read to her how Orwell had pulled the trigger of the rifle, aiming the first bullet a few inches in front of the elephant's earhole, where its brain was. The elephant sagged to its knees and Orwell fired again at the same spot and then again for the third time and how, finally, the elephant trumpeted and came down completely—but it was not dead. And Declan went on: "*I sent back for my small rifle and poured shot after shot into his heart and down his throat. They seemed to make no impression. The tortured gasps continued as steadily as the ticking of a clock . . ."*

That had been when Shanshan had started to cry. Her hands covered her face and the tears streamed down along her arms. She cried out loudly, almost howling. Her body shook.

"Mama, mama, mama," she cried, in Chinese.

Mama.

之署月果脩合增不須攜

乙肩竹面二下為樞山舊廬面

右扃止層書箱一紙筆墨硯剪刀韻略雜書冊

樞巾食碗楪各六七箸各四生果數物削果刀子

右兩上層琴一罅匣貯之摺疊棋局一樞巾棋子茶二□

而臘茶即碾熟者盞托各三　孟踏七箸

附帶　雜物

小斧子　研刀　劃藥　鋤子　臘燭二　柱杖　泥靴　雨衣

鐵笠　食銚　虎子　急須子　油筒

WHEN TRAVELING IN SUMMER

W hen traveling in the summertime," Shen Kuo wrote in the year 1095, "there's no need for assorted fruit platter, savory cakes, and raisins. On his back Servant Yi carries bamboo luggage, which consists of two sections. The lower section is a compartment while the upper section an open shelf. On the left side of the shelf is a bookcase, which contains a stack of rice paper, a couple of ink brushes, a bottle of ink, an ink stone, scissors, *A Brief Guide to Rhyme*, and some other books. In the compartment, there are six or seven bowls and plates, four pairs of chopsticks, a few pieces of fresh fruit, and a fruit knife. On the right side of the shelf is a zither, stored in a bamboo case. There is also a folding go board. The stones for the game are kept in the compartment, alongside three kinds of tea, including a fermented one, three sets of teacups and saucers, and seven tea mixing bowls and spoons."

It was January when Shen Kuo was writing in his study and the snow was about to fall. Seven braziers burned brightly in the room. Amid the cracking sound of firewood, he looked outside the window at a plum blossom tree and thought of the midsummer days, all the perspiration and light-headedness that would occur during travel. The imagined heat made his throat dry and itchy. He drank from the teacup. Then he dipped the brush into the ink stone, made a fine stroke on the rice paper, and carried on in a dancing rhythm: "Another few bits and pieces to bring: a small axe, a machete, a pick for blocks of Chinese medicine, two candles, a cane, a pair of rain boots, a raincoat, a conical straw hat, a teapot, a tea whisker, and a flask of oil."

He finished writing in the small hours when five of the seven braziers had dimmed. He stood up from the desk, closed the ink bottle, and washed the brush in a brass basin. Afterwards, he dried the brush, trimmed the tip with scissors, and carefully hung it back on the penholder.

Must travel light in the summer, he thought as he blew out the candles. Bring only the essentials.

On January 5, Shen Kuo's old friend Huang arrived from the capital with his two wives, six concubines, and forty servants and maids. His caravan congested the main street outside Shen Kuo's estate. As the servants scurried back and forth, unloading the luggage, Huang got off his carriage and stepped languidly to the front gate.

In front of Shen Kuo's estate, Huang stopped and looked up at the mahogany gate. A pair of stone gods stood on each side. The one on the right had the head of an ox, eyes protruding. It held a pair of axes. The left one, whose face resembled a horse, bared its teeth, letting out a soundless scream. Its arms extended forward, thrusting a machete at the visitor.

Huang smiled at them. His gaze moved to the top of the gate, where a thick wooden plaque hung. On the plaque, the name of the estate was engraved: *Mengxi*—Dream Creek.

Huang stared at the plaque, eyes narrowed. "Knock on the door," he ordered.

A broad-shouldered servant walked up and pounded the gate. "Here arrives the prestigious third-class officer, the grand minister of the supreme court, Master Huang! Come greet him immediately!"

The call repeated, each time louder. It finally reached to the end of the estate, and the gate opened. Behind the gate stood a young man in a white robe. His eyebrows were thick and dark, his eyes firm and bright. "Welcome." He bowed. "Master and Madam are expecting you."

Shen Kuo and his wife, Woman Zhang, stood at the center of the great hall as Servant Yi guided Huang in. Huang stepped over the stone threshold and smiled warmly at Shen Kuo. He was smaller and older than Shen Kuo remembered. His face was wrinkled like the dried shell of a cicada.

"It has been eight years, Mr. Shen." Huang bowed. "I hope you haven't been ill since."

"I've been healthy. Thank you," Shen Kuo said. "I'm glad to know you are ranked third class—a grand minister."

"It's the mercy of the emperor." Huang held his hands together and bowed to the north. "It's my honor to serve before His Highness."

"A great honor, indeed. Think about all the low ranks who died without seeing the face of Heaven's son. I must say congratulations."

Huang smiled wryly. "It's hard to say if it's an honor or curse; to serve the emperor is like serving a tiger."

"I always feel blessed to have served His Highness, who is most wise and fair." Shen Kuo bowed deeply to the north. "Eight years ago, when I resigned, my heart was saturated with reluctance and sorrow. However, I had to leave because the calling for me to write was imperative."

"I understand. And I truly admire your passion and determination. Tell me about your book, *The Notes in Mengxi*. Everybody in the capital is talking about it. Have you finished it?"

"I have," Shen Kuo said. "It was finished two years ago. A printing house in Yangzhou took the job. The types are ready, more than five thousand of them. The print plates will be finished this year. The book will be available next year, thirty volumes in total."

"Marvelous!" Huang said. "I heard it's so eclectic that it contains everything in the world."

Shen Kuo shook his head. "My old friend, I trust you not to be deceived by the hyperbole of salesmen. The world exists without limit or end. No one can elucidate such infinity. *The Notes* was finished two years ago and I've been recognizing its omissions ever since. Now, this new book I'm working on . . ."

They carried on talking while the wives chatted in indistinguishable voices. Their servants and maids stood still, like two rows of poplar trees. Servant Yi was at the head of the row, so close to Shen Kuo that he noticed his master was circling his index finger on his gown.

"Master." Yi stepped forward. "I deserve to die ten thousand times for interrupting you and Master Huang. But Magistrate Sun is visiting to consult you on the new irrigation system this afternoon."

"You are right, Yi," Shen Kuo said. "I must go now. Mr. Huang, my wife will see you to your accommodation."

The two of them left and walked along the nine-turn corridor. "Good that you mentioned the magistrate," Shen Kuo said to Yi. "Huang needs to know that I'm respected here. Where am I going to meet him?"

"You met with him yesterday, Master," Yi said. "I saw you circling your finger and thought you probably wanted to go back to your writing—I deserve to die ten thousand times for presuming your intention."

Shen Kuo smiled. "Nobody deserves to die ten thousand times. Once is enough. We shall go to the study."

The project Shen Kuo was working on was *The Book of Forgetting*, which would further complement *The Notes in Mengxi*, elaborating on earlier omitted items on agriculture, medicine, and geography. His plan was to finish it in June before visiting the Taoist temple on Burnt Mountain for a fortnight.

However, Shen Kuo wouldn't be able to make it to Burnt Mountain because he didn't have long to live. In fact, he would die in less than five months, but he was not aware of it—even if he had known, he probably wouldn't have allowed himself to be preoccupied by the notion of mortality.

"If anything happens only once, it is meaningless," he used to say.

———

Growing up in an upper-class family, Shen Kuo revered the values of Confucius and did not believe in the afterlife and reincarnation. His wife, Woman Zhang, on the other hand, was extremely superstitious. Before the New Year, she had drowned Shen Kuo's seventeenth son—born to his sixth concubine—because a Buddhist monk had discerned that the baby was the reincarnation of an enemy from Shen's previous life. The concubine had killed herself shortly after.

Shen Kuo was initially oblivious to their deaths. The concubine had been a quiet woman and had lived at the west end of the estate. Had Shen Kuo not gone over to admire the blossom of the Fragrant Snow peony last spring, he wouldn't have sauntered into the concubine's residence and spent a night there and impregnated the woman.

Two days after Huang's arrival, Woman Zhang organized a welcome banquet. A long table was carried out by six servants and placed in the middle of the great hall. Shen Kuo and Huang sat at the head of the table; along the sides their wives and concubines sat like two strings of pearls.

"What a prosperous family you have," Shen Kuo said. "I'm very glad to see this."

"Likewise." Huang smiled. "How many wives and concubines do you have? And how many sons have they borne you?"

Shen Kuo put down his chopsticks. Servant Yi stepped forward and whispered in his ear: "Master, you had one wife, nine concubines, and seventeen sons last year. Now you have one wife, eight concubines, and sixteen sons."

"What happened?" Shen Kuo turned around.

"The sixth concubine threw herself into a well because her

newborn drowned in Wenxin Lake at the west end of the estate," Yi said as Woman Zhang sipped lamb soup slowly. "It was an accident."

"All right," Shen Kuo said, turning to Huang, "it seems I have one wife, eight concubines, and sixteen sons."

"How inappropriate. You were a second-class officer who should own at least nine concubines—not to mention you were much valued by the late emperor."

"This is my fault." Woman Zhang put down the bowl. "I should have filled up the vacancy immediately, but it's been quite busy with the New Year celebration—anyhow, there should be no excuse. I beg for my punishment, Master."

"You may be pardoned," Shen Kuo said. "I appreciate that it takes incomparable effort to manage this house."

They dined until late in the evening. Afterwards, Shen Kuo went to the study with Servant Yi. When Yi prepared the ink on the inkstone, Shen Kuo sighed loudly.

Yi looked up. "May I spare your worry, Master?"

"Thanks to you, now Madam will acquire me a new concubine."

"A great man like you should have more women bearing your descendants. So your name of prestige will be passed on."

Shen Kuo didn't respond. The fire was burning. The fragrance of the ink pierced through his mind. He stared at an old letter on his desk, which he had retrieved from a bamboo case after Huang's arrival. It was the last letter from the late Prime Minister Wang. *To be viewed by my kind brother Shen Kuo*, it began.

Shen Kuo picked up the letter, held it above the burning brazier, and released his fingers. Instantly, the flame caught the paper and turned it to ashes.

Then he sighed for the second time. "The material appearance is fragile and the name the most ephemeral," he said slowly. "Even if my name is remembered by later generations, who knows whether it'll be praised or condemned. In all respects, one should disregard his name the way the cicada sheds its carapace."

When Shen Kuo finally met his new concubine, the fifth daughter of a medical practitioner, it was a fortnight after the girl had moved into the estate of Mengxi. Having received three urgent messages from Woman Zhang, Shen Kuo savored a well-prepared dinner by himself before heading to his wife's residence with Servant Yi.

It was around six in the evening, but the sky was still bright. He walked into the chamber and saw Woman Zhang sitting beside a zither, staring at it like a bird. Upon his entry, she lifted her head and said, "Welcome, Master. Come meet Ping."

In the golden light, Shen Kuo saw a small woman sitting on the bed in a red dress. The dress was massive, the red silk shone flamboyantly under the sunset. Inside the dress, the girl looked like a faint stream of exhalation.

"Master, please lie with this poor girl." Woman Zhang stood up, retreated from the chamber, and closed the door behind her.

Shen Kuo seemed to have vanished behind that door. In his study, the braziers had dimmed and gradually gone out. The room grew bigger and the walls whiter. When he finally reemerged from his time with Ping, it was nearly the end of February.

Shen Kuo walked into the study with Servant Yi and saw Huang was there, sitting by the low table, reading.

"Mr. Huang." Shen Kuo bowed. "Why are you here by yourself in this cold room? You should have got someone to light the fire."

"It's fine." Huang put down *A Brief Guide to Rhyme*. "I don't like the heating. It's only natural to feel cold in the winter."

"You're right." Shen Kuo went over and sat down across the table. "We should allow ourselves to thrive and wane, like the moon and the flowers."

Yi brought in the wood and lit the fire. "Make tea for us," Shen Kuo said.

The pair of old colleagues chatted as the kettle started to bubble on a brazier. Shen Kuo asked Huang how he had found his stay so far.

"Marvelous," Huang said. "I'm being spoiled. I've been treated with the finest tea and wine, even better than the ones we have in the capital. You're truly a connoisseur of exquisiteness."

"You are embarrassing me with such a false statement," Shen Kuo said. "We all know that the capital is the home of Heaven's son—it has the best of the best."

As they reminisced about their old days at the royal court, Servant Yi unpacked a sixty-year-old fermented pu'er tea brick. Holding the brick with one hand, he maneuvered a golden pick with the other, breaking the tea leaves off the brick painstakingly and laying them into an iron teapot. When the kettle came to a boil, Yi poured hot water into the pot, turned it six times, and dumped the first-time tea into a large mixing bowl. Again, he poured in water, turned the teapot nine times, and tilted it skilfully into two cups: one jade green, the other ocher red. He placed the cups on their matching saucers and brought them to the masters.

"What incredible subtlety!" Huang sighed after taking a sip. "So well aged and delicate."

"It's a gift from a friend." Shen Kuo smiled. "There are still a couple of bricks in storage. I'll be glad to give you one when you leave."

"Oh, I don't know when I'm leaving." Huang laughed.

Shen Kuo put down his teacup. Yi leaned over and poured more tea.

"Before the New Year, the emperor had a dream," Huang said. "In the dream, he was traveling southward from Yangzhou. It was very hot, so he fetched some water from a creek. As he sat underneath a tree, drinking, he saw something glinting in between two rocks. He went to check what it was. It turned out to be a small turtle. The emperor picked the turtle up from between the two rocks, realizing it was eerily heavy. He was just about to take a closer look at this peculiar creature when the turtle bit him on the hand in the most ferocious manner. The emperor woke up shivering and his left hand was swollen. He had to stay in bed for days."

"I'm petrified by this horrific news. I hope His Highness has regained his health by now," Shen Kuo said, bowing to the north.

"Yes, he has." Huang tapped the table as Yi poured him more tea. "The royal doctors took good care of him and he's as strong as an ox now. However, his spirit is still disturbed. So His Highness summoned me and entrusted me with a secret mission." Huang paused for a long while before he continued. "The emperor gave me an edict, ordering me to travel to the south, find that turtle, and sentence it to death."

It was at this moment Shen Kuo fully perceived the purpose of Huang's visit. He moved the teacup away from his lips and put it down on the saucer. The cup tipped and the tea spilled out. Servant Yi reached over. "I'll get you a new cup, Master."

Shen Kuo sat in silence. He looked outside the window at the plum tree. The blossoms had withered and fallen.

Eventually he turned to Huang and said: "So, my old friend, when are you planning to return to the capital and report back to the emperor?"

"I know you're still working on the book," Huang said, smiling. "And I've known you well, my friend. Even though we weren't on the same side during the years of Prime Minister Wang's reformation, I'd always admired your courage and felt sorry when the reformation fell through. It'll be well suited if I could go back in June, after you finish the book. What do you think?"

Through the sharp tip of Shen Kuo's brush, the ink contacted the rice paper. It floated on the surface for just a passing second and permeated the paper. An imperishable entity was forged, and it would exist until the end of the universe.

It was this sense of profundity that propelled Shen Kuo through his decades of writing. His study was that of a totalitarian state where he held the utmost power, announcing in a singular voice the rules and facts of the world: how to deliver a calf; where the first Tang Sancai ceramic plate was cast; how many species of insects had gone extinct during the Wars of the Three Kingdoms; who assassinated Emperor Zhaozong of the Tang dynasty and his nine sons; and how to eliminate the wheat pests in Bianjing Province.

"What's this character, Master?" Ping asked, leaning over the desk. She pointed at the rice paper Shen Kuo had just finished writing on, at the second character in the first column on the right.

"It's shu," Shen Kuo said, "means 'summertime.'" He took out a fresh piece of paper and wrote down the character at a large size: 暑. "You see. The upper radical is ri which means 'the sun.' He gestured at 日. "And the lower radical is zhe, which means 'people.'" He moved his hand towards 者. "So what this character shows is a man standing under the sun."

"Fascinating," Ping said, resting her hand on his arm. A coolness passed through her fingers.

"Do you want to learn how to read? I can teach you," Shen Kuo said.

Ping's face lit up. "Thank you, Master. I'll be in gratitude forever."

It was Ping's last word that reminded Shen Kuo of his doom. He turned away from Ping and saw Servant Yi sitting by the low table, playing go with himself.

"Yi," he called.

Yi put down the stones and stood up. "Yes, Master?"

"Why don't you teach Ping to read?" he said. "Look." He took the page he had just finished and handed it to Yi. "Read this to her and teach her the characters."

"Thank you for your generosity, Master." Yi received the page with two hands. "We're blessed to serve you."

The two of them went to the low table. Yi pushed away the go board, laid down the paper gently, and placed two go stones on the top corners to secure it, one black, the other white. They sat down by the table beside each other, eyeing the paper.

Yi perched his index finger on the first column and moved

down slowly as he read out loud: "*Zhi shu yue guo xiu he jie bu xu xie*—this means: 'When traveling in summertime, there's no need for assorted fruit platter, savory cakes, and raisins . . .'"

Shen Kuo felt a hazy pain in his chest when he recommenced with his writing. If I were Servant Yi . . . , he thought, and picked up his pen again.

In mid-March, when the rapeseed flowers shrouded the farm fields, rippling under the sun like a golden desert, Woman Zhang sensed something was off.

She asked the maid to prepare her a bath, to which saffron and cinnamon essences and fresh rose petals were added. She then removed her dress, stepped into the aromatic water, and savored a bowl of stewed hasma and dates while the maid gently scrubbed the dead skin off her back with a piece of dried luffa. After the bath, she applied makeup, got dressed in a silk floral gown, and sent the maid away.

It was around four or five in the morning when the bottom of the velvet sky began to illuminate. In silence, Woman Zhang sat in her chamber until there was a knock on the door.

"Come in," she said.

Servant Yi walked in and bowed to her. "Madam, you sent for me."

"Yes," she said, standing up and walking towards the bed. She removed her gown and lay down. "Come lie with me," she said. "I long for you like the clam longs for the eel."

They slept together. Afterwards, Woman Zhang asked Yi if there was anything unusual going on with her husband. Yi informed her of the conversation Huang and Shen Kuo had about the emperor's dream and the emperor's edict to kill the turtle.

Woman Zhang sat up. The color on her face faded. "We're doomed," she said. "Huang is here to sentence Master to death."

She shivered like a leaf in the wind. "With the edict, I will be killed and so will the concubines," she murmured. "I must send my sons to my father immediately—or shall I run away as well?" She turned to Yi and looked at him—she must have been mesmerised by Yi's young and handsome face before the revelation came to her.

"Wait," she said. Her eyelashes flickered and the tears dropped along her cheeks. "Did Huang say he'll wait until June when Master finishes this book?"

"That's what he said."

Woman Zhang closed her eyes. She put her palms together in prayer. Her lips moved soundlessly. Eventually, when she opened her eyes, her face was flushed like the plum flower.

"The Buddha has guided me and I see a clear path in the darkness." She held Yi's hands as her words streamed out. "The only way for us to survive is to kill Master before Huang announces the edict. And we must convince Huang that Master's death is of reasonable cause. It mustn't be seen as a conspiracy against the emperor's edict or we'll all be killed."

"I'm truly lost before your insurmountable wisdom, Madam," Yi said. "Such a thing seems impossible to achieve."

"The wisdom belongs to the Buddha." Woman Zhang smiled and kissed Yi on the mouth. "I'm merely his messenger," she whispered. "Now, what the Buddha thinks is wise to do is for you to lure the new concubine so she could serve as his tool . . ."

———

Shen Kuo had not been unfamiliar with Woman Zhang's foul reputation even before they were married. She was the only daughter of Chancellor Zhang, who supervised Shen Kuo when he worked in Yangzhou as a local prosecutor. Having seen potential in the young man, Chancellor Zhang praised Shen Kuo cordially in front of the late emperor and eventually facilitated Shen Kuo's promotion to the royal court.

Looking back to the year 1069, it seemed clear that everything was predestined: as an ambitious young politician, Shen Kuo had to move from Yangzhou to the capital; his first wife, Woman Ye, must die during this trip for some unclear reason; he would then express to the chancellor his irrepressible admiration towards Woman Zhang and her widespread virtues; they would get married the next spring.

However, on their wedding night, when Shen Kuo lifted the bride's red veil and saw her face for the first time, he couldn't help but think: she really looks like a gray egret.

In spite of this likeness, Shen Kuo always found Woman Zhang a dutiful wife. For more than twenty years, she treated him sensibly and respectfully while managing the subordinates with justice and strictness. He would not say he was not pleased with their marriage. So, when Ping asked him if Woman Zhang beat him regularly with a cane, he laughed.

"This is why people say rumors end in the ears of a wise man. I've heard more absurd things about her. You don't need to worry. She's a reasonable woman," Shen Kuo said, reaching out his hand to adjust Ping's right elbow.

He was teaching Ping to write. She stood by the desk, holding an ink brush firmly with her right hand while trying to relax the wrist. She pressed the rice paper with her left hand, dipped the brush onto the inkstone, holding her breath, and wrote: 乙.

It was mid-April. Ping had finished practicing the characters on the first column of the page and moved on to the second column. The first character was easy. She wrote five in one stretch: 乙乙乙乙乙.

"Did Yi tell you what this character is?" Shen Kuo asked.

"It's yi," Ping said.

"That's correct. It's his name. It means 'second.'"

"Yes. He told me you named him Yi because he is your second servant. The first one died before he came."

"That's right." Shen Kuo smiled. "He was only nine years old when I bought him—that was almost fifteen years ago."

"Can you teach me your name, Master?"

Shen Kuo was bemused. "Why do you want to know?"

"Names are important, aren't they? I heard our fates are concealed in our names. I've learned that my name means 'ordinary,' Yi's name means 'second'—I want to know what your name means."

"Well," Shen Kuo said, "mine is a bit complicated." He took a piece of paper and wrote down the first character: 沈.

"This one is the name of my family, Shen," he said. "It's a phonetic loan character of Chen." He wrote: 沉. "It means 'heavy.' And my first name is Kuo." He wrote: 括. "Which has various meanings. So I gave myself a stylized name to specify the meaning of my first name. And my stylized name is Cun Zhong." He wrote: 存中. "They mean 'exist, in between.' My name Kuo basically

74

means 'existing in the middle.' It manifests the Confucian doctrine of impartiality, reconciliation, and compromise."

"Incredible." Ping exhaled, staring at the characters on the paper. "I wish one day our children could have fine names like this."

Shen Kuo's heart sank. As the days got warmer, *The Book of Forgetting* was about to come to its last chapter.

"I've been wanting to ask you," he said. "What do you think of Yi?"

Ping's wrist shook and the pen dabbed on the paper, leaving a black stain.

"He is a dutiful teacher," she said quickly. "He always speaks of you with the utmost loyalty."

"Good," he said. "I have an arrangement for the two of you— I'm afraid an extraordinary plight will befall me and this family. And I want you to run away with Yi. I've prepared some gold and a carriage. I'll inform Yi about the arrangement soon, and you need to go before the summer."

Ping stared motionlessly at the ink stain on the paper while Shen Kuo explained the purpose of Huang's visit and the imperial edict that would terminate the lives of everyone in this estate. When Ping lifted her head, her eyes were filled with tears.

"You are truly kind, Master," she said. "You do not deserve to die and I will not abandon you in such adversity. I must think of a plan—a plan that will change your destiny."

Shen Kuo reached out his hand and touched her cheek gently, as if he were touching a reflection in water. "Thank you," he said. "Although I've failed to see any way out. The emperor wants me to die. Therefore, the death of Shen Kuo is but inevitable."

Shen Kuo did not mean what he said. In fact, ever since he had heard about the sprouting love affair between the servant and his new concubine, he realized there was hope for his escape. He had been observing, waiting patiently for the right moment to talk to Ping. After all, he had always been proud of his comprehensive understanding of the universe, his ability to see how everything was inherently connected and how, with perfect timing, the constellation of destinies could be shifted with the faintest nudge.

When Shen Kuo smelled the familiar scent of moxa in the air and saw vases of pomegranates, sunflowers, and gardenias blooming in the estate, he realized in surprise it was the Double Fifth Festival already. He could not believe it was May; he still sensed the remains of January.

Woman Zhang had always been fond of festivals and this time was no exception. Every room teemed with flowers. Every wall was hung with bundles of moxa grass. A huge golden Buddha was invited from White Horse Temple and enshrined in the great hall, in front of which three pagodas of rice dumplings and fragrant sachets were presented on cloisonné plates.

On the afternoon of May 5, the festival dinner began. Shen Kuo sat at the head of the table and looked around at the faces of his guests, wife, and concubines. He raised a glass of wine. "Happy Double Fifth Festival to all, especially my prestigious guest, Mr. Huang."

"It's my honor to be here, I've been indulging myself in the marvelous book collections of the estate," Huang said, raising his glass and finishing the wine.

"We're very pleased to have you," Woman Zhang said. "I wish you and your wives could stay until the Mid-Autumn Festival."

"Thank you for your hospitality. I'd love to, but I have my imperial duties."

"Then let's drink to your departure." Woman Zhang filled up their glasses and drank with Huang.

Under her orders, Shen Kuo's concubines—Jin, Ying, Yue'er, Su, Lan, Ping, Lian, Mei, and Wei—went to drink with Huang one after another, finishing six bottles in no time.

As Huang stood up from the table and staggered to the toilet outside, Woman Zhang gave a cough, nodding slightly at Servant Yi.

On Huang's way back, in the nine-turn corridor, he saw two figures cuddling. When he got closer, he recognized they were Servant Yi and one of Shen Kuo's concubines.

"You damn lackey!" Huang shouted, gripping Yi's arm. The concubine collapsed to her knees.

Huang hauled them both back to the great hall and threw them in front of Shen Kuo. "Look at what I found outside," Huang said. "Mr. Shen, these two lowlifes have brought shame on your house."

Shen Kuo looked at the young pair. Before he said anything, Woman Zhang stood up, yanked Ping's hair, and slapped her fiercely. "You deserve nothing but a piece of white silk robe," she said. "I order you to hang yourself immediately."

Tears streamed down Ping's face. To everyone's surprise, Yi jumped up like a leopard and pushed Woman Zhang away. "Leave her out of this, you despicable cow!"

This was the only moment Shen Kuo felt sorry for his wife. Being gripped by a sharp sense of nostalgia, he averted his eyes and signaled to two other servants, who brought Yi under control.

"Take him to the stable," he ordered, staring at the golden Buddha. "I'll deal with him tomorrow. Ping, you go back to your residence. No one shall harm you."

And then Shen Kuo walked away by himself, in front of his guests, wife, and concubines. He disappeared behind the door, the sound of his footsteps vanishing along the corridor.

It was on this same night—the night of the Double Fifth Festival—that Shen Kuo died in his study. It was believed that Ping freed Servant Yi and the pair sneaked into the study with a flask of oil. They brought in all the firewood and set it alight before running away together. The fire burned for two days. When it was finally put out, everything was destroyed, leaving only the iron frames of seven braziers and a black skeleton.

His guest Huang left despondently with his caravan. His wife, Woman Zhang, became preoccupied after the tragedy and eventually slipped into Wenxin Lake on a starless night. A few days later, when the servant finally found her and dredged out her body, she was bloated and looked like a pregnant sow.

The traveler opens his eyes and thinks of the dream he had. It already starts to fade in the room. Pale light is cast in through the window. He hears the rain pattering on the pane and pushes himself up.

"You're up." The young woman sits by the table, wiping her eyes quickly with her hand.

"Is everything all right?" he asks.

"I woke up and couldn't go back to sleep," she says. "And I

thought I should start packing since we need to leave before the hostel gets busy."

"We're almost in the mountains. Nobody will recognize me there." He gets up, puts on his gown, and sits down by the table.

A fruit knife and orange skins lie on the table. The young woman is packing some medicine blocks. "I don't want to risk it. Not after everything that happened," she says.

"I understand. We'll go early, then." He disposes of the fruit skins, puts the knife away, and stacks the books together. Underneath one book he sees a piece of paper. He reads: *When traveling in summertime.*

"I didn't know you'd kept this page. I thought it was burned with the study," he says.

The young woman doesn't look up. "It's a souvenir." She puts the medicine into the lower compartment of the luggage.

He doesn't ask more. They pack item after item.

"Put on the boots," he says. "The paths are muddy in the mountains."

She puts on the boots and the raincoat. He squats down by the back of the luggage, puts the straps through his arms, and lifts it up. Quietly they leave the room and walk down the stairs. The owner is dozing behind the counter.

Outside the rain has gotten heavier, flowing down from the eaves like a mirror.

"The reason I kept that page is not because I have any affection for him," the young woman says. "I only feel troubled because I was the one who engineered his death."

The traveler sighs. "Your plan wouldn't have worked if they

were not, in the first place, trying to use you to kill me. I would not have been able to live if it wasn't for you. You saved my life."

She looks at him. Her beautiful face is soaked in sadness. "Thank you, Master."

"I'm not Master anymore. I shall remain nameless for the rest of my life." He puts on the conical hat and walks into the rain. She follows.

The rain hits the traveler's hat. The luggage on his back seems to be of great weight. The traveler walks hunched, like a mantis. The young woman is behind him, stepping lightly and rhythmically, like an oriole.

The summer rain pours down. They walk towards Burnt Mountain.

STOCKHOLM

In late November, I flew to Stockholm for a weekend to attend a literary event. My friend H, who had known me for ten years, was the organizer. H had convinced himself, after a long phone call in September, that I was suffering from postpartum depression. You need to take some time off from the baby, he had said. How about coming here in a couple of months' time and joining a panel to discuss women writers in diaspora? It'll cheer you up.

The event took place the day after my arrival in an old bookstore in Södermalm. I sat beside a spiral staircase and chatted with my co-panelists for about an hour. There were roughly twenty people in the audience, mostly senior citizens, all thoughtfully dressed, observing our conversation in a calm and benevolent manner.

Among them was a pale young man sitting in the back row, who smiled at me whenever I looked in his direction. After the event had finished, as I was gathering my coat and scarf, he approached me and wondered if he could ask a question.

Certainly, I said. Under his eyes were the worst dark circles I'd ever seen.

What is your favorite Chinese word?

His question was not at all what I had expected. It depends on the context, I said, and saw from the corner of my eye that H was miming drinking from a glass.

My favorite word is *lanshan*, he said.

I immediately recognized which word it was. You don't mean "blue mountains," do you? I said.

After a brief delay, the stranger laughed. No, I don't.

It's a very beautiful word, lanshan, I said. Oblique and melancholic.

He looked satisfied.

I saw H was tapping his watch at me before tilting another imaginary drink into his mouth. I really need to go now, I said.

Wait a second. The young man took out a pen from his satchel, gripped my wrist, and scribbled on the back of my hand.

I hope to see you again. He gave me back my hand and left.

Later, in a local pub, I ordered a double whiskey and showed H what the young man had written. That weird guy didn't give me his number but left his name, I said, as if this will help me see him again.

Delar, H said, reading from my hand. It's not a name, just a word. It means "pieces": like fragments.

The five of us sat around a long table, an unusual distance between one another, and sipped our respective drinks. Anna, one of my co-panelists, was narrating her typical day. H conversed with Jacob—a novelist and his friend—about their trip to Israel next spring. The other panelist, Olivia, who also happened to be H's girlfriend, sat in silence, slowly rotating her martini glass. As the pale liquid undulated, the olive swirled inside.

You must go to the library, Anna said. It's the most extraordinary place in Stockholm, in my opinion.

I nodded, trying to ignore the pain thrusting across my left breast.

I often tell my readers, Anna said, I am Swedish in the sense that the city library is my birthplace in this country. It was in the library I learned the language and later where I wrote my first novel.

The book was a huge success, H swiveled around in his chair to comment. It was short-listed for the August Prize. Then he returned to his conversation with Jacob.

I'm very lucky, Anna said. Although I will never be able to write Swedish as finely as some of the great writers here, and occasionally some newspaper will refer to me as an Armenian writer. But I'm truly grateful.

I smiled at Anna and quickly touched the top of my left breast. The damp patch was expanding. Sorry, I need to go the bathroom, I said, standing up and picking up my tote bag.

Oh good, you brought your pump today, H said. Olivia had to send her back early last night, he announced to the table in general, so she didn't end up flooding Madeleine's poetry salon.

Nobody told me that Madeleine's still running her little parties, Jacob said. How is she?

I retreated to the bathroom and shut the door. It was cramped, all the walls painted red. Sitting on the toilet, I realized that if I pressed my hands against the walls and feet on the door, I could easily elevate myself from the seat. Instead, I assembled the pump and latched the flange on to my breast. In the low and soothing electric beats, I thought of a perpetual motion machine and then imagined a postapocalyptic world where Earth was struck by countless asteroids, and all the creatures were annihilated, all the lands scorched. The last human alive was a woman, who woke up in a deserted cottage without any sustenance at her disposal. Fortunately, this woman was still in her postpartum period. So she found a jar, and began to hand-express from her engorged breasts. And just like Kevin Costner drinking his filtered urine in *Waterworld*, this woman pulled through with her rich-with-protein-enzyme-and-antibody breast milk.

I returned to the table and people had swapped seats. Olivia and Anna were sitting next to each other, whispering. Come sit with Jacob, H said, waving at me. You must talk to Jacob now that you are in Stockholm.

As I slid down onto the designated chair, H stood up to get another round. I tossed my bag on the floor and asked Jacob how he had found the evening so far.

Jacob smiled, his mustache impeccably trimmed. Is it correct that you were expressing your milk in the bathroom?

You'd hope so, I said. Otherwise I must have been critically constipated.

I want to ask you a question if you don't mind.

Certainly, I said. H beamed at me from beside the bar and gave me a thumbs-up.

I'm curious to know what you did with your milk there, Jacob said. Did you dump it, or did you drink it?

I had informed H and Olivia, when I had arrived at the airport, that I was going to drink carelessly for the next two days.

Bless you. H spread his arms wide and squeezed me, which had really hurt my breasts.

Actually, just one day. I need twenty-four hours to detox before I go back to feed the baby.

So how is the baby? Olivia asked. She looked fresh, as if having just stepped out of a shower, her straight black hair glowing.

I had not met Olivia before but had read a great deal about her. Her name is Olivia Tanaka. She's doing a PhD in comparative literature. She speaks four languages, writes fiction in Swedish, poetry in Japanese, and owns the most exquisite pair of tits. It would have been a crime not to sleep with such a woman when the opportunity had presented itself. The email had arrived a couple of days before the baby had been born.

H had been writing me these emails for about eight years, in which he would delineate every woman he'd encounter and then fostered a dalliance with. These emails were meant as preparation for his novel, a book he was planning to write when he turned fifty, about a man who corresponded with an elderly female friend, reminiscing about all the romances he'd had in his youth. I had noted that I was not much older than him. He had responded that it was just fiction.

In the taxi to Madeleine's poetry salon, Olivia and I sat in the back seats. She asked me what kind of fiction I wrote.

Mainly about small towns in China, I said. The unspeakable natures of their residents. Gossiping, bickering, pilfering, and fornication. Basically, a bunch of faithless people indulging in petty crimes.

Olivia thought for a few seconds. Petty crimes, she repeated. Would you see the lack of faith in China as a regrettable consequence of the Cultural Revolution?

H was texting intensely in the passenger's seat. Outside the window, the rain drizzled, the city soaked in darkness.

I tend not to politicize my writing, I said.

Olivia raised her eyebrows slightly. All writing is political, she said. To narrate is to make choices, to cut out the insubstantial and to inaugurate order. Essentially, those who are written onto the page and therefore dominate the narrative hold the power. Wouldn't you agree?

Hey! H turned back from the front. Do you fancy meeting someone while you're here?

I stared at him.

I have a friend who's an illustrious novelist, H said. I was telling him about your event tomorrow and he said he'd come over. Jacob. Jacob is nice, isn't he?

Olivia chuckled, as if hearing a joke. Yes, Jacob's terrific.

Madeleine's apartment was palatial, filled with guests in monochrome clothing. Two blond waiters cruised from room to room, carrying trays of drinks. H had been caught in a conversation as soon as we entered the sitting room. Olivia and I stood in front of a wooden mask and drank our gin and tonic. The mask was erected on a plinth and bore no distinctive gender or racial traits. It seemed expensive.

How do you feel about H's proposal? Une aventure? Olivia asked, studying the mask.

I could sense a hard lump distending insidiously in my left breast and regretted leaving the pump at the hotel.

I suppose he was not entirely presumptuous, by trying to set me up with someone who's not my husband, I said. The other day I was pushing the baby in the park at about seven a.m. He wouldn't stop crying, so I had to take him out of the house even though it was freezing. I saw a piece of rusted bolt by the road, abandoned in the grass. Then I was seized, just in that moment, by this savage craving to get laid.

Olivia looked at me. Wow, she said.

A young woman in a slick bob approached us, holding a notepad and a pen. Hello, ladies, I hope you're enjoying the evening, she said.

Thank you, I said. Can I get a sandwich, please?

The woman seemed baffled.

I think Cara's here to ask us what we're going to read, Olivia said. Hi, Cara, how's it going?

What? I said.

I'm well, thank you. What poems would you like to read later? The young woman gripped the pen, its nib suspended precariously above the pad.

Shall we read together? Olivia said, saving me from the predicament. How about . . . Maybe we could read an Audre Lorde, "Who Said It Was Simple."

Excellent choice. Cara nodded and wrote on the pad. And any preference for the background music?

Jacob laughed so hard he began to cough. He asked me what music we ended up picking.

I can't tell you. It's just embarrassing, I said.

We walked to my hotel, the searing wind blowing in my face.

Jacob had suggested a taxi but I had said, Well, if it's only ten minutes' away.

Now time was being slackened by the frosty air. We passed a brightly lit subway entrance and strolled along the wide, foreboding street. On both sides, the concrete buildings stood in the wind like petrified giants.

So, you're going to Israel?

I am, Jacob said. My second time already. Then I'll be in Buenos Aires in May for a three-week residency. Early June, going from there to Bogotá for a literary festival and then to New York City to visit a few friends. August in Budapest and Warsaw.

You're busy.

I'm in a phased exile, said Jacob. I'm not particularly liked here, just in case you hadn't noticed. The liberal minds of the literary circle aren't open to having a conservative man among them. It's pure ostracism. Anyway, what can an old bachelor do besides drift from one hotel to another? Fine lines, like thistledown, emerged around his eyes when he smiled.

At least sometimes they put you up in good hotels.

That's true, Jacob agreed. Earlier this year, when I went to Macau, I was installed in the most extravagant hotel and taken to Michelin star restaurants. They even gave me free tokens for the casino.

I was there too, I said, checking his profile and his long black coat. Two years ago. Do you know Susie Tse?

Of course I know Susie. She is the sweetest. Jacob gently placed his hand on my shoulder, guiding me to make a turn.

We walked along a small road lined with tall and bare-branched trees, exchanging fond memories of our mutual friend. We realized we'd both been at a festival in Sydney but three years apart. Klara, who had taken care of me in Budapest in 2016, was inviting Jacob to go this year. And in 2015, we were both in Frankfurt. A few times Jacob repeated: What a small world.

He then asked me why I had lived such a life, to be a writer for foreigners instead of for my own countrymen and now dwelling in England. Are you also in some kind of exile? What problems did you have in your country? Did you write censored books? Were you persecuted by your government?

I laughed. Not everything is political. I had some personal issues and made certain choices.

Nothing is personal after modernity. Jacob held my shoulder again. We're all fractions lost in the public machine.

I checked my phone. The hotel was two minutes' walk away from the blue dot that was my projected being. It was nearly midnight. Well, in thirty minutes, I need to pump my milk. Is that personal or public?

Jacob smiled innocuously. The travail of women, he said. But there's lots of hardship in being a man, too.

Like what?

The novelist sighed, halting. For instance, our doomed compulsion to penetrate.

I had not slept since arriving in Stockholm, while the city itself never seemed to be fully awake. The sky would remain hazy for a few brief hours before returning to darkness, in which our exhausted bodies would be hidden, without leaving a trace. Fortunately, since childbirth, I had been used to long, insomniac nights.

After closing the door and kicking off my shoes, I stood alone in my immaculate hotel room, strangely free of the infant's crying, and a formidable fear crushed me like the arrival of a god. Immediately, I regretted my decision not to invite Jacob in and checked my phone for messages.

H had emailed, notifying me about an interview I would be doing tomorrow. He admitted that it was rather a last-minute request. But he thought I could use some company at lunch since he wouldn't be available until 3 p.m.—at which point, he and Olivia would meet me in the hotel lobby and accompany me to the airport. He also congratulated me on the success of the event. It was an absolute delight, he wrote, to see three beautiful and talented women participating in an inspiring and scintillating conversation.

It was hard for me to read H's comment without hearing a note of sarcasm. I could not recall what I had muttered during the event. I had read the opening paragraph of an old story of mine while engaging my core to prevent myself from falling off the murderous stool. I'd also watched my fellow panelists talking, mainly Olivia, since she and I were sitting in symmetrical positions while Anna was two steps back in the middle. Olivia had been wearing bright scarlet lipstick, the contour of her lips beguiling and sensuous as she spoke.

I took care of my breasts, showered, and walked to the guest lounge to make myself a double espresso. The lounge was empty, saturated with a sharp smell of bleach. I sat down on a sofa with my coffee and texted my husband.

In spite of the late hour, he called me back right away. He said he had just given the baby a bottle and rocked him back to sleep and he was now wide awake.

Me, too, I said. I haven't slept since I got here.

You'll be home tomorrow. Then you can rest, he said.

I laughed. How's the baby?

He's good. He only woke up twice last night.

I miss him so much, I said. And I miss you.

We miss you, too, he said. How did the event go?

Disastrously. I totally bombed, exhibiting no intelligence whatsoever. I have truly lost it, you know, the ability to write or to even perform like a writer. I'm simply disgusting. All I think about is feeding cues, clogged ducts, latch, nappies, pee, poop, solid poop, loose poop, and more poop.

It'll get better, my husband said.

You don't know that. I bottoms-upped my coffee.

I do, he insisted.

There is a curious phenomenon that the more ignorant a man is, the more confident he feels, Olivia commented after the male poet finally finished his lengthy lecture on poetry and the screen-reading era during which Olivia and I each downed two gin and tonics.

Doesn't it also apply to women, I said. After all, ignorance is an indiscriminate human condition.

You're right. But women are rarely confident, don't you think? We are more critical of ourselves because we're taught to be considerate of others.

I hailed the waiter who was passing by and asked for two more drinks. I need to sit down, I said.

Madeleine's sitting room was fully occupied. H and a few other guests had formed a tight circle, blocking the doorway to the balcony. Olivia and I went to the dining room, settled in the upholstered leather chairs, and sipped our third or fourth G&T. I told her I would rather not gaze through the lens of gender but see the world as an autonomous individual. Imagine that this cocktail is my fiction, and I, as the writer, am just the thing that contains it. I tapped my glass. All I hope to be is transparent and clean so that the liquid inside will not be obscured or contaminated. In this way, it can be delivered to its drinker as originally devised by its maker. I lifted and finished my gin and tonic.

Olivia winced. I hope you're not talking about God.

Ah no, I said. Remember, I'm Chinese, hence an atheist. But I do believe, in order to write, one needs to be humble and even fearful of a certain higher power.

I agree with you, Olivia said, on the idea of a higher power. *The branches shatter before they bear.* We are all deeply manipulated, in each culture, language, and society. The more marginalized we are from the center, the less we are allowed to talk, write, and think as ourselves. Even you would like to consider yourself an unbiased individual but you are perpetually negotiating with the coercions of collective identities. You're always seen, by others and by yourself, as a woman, a foreigner, an outsider, therefore the subordinate, the inferior, and the inauthentic . . . She stopped, frowning, and pointed at my chest. What's going on with your top?

I had completely forgotten about my breasts and now they had erupted. The milk had soaked through my bra and was permeating my blouse with vigorous force. Oh shit, I said, grabbing a napkin from the table.

Olivia laughed and swiftly downed her drink. Let's get you back to the hotel.

She held my arm and ushered me to the hallway. From the sitting room, the chorus of chattering and debating resounded. We dug out our coats from myriad carcasses of outer garments.

Shall we tell your boyfriend we're going? I asked.

What for? she said. We're all autonomous individuals.

H walked into the lobby in a black parka jacket. He glanced around before meeting my eyes. His face, despite being veiled by a thin smog of fatigue, was irrefutably handsome. He smiled at me, walked over, and sat down in the armchair opposite the coffee table.

How was the interview? he said.

I didn't need to ask him to know that Olivia was not coming. I ended up receiving a tour, I said.

H examined me. You look somewhat different.

I'm just wiped out, I said. Having talked about myself at length.

H disagreed. He said as far as he was concerned, I always seemed enchantingly inexhaustible, more of a river rather than a pond. After all, he had recognized, since the first time we had met, that I was one of those lucky writers who would be reinvigorated by speaking in front of an audience. He asked if he could be candid with me. After receiving my consent, he disclosed that for a long time, he had considered me as someone who was better at performing being a writer than actually writing.

He paused, replying to a message on his phone, and continued to say that I had inspired him so much, in the early days of our friendship, with both my public talks and our private exchanges on literature and writing. He then admitted that he had gone through a lot of trouble to order one of my books online, hoping to gain a deeper insight into the world of literature. However, he had been disappointed.

I was profoundly traumatized, H said. I couldn't believe that I didn't like your book because, honestly, at that point, I thought I had fallen in love with you. He stopped, clasping his hands, and looked at me like a petitioner in a courtroom, waiting for a verdict.

I considered his words. Then the receptionist called to me from the desk. Ms. Zhou, your taxi to the airport is here.

I stood up and thanked them. H took my suitcase and walked out with me. To get to the street, we needed to cross a cobblestone courtyard in which an old laurel tree stood. Its branches spread exuberantly against the taupe walls of the hotel and the flake-white sky. How does it feel to be an evergreen tree in the deep winter? I said, watching my exhalations condensing into murky clouds.

What a blessing to be impervious, said H.

I'm drowning, with the amount of coffee I've taken, I told him. My hands wouldn't stop shaking.

He took one and gave it an affirming squeeze. You'll survive, he said.

Later, sitting in the back seat of the taxi beside H, who was immersed in his phone, I was reminded, by our brief bodily contact, of a perfunctory kiss between us in the summer of 2008 and, while my nose had been pressed tightly against his face, a tenuous yet distinct scent that emanated from him. The smell was neither pleasant nor repellent, and I had never detected it since.

It was completely dark outside. The taxi shot along the gloomy highway, lit up occasionally by the oncoming vehicles returning to the city. In the sky above us, small red lights glinted as planes passed like albatrosses. I asked H if he planned to send me more emails.

He looked up from his phone. I don't know, he said. Things are going well between me and Olivia. But to say I'll never love another woman or that she'll never love another man seems obtuse, even hubristic. Who am I to assert, at this point, that our sexuality should be fully taken custody of by a contract of confinement and potentially to be absorbed in the solemn function of reproduction? He glanced at me the way a professor might take notice of his pupil during a lecture and, as if just remembering him, he said: Oh, speaking of which, how's Liam?

Without waiting for my response, H carried on expressing, enthusiastically, his admiration for my husband's work. He said the first time he had truly enjoyed my novel was when reading my husband's translation of it. Although he was not certain whether it was because Liam had triumphed in domesticating my impetuous style, or because, in English—his adopted language—his own perception had become untrustworthy. Nonetheless, H said, I often regard your relationship with Liam as a model one, a perfect union that will extend both your genes and fame.

I folded my hands together to stop them from shivering and thought of my husband and the baby. I thought I'd better pump my breasts before boarding the airplane. I thought I'd better find a clean and quiet bathroom cubicle and extract my milk with the machine. Then I would pour it down the toilet and flush it away. Yet, by the time I reached Heathrow, my once-emptied breasts would be replenished with milk, like a forever-flowing river.

———

When the interview had finished, the young man from the website had asked me if I wanted to go see the lake. He brought it up rather casually, while turning off the recording device and putting his notebook and pen back into his satchel, but the question felt momentous.

I knocked back my second coffee before asking him whether the lake was another inexplicable signifier, like the Swedish word he had left on the back of my hand.

He looked up from his bag. No. He smiled. I meant literally *hu*, as in we are on an island and surrounded by lakes.

I didn't know this.

You have to see it to believe it, the young man said, standing up from the sofa. His face was gaunt and pale, no different from when I last saw him at the bookstore, except the dark circles under his eyes had grown even more dire.

We walked out of the café together and descended the sloping, narrow street. The buildings on both sides were tall, creating a sense of oppression. It was midday and there were a number of pedestrians on the street. When I looked at them looking at us, I wondered what speculations they were making about the relationship between me and my companion. The young man had been quiet for a while. In fact, everybody passed by in incredible silence. A man carried groceries, a woman held her phone against her ear, and a young couple pushed a black buggy. There was no sound of chatting or whispering nor the slightest shuffling of soles, as if we were all actors in a mime show. I could not be certain if there was an infant in the pushchair.

The young man gestured to turn into a small alleyway between two large buildings and we walked on in single file until the edifices vanished. I stood facing an opening of wild land. Tall, shriveled grass swarmed up around us, and a muddy path wound towards the rugged rising mound in the distance.

Is this the right way to go? I asked, breaking the long-sustained silence, my lips stinging in the cold air.

It's a shortcut, he said.

I glanced at my interviewer, who was much taller than me. His jawline was sharp and bony, reminding me of a crowbar. I thought of my husband, holding and cooing the baby, as he read online the news that a Chinese woman writer had been murdered in Stockholm, her body bagged and buried in the weeds.

We carried on walking along the path. The clouds thickened. The sun dimmed to a smudged circle. Do you miss speaking Mandarin? he asked me.

I try not to, I said.

I have to admit I was a little bit disappointed at the event, he said, smiling apologetically. You didn't talk in Chinese. And you only read the English translation of your story.

My chest was swelling up again hopelessly. I did speak Chinese at the event, I told him. Thanks to you I said lanshan.

He chuckled. Right, the blue mountains.

We began to walk up the hill along the stone steps. Gray lilac flowers pushed their way through the cracks in the stones. Blotches of dry dwarf shrubs were scattered across the mound. A few seagulls hovered above us, drawing invisible lines in the sky. When we finally reached the top, a massive body of water filled the panorama before us, like a cosmos of blue ashes.

On the other side of the water floated a string of elongated islands, on which varicolored buildings stood next to one another.

Rising above them were the copper domes of cathedrals, their bright patinas gleaming through the mist.

We stood watching a white ferry move slowly across the lake. Beneath the overcast sky, the whiteness of the ferry seemed other-worldly, making me think of Charon. In Chinese mythology, the one who would help the deceased cross the river to the afterlife was a woman. She would take you to a raised terrace from which you could look back to the world of the living one last time, before you drained the soup of forgetting and traveled to the underworld.

Can I tell you something?

The abrupt utterance startled me. Of course, I said.

He told me that during his last year in China as an exchange student, he had lived in my home city, C. Through an online forum popular among the homosexual community, he had met a local man who was about ten years older than him. Soon he began to see this man regularly. They would meet in a pub, have a few drinks, go to a cheap hotel, and have sex. One night, in the middle of intercourse, the man, who'd had too much drink, started to shudder. Realizing his lover might be having a seizure, the young man tried to call an ambulance, but the older man gripped the phone and assured him he would be better soon. However, it didn't happen like that. Shortly afterwards, the Chinese man died in the hotel room while my inter-viewer fled, leaving the country on a red-eye flight.

After returning to Stockholm, the young man told me, he had searched on the internet and read in the *C— City Evening News* that his lover's body was found in the hotel room the next day and sent to the hospital. His pregnant wife had come to identify the corpse and had wailed in devastation until she passed out.

———

In the taxi back to the hotel, Olivia and I had laughed so irrepressibly the driver checked on us in the rearview mirror. Oh my god. She wheezed, her body shaking like an aeroplane about to crash. This is the funniest story I've ever heard.

I know, I cackled, pressing the milk-soaked napkin on my chest as if I'd been shot.

The taxi arrived. Olivia tapped her card and climbed out of the sedan with me. The world swirled as I stood up straight while Olivia clutched on to my arm to steady herself. I think I'm getting sick, she said. Urgh, too much fun and alcohol.

Do you want to come in and use my bathroom? I asked her.

Is it okay? If you don't mind. She crunched her face. Her black hair was mussed and stuck to her cheek.

We stumbled across the courtyard, passing the laurel tree, and down the corridor into my room. Olivia went straight to the bathroom and shut the door while I unhooked my bra and dug out the breast pump from my suitcase.

Shortly after I had switched to my left breast, Olivia reemerged from the bathroom. She looked renewed, her face luminous, her long, slick hair draping down her shoulders.

Did you just vomit in there, or were you taking a beauty nap? I said, sitting in the armchair and holding the flange in one hand and the motor in the other like a woman warrior with her sword and shield.

Olivia ignored my joke. Instead, she stared at my breast, which was being repeatedly tugged into the plastic tunnel of the flange, the motor beating. A stream of pale liquid plunged into the half-full bottle, spattering before more ensued.

Holy shit, Olivia said, walking to the armchair and sitting down cross-legged right in front of me. She held her chin with both hands and looked up at me like a child. This is amazing, she said. So powerful and poetic.

It's more like clogged ducts and mastitis, I said.

She didn't respond, but watched my milk amassing in the cylindrical container. I don't think I'll ever have a child, she said. But this is something else. You should write about it.

What? I said. No. How can I write about *this?*

Olivia frowned. Of course you can, she said. In fact, you must. You must write about this—she raised her hands towards my chest—the only reason you feel you can't write about it is because you don't think it's worth being written about. And the only reason you think lactation is not literature is because it has been cut out, for centuries, from the literary narrative. And who has ordained for us the distinctions between the canon and the censored, the classic and the vulgar, the speech and the noise?—she let out a burp—So I say now: You must write your boobs into literature. Make them heard. The need to redistribute the perceptible is pressing and we must take action *now*.

God, you're wasted, I said, shaking my head.

She laughed. We giggled intermittently until my milk filled the bottle and I turned off the motor. Gazing at the light-white liquid, Olivia sprang up, fetched a pair of glasses, and divided the milk into two portions, which we each drained in one long haul.

Afterwards, we sat on the floor, leaning against each other and began to talk. She told me about her childhood in Nagasaki, her short-lived career as a Japanese teen model in Sweden, and the time, when she was an undergraduate in the States, a professor asked her to touch his penis. I told her that, speaking of penises, I remembered when I had been about five years old and was taking a nap with my grandfather one day, he had drawn my hand onto his erection. Although I could not be one hundred percent sure if it had actually happened. Nonetheless, my counselor had concluded that this incident was the root of my low self-esteem, which had then deteriorated into body dysmorphia after the birth of my child. I was disgusted by the smell of my armpits, the fat on my abdomen, my cracked and blistered nipples, and most sickeningly of all my cut-and-sewn-back vagina.

When I had confessed this to the counselor, I said to Olivia, she asked me to take a look at my vagina when I got home. She said I needed to embrace the changes in my body as the first step towards healing. Then I told her these days I only had time to embrace the baby.

So, did you look at it?

Of course not, I said. Why would I do that?

After pausing for a few seconds, Olivia asked me if she could check it for me. It might help, she said, if I received, instead of the visual image in the mirror, a description in words. After all, I had been intimate with words for years.

I thought about her proposal. It does make sense, I replied.

Then I pulled myself up from the floor, climbed onto the bed, removed my pants, and parted my legs before Olivia. She smiled at me, craned her head, and, after a long and careful gaze, kissed my labia.

FREE WANDERING

The moment I open my eyes, a savage pain cuts through my body. Fucking Christ. I push myself up. Sitting beside me is a foreign woman, her skin white as a sheet, her irises unreally blue, almost like glass. She stares at me.

"We're nearly there now," she says, to my surprise, in Mandarin. "You might want to put that on." She points at a yellow safety helmet on my lap, its surface badly scuffed, its strap broken.

I follow her instruction. The bus we are in is freezing and reeks of urine and blood. Outside the window, fluorescent light flashes in a long white tunnel.

"Where are we?" I ask my neighbor.

"Crossing the river," she says.

The hair on the back of my neck stands up. "The river?"

She gives me a look. "We are in the underwater tunnel. Should get to the City soon." She shows me the map on her phone, on which a blue dot is moving along a thin stripe connecting two planks of land.

Then I remember. Getting out my old Nokia, I text my cousin. Hi Linda, I'm arriving soon. See you at the bus terminal?

"I can't believe I'm actually here," I say.

"I know," my neighbor agrees, swiping her screen. "Guess you're super excited to see your cousin, huh? You two haven't met for how long now? Ten years?"

Jesus, I have to stop oversharing. "Fifteen years."

"Wow, you think you'll recognize each other?"

"Here." I retrieve a folded photo from my trouser pocket. "It's us when we were thirteen."

She leans over. "What a cute pair. And you took this at the Statue?"

I tell her it is only a fake. The photo was taken in a theme park that my cousin and I visited before she left China. "She promised when I came to the City, she'd take me to the real thing."

My neighbor cracks up. "Don't get your hopes up. It won't be much different from this one." She taps my photo.

My cousin is not at the bus terminal. She's still in a meeting and texts me to wait for her at M— department store. Take any southbound line and get off at 34 St. Then M— is just one block away, you can't miss it.

All the other passengers have disembarked. I grab my backpack and walk out of the terminal.

In my twenty-eight years, I've never left my hometown, let alone arrive in another continent and now the City. Nonetheless, I have seen it myriad times, images collected from the movies, magazines, and documentaries. In my mind's eye, I have always pictured the City as a panorama, towards which I would glide from the sky.

In the light of the setting sun, all the high-rises would stand along the river, glinting like giant fish leaping out of water, their windows silver scales.

In reality, when I enter the City from the ground, walking along the concrete sidewalk, there is no glorious light but a hellish gust of wind that nearly blows away my helmet. A mechanical screaming blasts overhead. Pressing down my helmet, I scurry back and forth along the narrow streets, looking for a subway entrance.

Pedestrians shoot past me like wild horses, imperturbable determination written on their faces, which thwarts my attempts to ask for directions.

"Watch where you're going!" somebody shouts at me.

"Sorry!" I hop aside before being shoved over by the oncoming person.

I struggle to catch my breath. Then I see across the road, outside a building enclosed by scaffolding and netting, a large letter M gleaming in gold like a miracle.

McDonald's.

I scuttle inside, carrying the backpack in which I've brought my late grandmother's last batch of homemade spicy cabbage pickles—a present for my cousin—in a carefully wrapped lunchbox. And I suspect, from the distrustful looks I get as I enter, that the pickle juice might have leaked from the supposed-to-be-airtight lunchbox. I decide not to check.

Sitting down at an empty table, I remove my backpack. Before me, the large window frames a rectangular screen, showing the same swarming scene on the street, only, through the glass, the image seems flat and serene, even hypnotizing.

Am I really here now, in the City? I steady myself against a sudden and paralyzing exhaustion.

My phone rings. It's my cousin. And she says, in a sweet voice, that she's at M— department store and has searched through three floors and only seen an oldish Chinese man who also happens to be bald. "Don't tell me that's you."

I apologize, explaining I have ended up in a McDonald's.

"All right," she says. "Got ya. Stay where you are. I'll see you in a minute."

Yawning, I flip through our exchanges on my phone while waiting.

So great to hear from you, cuz, one of her early messages reads. What have you been doing all these years? Can't wait to catch up soon.

The door to the McDonald's clanks. A group of tourists flock in. All of them look Chinese and wear identical orange vests. They quickly occupy a number of tables, unzip their suitcases, take out white buns and jars of spicy pickles, and, with a loud munching sound, begin to eat.

As I watch them, saliva surging, I realize that I actually know these people. They are my co-workers, their vests crossed by hi-vis reflective stripes.

One of them turns and looks me up and down. "Do I know you?" he asks, in my local dialect.

Seeing clearly that he's my foreman, I freeze as he gets up and walks towards me. "Wait, are you that scaffolder? Why are you here? Shouldn't you be with us, going to the renovation project at the Empire Building?"

"I, I'm not," I mutter, my face hot. "I'm here to see my cousin. You must have mistaken me for someone else."

The foreman laughs. "You're not very good at lying, kid. And what is your name again? Xiao . . . Xiao . . ."

"Xiao Peng! Xiao Peng!" a man's voice calls in Mandarin.

With a jitter, I wake up.

A Chinese man is standing in front of me, wearing a corduroy jacket. His face hides behind a pair of black-framed glasses and a head of mussed medium-length hair. I can't tell if he's older than me or around my age. But he is smiling at me.

"Are you Xiao Peng? Linda Chow's cousin," he asks.

"Yes, I am." I wipe the dribble from my mouth.

"Good." The strange man nods. "Linda needs to run because there's a situation. She asked me to come here to pick you up and bring you to meet her at a party in Borough Q——."

I stare at his face, which remains obscured behind the glasses and beneath his hair. My ears are burning under the gaze of other customers, among who—I suspect irrationally—are the builders from my dream.

"I'll go with you," I say.

"Excellent." The man picks up my backpack. "We'd better leave now. The F line's ridiculous. Have you eaten?"

I tell him yes and walk out of McDonald's. The daylight is now gloomy, the street busier than before. The crying of sirens interweaves with the thrumming of helicopters, the pavement flooded by people.

"Come on! Xiao Peng!" Before I know it, the man skips into the stream of pedestrians, and I follow, fixing my eyes on his back and my khaki rucksack he's carrying. We arrive at a narrow iron gate leading to a flight of stairs extending downwards. The man stops abruptly. He turns back and steadies my shoulder as I'm about to stumble.

"By the way," he says. "My name is Simon. And you should know I'm totally trustworthy."

The subterranean world is long and narrow, cluttered with humans, pervaded by the stench of perished food. Right away, I regret my decision. I should have told Simon that I am actually starving.

At the thought, hunger wrings my stomach like a python. But there's no way to turn back. One by one, the passengers are drawn in by the cold arms of the turnstiles and gulped into the deep, low-ceilinged tunnels. We congregate like overcooked dumplings, countless heads, hair, and shoulders melting into each other.

Where the hell is Simon?

More people flush in from behind, sweeping me down to the end of the staircase, where the tunnel forks. I feel I might be sick as the mass swirls around me before rushing out in two opposite directions.

"Xiao Peng!" I hear Simon calling. "This way!" I try to turn, but my body is trapped in the left-surging current, crushed and heaved by frenzied commuters. "Xiao Peng!" The calling is moving farther away.

Suddenly, a ridiculous terror seizes me. No, no, I don't want to die here.

"Excuse me!" I call out, in English, pushing my arms in front of me, trying to squeeze through tangled human limbs and torsos. I hold on to my helmet. "Excuse me, please!" My tears are welling up when finally, forced out from the passageway, I land on the solid surface of the platform, panting.

About a dozen passengers are dotted along the platform. Simon is standing at the far end, waving at me with a grin.

"Ah, thank goodness!" I dash towards him. "I thought I'd lost you."

Three tall and well-built men stand coolly and squint at me as I pass by. I look away. Beside the platform, the hollow subway tunnel extends into the darkness.

"Watch out, Xiao Peng!" The next moment, I trip on something and plummet to the ground, my helmet flying off. With a piercing pain, my head hits the concrete. The three men roar. Their laughter almost sounds like cries of horror.

Footsteps approach. The helmet rattles away. The aroma of my grandmother's home-made pickles. "Nainai . . ." I mumble before passing out.

I open my eyes in dim orange light. The space smells faintly of sandalwood—the very scent that used to diffuse through my grandmother's apartment. But I can tell, by the width of the bed I'm lying in and the height of the ceiling above me, that I'm elsewhere.

I prop myself up. On the opposite wall hangs a long calligraphy scroll, on which is spread an enormous character: 鯤.

I can't recognize it. Blinking, I try again, scrutinizing it stroke by stroke, only to see its radicals orbiting away from each other, turning into a senseless heap. My head aches violently as if it has just been stapled back together.

Where the hell am I? What happened? Did I break my head open somewhere?

A knock comes through the door. Followed by another.

The door opens and a man walks in. He is my build but could be slightly taller. He wears a pair of glasses; his hair is tied to the back of his head.

"How are you feeling, Xiao Peng?" he asks.

I look at him in a daze.

"I'm Simon," he says. "Your cousin's friend. We just met at McDonald's. We were taking the subway to Borough Q——. Then you passed out."

The images flash before my eyes: the white tunnel, the towering buildings and the scaffolding, the big, glowing window and my yellow helmet, the dark underground world. I see myself dropping to the ground like a stone.

"Kun," I say.

"What?"

"The character." I gesture towards the scroll. "It's kun, right?"

Simon inspects the suspended calligraphy. "Right," he says. "Not many people know this character. It's from Zhuangzi."

"*In the northern darkness there is a fish whose name is Kun. Its size so immense that I don't know how many thousand miles it extends,*" I spew out the lines.

"Wow, that's impressive."

I tell him that, back at high school, "Free Wandering" was my favorite essay in Chinese class.

"It was my favorite too," he says. "Do you want to eat? I cooked some fish balls."

My stomach lets out a croak.

He laughs and guides me to the living room, which is fairly big. A floor lamp glows in the corner. Three tall windows reach up to the ceiling, letting in the soft light from the street. I feel like I'm walking into an underwater palace.

"Sit, please." Simon reappears with two bowls. I settle myself in an armchair and take one.

The pearl-white fish balls are cooked in a clear soup, seasoned with soy sauce and sesame oil, and topped with finely chopped spring green leaves.

Without a word, we eat. When I finish, I exude a long sigh and tell Simon that my grandmother used to make me these when I got full marks at school. "And every time, I had to save some for my cousin who never did great in exams." Then I remember. "Aren't we supposed to meet Linda?"

"Yes, we were," my host says, and explains he has messaged my cousin to let her know about the accident and told her that he carried me back to his place since I was unconscious. "Perhaps you should give her a call now?" He stacks up the empty bowls and leaves the room.

I call my cousin. Right away, she picks up.

"Xiao Peng, you poor thing!" she calls out. "Simon said you fell in the subway."

"On the platform," I say. "I tripped on something."

"Eew!" she says. In the background, I hear hubbub and laughter.

"I'm okay now," I say. "Tell me, how shall I get to your place? You can just text me the address, I'll figure out the rest."

"About that"—she pauses—"I'm sorry, cuz, I meant to tell you earlier, but I didn't want to sound unwelcome plus I didn't want to jinx it—but, actually, my boyfriend Stanley just moved in with me—and this is a really big step for us, you know? So I'm not sure if it's a good idea for you to crash on my sofa right now . . ."

While my cousin talks, my eyes alight on the vista outside the window. The City's signature skyscrapers are glittering, piling on top of one another into the distance, where their silhouettes blur, suffusing into the dark, cloudless sky.

My heart palpitates with a strange uneasiness. Did I forget something, something very important?

Into my ear rings my cousin's disembodied voice: ". . . What do you think, Xiao Peng? Will it be okay? Simon said there's no problem for you to stay with him. But of course, if you still don't feel comfortable, you can come here to my place. I'll explain to Stanley, he'll understand."

"It's okay," I say, getting up from the armchair and pacing towards the window. Outside, almost at my fingertips, the canopy of a nameless tree is rattling, its wide leaves catching the early autumn breeze and the streetlight below.

I tell my cousin not to worry. "I'll stay at Simon's and let's meet in town tomorrow."

In the morning, I wake up with a tightness in my chest as if having spent the whole night underwater. I put on my clothes and walk out of the bedroom.

A metallic noise blares down the corridor. In the kitchen, Simon is standing in front of the counter, topless, operating a food blender. His hair is tied up into a high bun, sweat dribbling down his back. Thick white vapors rise from a black pot on the hob. At the other end of the counter, a great pile of things lies in disarray:

glass jars of red and yellow powders, white and purple crystals, bundles of dried herbs, a velvet antler, and other parts of unidentifiable animals.

The food blender stops. Simon turns around, his face flushed and clammy with sweat. "Xiao Peng!"

"Good morning," I say reluctantly.

"Come in!" He waves at me.

"What are you busy with here?" I step into the kitchen.

"Cooking meds." He pours the sludge into the pot and closes the lid. "What would you like for breakfast?"

"Uh, coffee?" I say, swallowing. "I'm not really hungry."

"Come on! A big man like you needs to eat more," Simon says, opening the double-door fridge and taking out an armful of food. Then he begins to cook, to my relief, normal-looking steamed buns and noodles.

He moves around the kitchen while chatting with me, asking if I slept well last night and if I have any dietary requirements.

I tell him I have been feeling tired since I arrived, possibly because of the jet lag, and I eat everything.

The food is brought to the table, all in impressive quantity. My host sits down across from me with a large white plastic bottle that seems to contain nutritional supplements.

Still flushed, he drains half a glass of water before screwing open the bottle. "Now, this is good for fatigue." He scoops out a full spoon of brown powder and, before I react, dumps it into my breakfast.

I watch the powder dissolve into my noodles, which have been topped with minced pork. "What is this?"

"Cold Food Powder," he says, shaking another spoon into his

own bowl. "But it makes you sweat, brilliant to take in the morning to get a full day of energy."

I wait for him to eat a few bites before digging into mine. "Thank you. It's delicious. It reminds me of the noodles from this old shop in my hometown."

My host nods, gobbling. "So tell me, Xiao Peng, did you come all the way here just to see Linda?"

"Um," I say, swallowing the food in my mouth. "No, of course not. I'm here for work. I'm participating in the renovation project at the Empire Building."

Simon cracks up. "Good man," he says. "The Empire Building, if you don't mind. So you're an architect or something?"

"Sort of," I mumble as a heat rises from my guts. I bury my face in the bowl.

We continue our breakfast. The hotness in my body intensifies as if something is burning out of my chest. To distract myself, I ask Simon why he came to the City and what he does for a living.

"I came here in the eighties, pursuing a PhD in history—history," he repeats in a sarcastic tone. "Long story short, I didn't get the doctorate and now work in palliative care."

"What does that mean?"

"It means I deal with people who are on their way out," he says, and chuckles when he sees the expression on my face. "No need to feel sorry for me, Xiao Peng. We all came here for one thing and ended up with another. And I actually enjoy spending time with my clients and getting to know their life stories. It turns out that rather than fabricating a collective narrative as a historian, I prefer archiving personal memories." He stands up, walks to the hob to switch off the flame. "I need to run now. Got an early appointment today. What's your plan?"

I tell him my cousin and I are meeting near her office for lunch.

"Excellent," he says, wrapping the pot up carefully and lowering it into an insulated bag. "Before I forget: the spare key should be in the drawer of your nightstand. The Wi-Fi and the gate code to the lobby are written on the fridge. To get to midtown you can either take the subway or the bus. But I guess you'd probably prefer the bus after yesterday. The stop is by the Avenue, on the side of the Park, one block to the west. You can't miss it."

Outside the empty lobby, the street is quiet. The dove-gray buildings are old and tall, obscuring the sunlight from above. Marveling at the edifices, I recall my conversation with Simon earlier. Me, an architect? I shake my head as I walk on.

I must have seen a similar story in a movie: the poverty-stricken young man arrives in a city and is mistaken for someone else and, instead of clarifying the miscomprehension, he reinvents himself and embarks on the journey towards a great future.

As if echoing my thoughts, the Park emerges gloriously at the end of the road, beyond the bustling Avenue. Under the azure sky, its renowned autumn foliage blooms. The florid leaves flutter in the sunlight, their colors dramatic and vivid, as if enhanced by a filter.

Mesmerized, I pause. My phone rings. It's my cousin.

"You wouldn't believe what I'm looking at," I say.

"The traffic?" she says. "If you're crossing a road."

I tell her I am indeed about to get the other side of the Avenue to catch the bus to midtown.

"Oh, good," she says. "I just found out that I have an early meeting in the afternoon, so make sure you get here before twelve."

"It should be okay." I check the time on the phone. "I've got nearly two hours."

My cousin agrees. "If you get lost again or something," she adds, "you can always ask for directions. Call me to put me on the phone if you need me to talk to the other person, you know?"

"No worries. I speak English, at least the basics."

"Of course." She chuckles. "I forgot you're the brainy one. See you in a bit, then. You are gonna love this Korean place I'm taking you to. Their kimchi tastes exactly like what Granny used to make."

Ah no, the cabbage pickles. Hanging up the phone, I realize I've left the present at Simon's place. At least I haven't gone too far.

As I return to Simon's place, in the opposite direction, the scene along the street looks somewhat different. A nervousness accumulates in my stomach. I tell myself to relax. Before long, I see the familiar gray facade of the apartment building, the elegant cornice above the entrance. On the wrought-iron gate, a slim code lock blinks slowly red.

The gate code. Christ, did Simon say something about the gate code? Now my stomach is cramping.

"Excuse me." A small woman in a pink tracksuit walks up, Southeast Asian–looking, a grocery bag dangling from her arm. She presses the code into the lock without looking at me. The gate clicks open.

Relieved, I follow her into the lobby and she swivels around. "May I help you? All parcels should be dropped off at the back gate."

"Huh." I swallow, searching my head for a good answer in English. "I, I live here, in Five B."

Her almond eyes widen like a chihuahua. "No way," she says. "I'm the vice chairwoman of the residents' committee of this building. And I don't recall receiving any applications for new tenants."

What is she saying? "Sorry, what . . ."

"Jackie? Jackie!" she barks into the lobby and a dark-skinned Asian man in a claret uniform appears. "Hello, Mrs. Goldman," the man says, waving. "I was just helping Mr. Levin get his wheelchair into the lift."

"Do you know this man? He says he lives in Mr. Chow's apartment," the woman asks.

The doorman examines me. He has a big nose, his eyebrows thick like weeds. I have never seen him before.

"I have never seen him before," he says.

Sitting on the couch, I stare at the vacant doorway from the doorman's cabin. The doorman himself is in the lobby, talking on the phone in a language I don't understand.

The chihuahua-like woman instructed him to escort me here and to watch me while she reports the incident to the chairperson.

On the wall, there's a large poster of three broad-shouldered men in white jerseys and black caps standing in a row. In their hands are long wooden bats. Beside the poster hangs a clock, its ticking sound prodding my head.

Time. Time is running out.

I get up and slink out of the cabin. The doorman has his back to me as he laughs into his phone. The marble tiles are lustrous, leading me to the exit.

The elevator door opens, and the chihuahua-like woman walks out with another person who is almost made invisible by the long black coat they are wearing. "Jackie," Chihuahua says. "You're supposed to be watching him."

Shoving the phone into his pocket, the doorman turns back to me. "Hey! You're supposed to stay inside!"

"Sorry." I retreat to my seat.

The chairperson enters and sits down on the chair by the desk, followed by the deputy and the doorman, who stand guard either side of their superior.

"This is Mrs. Walsh, the chairwoman of our committee," Chihuahua says.

I look up. The woman in the middle is old, and strikingly East Asian–looking. Her face is long and haggard, run through with countless deep creases. One of her eyes bulges, a translucent white film clouding its iris.

I freeze.

The old woman turns to her deputy. "So this is the Chinaman you mentioned." Her voice is weak and gruff, just like the way I remember.

"Nainai!" I call out.

The trio looks startled. "Could you speak English, please?" Chihuahua says.

"Nainai, it's me!" I cry in Chinese. "I'm Xiao Peng, your grandson! Please let me go, I need to meet Linda for lunch!"

The old woman sits like a statue, unimpressed. Only her eyebrows move, wringing violently against each other. "What is he growling about?" she asks the doorman.

The dark-skinned man purses his lips. "Honestly, I don't quite know. I only speak Cantonese. He seems to be saying something about a Linda?"

"Never mind Linda," the chairwoman announces. "You'll be here with us for as long as this investigation takes." She watches me with her one good eye.

Her gaze makes me shiver. I look away. On the wall, the clock reads *11:40*. Oh no. "Look, I have to go!" I shout the words to drum up my courage. "I'm sorry but I'm running late. I need to leave now!"

As soon as I get up, the doorman darts over like a tiger and thrusts me back into the chair, his arm tough as iron. I blast out a long series of coughs.

"God, this thug's trying to escape! Keep him under control, Jackie," Chihuahua says.

Isn't this a bit too theatrical, I think in a trance as the doorman crushes down on my chest, forcing more coughs out of me. A sour taste rises from my stomach. I shudder, sinking into the chair.

Jackie glowers at me. He might have loosened his arm, but the air around me nonetheless continues to drain no matter how hard I inhale. "Please, Nainai, please . . ." I murmur in gasps, eyeing the old woman.

Frowning again, Mrs. Walsh pushes herself up.

"Chairwoman, you stay back!" In spite of her deputy's warning, she walks over and stands right in front of me. She watches me, drops of turbid liquid leaking out of her sick eye, her face exactly like my grandmother's.

"Don't you try to get rid of me," she says. "We're stuck with each other."

Tears pour from my sockets. I try again to breathe in, but my chest spasms as if something is thrusting from inside. I retch, sticking out my tongue involuntarily. A rancid reek permeates the cabin.

"Jesus, Mary, and Joseph." Mrs. Walsh recoils, crossing herself. Chihuahua bursts out screaming.

A man strides in. He is wearing a tunic suit and a pair of fine golden-framed glasses. His grizzled hair is combed back.

"Xiao Peng!" Simon kneels down beside me. Swiftly, he retrieves the stone pot from the insulation bag, digs out a small lump of black balm with his little finger, and feeds it into my mouth. Then he grips my arms, holding them down, as if preventing them from exploding.

"What the heck? Carol and Helena?" he asks my interrogators. "This is my friend who's a very reputable architect. He's in town for a job at the Empire Building and is staying with me. Now what do you have to say for detaining someone like this for no good reason?"

The balm dissolves behind my teeth and slowly the shiver recedes, air traveling up my nose. "S-Simon," I mutter as my host turns to me, my shrunken reflections in his dark pupils: pale and defeated. "I'm gonna miss my lunch with Linda."

"Don't be too hard on yourself." Simon pushes open the front door of the apartment. "I mixed them up all the time when I first came here. *Stay, live, live, stay*—they're confusing. The only person to blame is that old crow."

"I can't believe I made such a stupid mistake. I used to be good at English. It's just that I haven't practiced for ages." I follow him into the kitchen, still trying to shake off the physical resemblance between the chairwoman and my late grandmother.

"It's not your fault. That woman is getting increasingly insufferable since her husband died." Simon opens the fridge and shoves in the black pot. "Something to eat?"

I tell him I'm not hungry and text my cousin. My lengthy apology disappears with a whooshing sound.

"Linda's probably back at work now." Simon sits down beside the dining table with two cans of Tsingtao, pushing one over to me.

I stare at my phone, cold and silent. "Maybe I'll never see her again."

"You just got here yesterday," Simon says. "You are going to see her when you see her. Don't beat yourself up about it. It's not like this is the most important thing in the world."

"It kind of is." I open my can and take a swig. "It was the last thing my grandma wanted, to see my cousin again. She was in so much pain, that tumor in her head pressing her optic nerves, giving her hell. And that was probably why she began to see her— my cousin—and she'd talk to her as if she were right there in the room. *Linlin, you're back*, she'd say. *I thought I'd never see you again*. I can still hear it now, *Linlin, Linlin*, my grandma crying the name, again and again." I stop, a lump in my throat.

My host sighs. "You poor kid," he says. "I hear you. But you needn't feel dejected. As long as your grandmother believed in their reunion, didn't she die without regrets? Besides, she was fortunate that you were there with her. Trust me, I've seen too many people, who, as they drew their last breath, had no one around."

For some reason, his words stir up tension in the pit of my stomach. "It must be the most terrifying thing, to die by yourself."

Simon takes a gulp. "Yes and no," he says. "It depends on how you view the idea of death. Think about this: when Zhuangzi's wife dies, he celebrates. He sings and drums on an upturned basin."

I glance at him. "I've been actually thinking about that story a lot myself. But I couldn't get it. Isn't it a bit insane?"

"It makes perfect sense," says Simon. "The way Zhuangzi saw it, we don't really live our lives. Instead, life is just a brief stop on our long, infinite journey. Our transformation into life is merely an accident and it is our ultimate destiny to be released back to nature by our death. You must have heard of this: *The Way that can be told is not the true Way; the Name that can be named is not the true Name. It is from the Nameless that heaven and earth spring, while the Named is the mother that rears the tens of thousands of creatures . . .*"

"Is it the *Tao Te Ching*?"

"That's right!" He claps. "You see, we're made who we are by our names. In the beginning, all of us are adrift, without forms or spirits, and then we are given names, and henceforth confined in the set idea of self, ego, and desire. Now, the good thing is, when you die, you are given the chance to be nameless again, to free yourself from the prison of self and become one with nature, where you can breathe with the sun and the moon and thrive between heaven and earth—you get what I mean?"

"Uh . . . no," I say, emptying my can. "Do you think perhaps I should go into town now and wait for my cousin until she finishes work?"

He laughs. "Come on, Xiao Peng! Did you not hear what I just said? Forget about your cousin for now and focus on yourself instead, will you? I say you need to rest after that whole drama. Plus, the medicine I gave you will make you drowsy soon. How about this: I'll invite Linda to come here for dinner tomorrow, so you don't need to worry about it." He finishes his beer and throws the can into the bin.

Watching the perfect parabola, I feel my eyelids grow rapidly heavy as if being weighed down by stones. I let out a yawn.

"Right." Simon stands up. "So it's settled. I'll contact Linda about dinner tomorrow and you go take a nap."

I thank him for his help and walk to the guest bedroom. My bed is made, its surface smooth like a breezeless pond. I collapse into it.

●

It is bright outside when I wake up. The City hums with traffic. Fetching my phone from the nightstand, I check the time.

9:21 a.m.

Have I slept for almost a whole day? Is it the medicine? Jet lag? Or is time going faster since I got here?

There are two messages from my cousin. Sorry to hear you were lost again, she says. Do you not have a smartphone? The second one was sent right after midnight: Simon suggested it might be easier for us to come to you. So Stanley and I will join you for dinner. See you then.

It did not occur to me until now that I am going to meet both my cousin and her boyfriend. The revelation jolts me wide awake. I spring up from the bed.

Simon is not in the apartment. On the dining table sit a small pot of congee, the white plastic bottle, and a note that tells me he had to leave early because of an emergency at work.

I sink right into the chair and mix a spoonful of brown powder into the melted rice before beginning to cram the sustenance into my mouth. My chest is lit up, my consciousness revitalized with each gulp, seeping like water through every inch of my skin.

I take a shower, shave, and change into some fresh clothes my host has thoughtfully left by my nightstand: a fine white shirt, a pair of beige trousers, and buff-colored leather sneakers.

In the elevator, the Chihuahua-like woman, now in a full white outfit, is on her phone. She looks up when I step in.

"Morning, Helena," I greet her in English.

She is taken aback for a second. "Oh, hi! Sha . . . shao . . ."

"Actually, you can call me Little Roc," I say.

"Little Roc!" She smiles. "What a cool name. And I nearly didn't recognize you. You look sharp today."

"Thank you."

"So tell me, Little Roc, what kind of work are you involved in at the Empire Building? My father-in-law used to work there."

I tell her it's something rather basic and she calls me too modest. We chat as the lift descends and cracks open at the lobby.

"Could you tell me how I get to the Statue?" I ask her as we walk out to the street, where the sun is shining. The air smells new, full of life.

"Of course." She nods amicably, pointing across the street. "It's a bit far but super straightforward. Just go down along the Avenue until you get to the sea. The Statue is right there in the harbor. You can't miss it."

I set about my excursion, one block west to the Avenue, then trekking southwards. Flocks of tourists are pouring out from the Park, swirling on the pavement like dust in a whirlwind. I weave through them. It is the third day since I arrived in the City and, finally, I begin to see it in a shimmering light. The broad path extends ahead of me and spectacular structures rise on both sides, museums sprawling like giant clouds, towers springing up, high as mountains, imposing sculptures of lions and swans, titanic plazas, arches and cathedrals.

My heart thumps at the changing scenery and I walk on jubilantly. Along the flow of pedestrians I stride, racing across the intersections amid the locals who take no heed of the traffic lights, picking up speed as the numbers on the crosswalk signs decrease. Below the street, the subway trains roar, blowing gusts of hot air up through the gratings, and I mount the wind, sailing all the way south.

I don't know how long I've been walking but eventually I arrive beside the sea and the Statue is there. The bronze goddess stands potently, in the misty light, raising her arm to the sky, just like I first saw her many years ago, in the theme park near my hometown, with my cousin.

"Don't cry, Xiao Peng," she said, holding my hand. "Promise me when you grow up, you'll come to the other shore, and we will meet again."

Through my tears, I watch the goddess as she transforms. The hem of her robe fans out. The spikes on her crown expand. Her arms lengthen, multiplying, and, at last, dense with foliage— she becomes a prodigious tree, prospering, *in the land of nowhere, the wild of nothing*.

The night is drawing in when I return to the apartment building. The streetlight is on and in the lobby the doorman greets me with a broad smile.

"Hello, Mr. Chow," he says. "How's your day been?"

"Terrific. And yours, Jackie?"

"Not bad," he says, pressing the lift button for me. "Have a wonderful evening."

As the lift creaks, making its way up, a hazy tiredness engulfs me. My phone buzzes, a message from my cousin: Sorry, we're still stuck in the traffic, should be there soon.

Oh crap, the dinner. I didn't prepare anything. I am losing my nerve when the lift stops. The door slides open at the fifth floor.

A wave of chattering and laughter sweeps out from Simon's apartment, the front door ajar. I double-check the door number before stepping inside.

"Little Roc!" A gray-haired man darts towards me and gives me a squeeze. "Helena told me about your new name. I love it!"

It is my host, dressed in a formal-looking black suit. He ushers me into the living room where about a dozen or so men and women, all in white clothes, stand or sit in groups, speaking to one another.

"Here comes Little Roc!" Simon announces, nudging me forward while the guests all turn to me at once. "Hello, Little Roc!"

"What's going on?" I ask, surveying through the crowd. They all seem to be Asian, their faces unknown to me.

He beams. "Well, I thought since Linda and Stanley are coming, I might as well throw you a party so you get to know more friends."

"What?" I say, sweat seeping onto my back. "I'm useless around strangers."

"Nonsense," Simon says, pointing to a woman by the floor lamp. "Surely you know Helena."

Helena waves in her sleek white dress. "Hi, Little Roc, isn't Simon the best host?" She walks over and rests her hand on my arm.

I'm searching for the words when Simon says: "Right, I need to go back to the kitchen and check the food before Linda and her plus-one get here. Helena, I'll leave Roc to you for now."

Holding me by the crook of my arm, Helena cruises the room with me, introducing the guests one by one: Roger, Chris, Andrew, Bruce, Jenny, Henry, Mark, Lucy, Maggie, and Ken.

"Nice to meet you, Roc." We shake hands and they ask me how I have found the City so far, if I have recovered from my jet lag, and if I plan to stay long-term.

"Do you have any other family here, aside from your cousin?"

"Ah, your uncle, of course I've heard of him. We were both at C— University. He and his wife arrived a year before me. And what a tragedy, the way he ended."

"I have to take you to this new Sichuanese restaurant on Sixty-fourth Street. They serve the most authentic hot pot there."

"Are you seeing anybody, Roc? I know a girl who is half-Chinese, she also studied architecture."

"We have this condo in midtown. The tenants just moved out and it's now a wreck. Would you like to come over sometime and give us some advice on how to do it up?"

As our conversations get into full swing, a racket emerges from the corridor. I turn and see three men in white suits, carrying a collapsible table and a large wooden box. They put the table in the center of the room, the box on top of it.

"Awesome, Henry is going to perform now," Helena says buoyantly, clapping.

The guests gather around the table. An old man in an ivory Tang suit steps up, opens the wooden box, and retrieves an inkstone, a thick brush, and a roll of rice paper.

Spreading out the white paper on the table, the man prepares the ink. "Now," he says, addressing the room. "This one is for our precious guest."

He dips the brush into the ink and moves his arm like a dancing crane, wielding the brush across the paper until a mammoth character stretches out:

鵬.

"This is my name," I blurt out. *Peng.*

"Yes," the old man says, looking up at me with a smile. Now his face is familiar, reminding me of a certain black-and-white photo I saw as a child. "I thought I must dedicate this to you, Little Roc, as a present, and also as an apology on behalf of my wife, Carol, for her insensitivity yesterday." He puts down the big brush, switches to a smaller one, and continues to write to the right of *Peng* columns of small characters one after another, from the illustrious passage of "Free Wandering":

Later, the fish Kun changes into a bird, whose name is Peng. Its back is so vast that it is a thousand miles long. When it soars, its wings move like clouds, obscuring the sky. The roc is traveling to the Southern Ocean, known as the Celestial Lake. In the Records of Marvels, we read: The roc flies southwards, the water is churned up for three thousand miles; the bird ascends, mounting upon the great wind, to a height of ninety thousand miles . . .

The guests hold their breath, watching the words as they appear under the soft tip of the old man's brush.

Wait, did he say "Carol"? I quiver at the sudden revelation. Is he the chairwoman's husband? Didn't Simon tell me that the husband died long ago?

"Helena," I call my company. But she is fully immersed in the

127

performance. Standing still like a statue, her face is rigid, sallow like wax.

A nausea rushes up from my guts. Without warning, my arms begin to shudder like the tentacles of an octopus. The ever-intense stabbing pain returns, blowing up in my head.

I hear screaming. A figure runs towards me through the crowd.

"Ah, shit," says Simon, lifting the lid off the black stone pot under his arm.

What's going on? Was that a dead man who was writing my name? I want to ask him, but my teeth are clattering.

I collapse on the floor.

I wake up with an earthy aroma in my mouth. The room is empty, no sign of the guests nor the table and the calligraphy, only Simon crouching down in front of me, the black pot beside him, lidless, its opening dark, wide like a mouth.

"What is this thing you keep feeding me? Are you poisoning me?"

"It's just a balm made from an ancient recipe," he says, "called Longevity. I give it to you to buy more time."

"More time for what?" I clutch my fists to stop my arms from jittering.

Simon glances at them. "For you to make the decision."

His voice is wavering. I look up at him and, for the first time, see the unclouded face of my host. He is old, his hair silver as snow. There are blotches on his skin, deep lines crisscrossing his face.

Simon stares back at me, profound sorrow in his eyes. Outside, it has gone completely dark. The City is glimmering, the sirens crying, just like the wailing of the dead, trapped forever in purgatory.

Am I . . . ? I'm about to ask him when there is a banging on the front door.

"Little Roc! Little Roc!" a man bawls.

"Open the door!" It's my cousin's familiar voice.

She is here. The door is at the end of the corridor, its brass knob trembling. I only need to walk up and turn the knob.

Yet I hesitate. Is this really what I want?

All of a sudden, the room begins to shake as if an earthquake is coming. A gale surges into the apartment, rattling the furniture; the upholstery of the armchairs begins to rip open. Wadding spirals into the air. The floorboards rear up like enraged snakes. Steadying himself on his feet, Simon hauls me up and drags me to the window.

"What's happening?" I cry.

"You've made your decision, Roc. Now it's time to go," he says.

"What? Where to?" I ask, my head spitting.

My host's eyes redden, the curtains flailing behind him. "Remember," he says. "The name that can be named is not your true name. It is from the nameless that heaven and earth spring."

Then I understand.

With that, a savage pain cuts through my body. My torso twitches as if my muscles are being yanked out sinew by sinew. From the tips of my fingers, my skin is peeling off, revealing my already rotten flesh beneath.

I turn with the last of my strength. Darting towards the open window, I leap onto the sill and jump.

The building is surrounded by scaffolding, cracked planks and rusty poles. In the distance, golden rapeseed flowers hiss. Under the overcast sky are the ramshackle houses of my hometown, and my cousin and I—a girl and a boy—sneak to the river for a swim, while our grandmother shuffles up and down the grubby street, calling out to us again and again.

I drop like a stone. The mud, mixed with cigarette butts, spit, and litter, rushes towards my face.

People are shrieking.

"A scaffolder just fell from the top!"

"Is that Xiao Peng?"

"Somebody call a doctor!"

Then I see myself, slumped on the ground. My orange hi-vis vest flaps open and my yellow safety helmet has rolled away, its strap broken. Blood flows from my head, forming a winding stream through the filth.

I howl as the unbearable headache crushes my skull, and I stretch out my arms. Pain slits my limbs. My chest expands as if something inside is bursting through my rib cage. Fucking Christ. I roar again, another long cry, beating my arms against the wind.

They are growing. Long, tough feathers shoot out of my skin, fluttering in the storm. In a swirling nausea, I pull myself up, rising from the corpse on the ground and mounting towards the sky. My wings spread, their shadows, thousands of miles wide, are cast across the skyscrapers of the City and millions of glistening windows.

I fly into the cloudless night.

NO TIME TO WRITE

I decide to write a story to explain why I literally have no time to write. I consider it important to make official my no-time status so it can be comprehended, interpreted, and remembered.

First of all, of course, time is an invented notion. It was introduced by the Power Structure so that we ordinary people could regulate our destructive primitive urges and find meaning on a day-to-day basis. Nonetheless, it's fake. Therefore, when I say I have no time to write, I neither have nor haven't time. In other words, time is not an order to which I choose to submit myself. Or I question the very notion of order. Because if we consider ourselves in terms of particles in the universe, we must acknowledge that the universe exists only in chaos. As explained in the second law of thermodynamics, our universe is a system where randomness is bound to increase. Any attempt to annihilate entropy and to create order is ultimately futile.

When I am typing these words on my laptop, I am a nameless object floating in the universe. And my laptop, too, another insubstantial item whose trajectory happens, at this particular moment, to be brushing against mine. And very soon, our collaborative effort towards generating order will be disrupted by the formidable power of randomness. And then we will be forced apart, orbiting towards and brushing against other objects respectively.

This is why my writing will, and has to, stop. It is not because of the lack of time or the failure to put in personal effort. The discontinuity is simply inevitable because of randomness.

I worship randomness.

Some less interesting facts:

In 1982, I was born in Singapore to Irish parents. When I was six weeks old, we moved to Hong Kong because my father was needed there for a big merger. Three years later, my younger brother was born. When I was eight, my family relocated to Shanghai. This time, my father was tasked with building the China branch of his company from scratch.

I spent the majority of my adolescence in China before my family returned to Ireland in 1999, when my father was asked to step down from the Shanghai office. I attended Trinity College in Dublin, studied linguistics and philosophy as an undergraduate and postcolonial theory for my master's. After graduation, I taught in a language school for four years and dated two East Asian girls. In 2008, when the language school had to cut back on its staff, I traveled back to Asia myself, freelancing and backpacking in Cambodia and Thailand. Then, this September, I moved back to Dublin, to my parents' house in Castleknock, and have been living with them ever since.

Like everyone else, I'm troubled by my life but cannot pin down specific issues. I was once accused of being self-absorbed. A girl I used to go out with told me this.

"You think you're a woman," she said. "But no, you are just a man trapped in a woman's body and horrendously straight. Cliona, you are shifting your sexual identity at your own convenience— so you can slip in and out of relationships. It's ridiculous and . . . exhausting." She closed her eyes when the tears escaped. The timing was impeccable, making me feel she was rehearsing for a play.

It was sad, and to some extent moving. But she was wrong. My biggest problem is neither that I'm a man trapped in a woman's body nor that I have trouble committing to my sexual identity. My biggest problem is I'm naturally skeptical of binaries: man-slash-woman, straight-slash-gay, single-slash-taken, occidental-slash-oriental, and more fundamentally, past-slash-present.

My father says I'm too smart for my own good. My mother says I'm just an ungrateful little brat.

"Won't you just get your bloody life together, Cliona?" she says, usually when she sees me in the kitchen, munching another bowl of cornflakes. "Just get out of the house and get a life, for Christ's sake."

"She has just come back, Fiona," my father says.

"From a bloody five-year-long holiday!"

My mother swears a lot at home. It is quite unusual considering she is a well-educated, upper-middle-class woman whose life has been nothing but comfortable. She is all right when she's under the gaze of friends and acquaintances, but once left with us, the poor woman can't help but spew streams of obscenities. My father says it's her way of releasing energy. "We all need to find a way to let it out," as he puts it.

I understand. Years of relocating and dislocating have injured each one of us in this family. Everyone except my little brother,

Ian. Ian lives in Porto with his girlfriend, Sara, and is as happy as a goldfish.

In response to my mother's accusation, I have been trying to get my bloody life together. It is one of the reasons I want to write.

It happened in Chiang Mai, just a few weeks before I returned to Ireland. It was near dusk and I was sitting on the rooftop terrace of Sunset Lodge with Mama Mei. I was drinking a bottle of Beer Lao; she was smoking. It was my favorite time of day, when the temperature had finally decreased and the city had gone quiet. The nuns in the nearby convent were chanting some Buddhist sutra while pigeons circled aimlessly in the coral-purple sky.

"Doesn't this feel extremely repetitive, in the way such repetition forms eternity?" I said to Mama Mei.

"Oh, not now, Cliona, not another round of your philosophizing. It's been a long day for me." She shook her head and took a drag.

I shrugged. "I'm just saying."

"Although I do like what you said the other day about the brushes."

"Not brushes. I was saying we don't really engage, we are merely brushing against each other. It's all transient and superficial," I corrected her.

"Yes, yes." She nodded along. "I heard you and Junjun are over?"

I shrugged again.

"What was wrong? She is a very nice girl," she said. "And you, too."

I drank a mouthful of beer. "She wouldn't like to be called 'a very nice girl.' She'd probably say niceness is one of the stigmas that oppress women, and go on for hours—but no, nothing is wrong. It's just not working anymore. Have you ever had this feeling, that we can't really be with another person even when we are physically with them? We're essentially dealing with ourselves all the time. And it's all repetitive. It haunts me, this idea that I'm just an object and she's a mirror through which I see increasingly only all the absurdity in myself—"

"Your body is not happy, so your mind keeps itself busy," Mama Mei said.

"That's true," I agreed. "There is too much going on here. It's like the bus to Bangkok." I pointed at my head.

Mama Mei laughed. "You have such energy in you," she said, "thoughts, ideas, memories . . . And you're a bit fixated with all of them, you know? It's important to forget. Forgetting is a gift."

"I know." I sighed. "Remembering is the perpetual curse. The recollections are colossal, ambiguous, and changeable. For instance, every time I think of the past, I essentially create a new version of it. It's an endless loop. A panopticon. I'm just trapped—"

"Why don't you write it all down?" Mama Mei interrupted me again. "The way I keep a book for the lodge. Who checks in when. Who drinks how much beer. I write everything down so I don't need to remember it all. On paper, out of head."

"On paper, out of head," I repeated as if it were a proverb.

"Exactly. Now if you excuse me, I need to go check on the dinner. Shall I get you another beer?" She finished her cigarette, stood up, and went down to the kitchen.

———

It was the end of August. The tourists were fleeing Southeast Asia, and people in Ireland began to realize the summer was over. "Your mother wonders if you will be home for Christmas," my father wrote in his email, and he said he'd be happy to book the ticket home for me.

It was the first time this offer had come up since I had been fired from the language school for dating students and, that same night, had told my parents I was gay. My father even came to pick me up at Dublin Airport. "Welcome home, Cliona," he said with a broad smile as he took my luggage.

"How is Mam?" I said.

"She's cooking you a full Irish at home. We're both glad you're back," he said.

Ever since, I've been living at my parents' house. My sole mission is to write, to go down into my memories like a miner, get my hands dirty, and dig out the nasties. I stare at my computer screen and type words, sentences, paragraphs. Things that happened. My opinions about the world. Terms, explanations, distinctions. And then I realize: I am actually not able to write.

One of the reasons could be Gemma. It had always been like this since we were in secondary school. Gemma wrote poetry. I replied with broken sentences.

The last time I met her was in Paris. Having just handed in my thesis for the postgraduate program, I flew there on a fifteen-euro Ryanair ticket.

I stayed in this miniature hotel room not far from the Sorbonne and texted to tell her I was there. For four days she didn't show up, saying she was busy with her essay. Every day, I walked up and down Boulevard Saint-Michel for hours in the whooshing February wind. I remembered she'd mentioned she usually got the bus on Boulevard Saint-Michel to go to the university and I was hoping I would bump into her somewhere. It didn't happen.

The fifth day she emerged. After "pulling two all-nighters in a row" she looked as glamorous as a new sports car. She smiled when she saw me and reached out her arms. "Hi, Cliona."

I walked up and hugged her. She was soft and smelled like fresh apricots.

"How's life?" she said.

"Not bad."

"And how's Fiona and Anthony? How's Ian?"

"They're all doing better than me to varying degrees," I assured her.

We then stopped talking. It was very cold. I looked at the top of my boots.

"Burgers?" she suggested.

"Sure." I nodded.

Gemma was obsessed with American fast food when we lived in Shanghai. She'd usually skip dinner at home and go to McDonald's with me. She could eat five spicy chicken burgers in a row, no problem.

That night in Paris we went to a Burger King near Luxembourg Gardens where we ate six double cheeseburgers and countless chips. Afterwards, we walked across the road to a McDonald's and bagged ten discounted chocolate croissants to go. We shared the croissants as she walked me back to my hotel.

"This could be Shanghai," I said.

"Shanghai forever," she said in a singsong voice, as if we were in a TV commercial.

We were both hiccupping when we arrived outside my hotel. It was numbingly cold, so I asked her if she wanted to go up.

"Sure. I need to puke anyway," she said. "You do have a bathroom in your room, right?"

We went upstairs. I pointed her to the bathroom and gave her a fresh towel. Then I sat on the bed, listening to her gagging loudly behind the door. It sounded like she was throwing up a baby.

She'd had bulimia for years. I thought she probably still did. Having missed it for quite a few years, I was slightly nauseated by the noise of vomiting. At the same time I felt hopeful. I thought that when she finished, we would have sex.

Eventually she came out. She looked very pale and sat down on the armchair.

"Can I have some water?" she asked.

I poured a glass and gave it to her.

She drank. "Believe it or not, I haven't done this for ages." She started to sob. Her face was in her hands and she said: "Why are you here?"

"Well." I felt my throat was excessively dry. "I miss you, I miss us."

She snorted out a short laugh and raised her head. "You're mistaking the pain coming from your personal failure for nostalgia. Last June, when I had an abortion, I thought about you a lot, the way you would always talk about those big deep ideas, your skepticism and how you said, after we slept together for the first time, that you wished you had never been born, at least not to your parents . . ."

I wanted to tell her about the fight I had with my father before this trip but instead I walked towards her, kneeled down in front of her, and began to unbutton her jeans.

"What are you doing?" she shouted.

"It's okay," I said, clutching her hand. I pressed my face in between her legs.

"Have you lost your mind?" She kicked me away. "Oh my god, you're so self-absorbed!"

I thumped back on the floor and she continued. "I really wanted to be nice to you. I told James I didn't want to see you but he said I should go. How stupid of me to listen to him, to think you might have changed!"

"Who is James?" I said.

"He is my fiancé," she said. "He is in my present and will be in my future. And what happened between us is all in the past. There is no point holding on to the past. It has nothing to do with the present. It's just in your head. And it's in everybody's best interest if you just keep it in your head."

She was wrong. Gemma Wong-Laurent is an extremely bright young woman but she was totally wrong on this. The past has everything to do with the present. In fact, the past and the present are a set of interdependent notions. The past only establishes itself as the past of the present. And the present needs the past as its reference so it can be defined. We can only determine whether today is the present if we check it against yesterday, or if this minute is the present based on the minute just gone. In other words, the past and the present are inseparable. The line between them is only relative and always in flux.

After Paris, I posted Gemma the full three volumes of *Time and Narrative* by Paul Ricoeur, along with a fifteen-page introduction I drafted. As a result, I missed the job interview my father set up for me and ended up working in a language school near Parnell Square. To which my mother commented: "I told you to stay away from the Laurents. They are an awful bunch."

Blaming Gemma or not, the situation is that I am just not able to write. I find everything dubious, bland, and problematic. In order to feel inspired, I eat as much as I can, day and night, awake or half-asleep. Propelled by an extraordinary sense of urgency, I hold a snack bar in my hand while I read about the origins of tribes, the structures of hegemony, the anatomy of animal bodies, etc.

It is when my mother finds out that I've been forcing myself to vomit at least three times a day that she decides we need to get help.

After consulting old colleagues, my father contacts a reputable psychoanalysis institute in Malahide. He drives me there for an interview.

A short-haired woman in her forties leads me into a room. Her handshake is affirmative, her smile alluring. She asks me my name, date of birth, and my history of allergies. She chats with me for about forty minutes in a soft and sympathetic voice. Two days later she phones me, telling me my application is accepted. I need to go in on Tuesday at 2 p.m.

On Tuesday, my father drives me to the institute, and I am directed to the same room. Behind the door, seated on the same chair across the room, not the woman but a fifty-something man.

"Hello, Cliona. My name is Noel. Come in and sit." The man nods at me.

I am not sure if the institute changed doctors or I totally made up the woman in my last appointment. I walk over and sit down, put my handbag on the floor.

"Hi, Noel." I greet him.

"We had a meeting on Friday, deciding who would be the most suitable person to work with you." He speaks very slowly, as if somebody is typing in his stomach and the voice comes out from his mouth. "We think I might be the best person and I am happy to be here, to help you."

I want to ask him who *we* are. "Thank you."

"Good. So, let's start. First, can you tell me why you are here?" he asks me.

I explain the reasons.

"I see. Can you tell me a little bit about your relationship with your parents? What is it like with your mother, and with your father?"

I answer the questions.

"Right. Then let's talk about your father first. Tell me more about him. What does he do? What's he like?"

I speak for a while, gesturing with my hands and laughing the odd time.

Noel waits until I finish, and then he says: "I've noticed one thing since you came in, Cliona. You withdraw your feelings. Every time that you're about to get emotional, you pull back. You analyze and ridicule yourself. Why do you do it?"

It's a tough question. I think about it and suggest a few possibilities.

"I don't know the answers," he says. "I'm just asking the questions. Now, let's continue. Do you want to talk a bit more about what happened in Shanghai? How did you feel about what your father did?"

I speak. This time I pay more attention to the emotional flow. I pose and pace my words carefully.

"You are kind," he says. "Another person would have been very angry. Or at least would have let him know how she felt."

I respond to his comments.

"I'm not the judge here. If you think your decision is right, then it is the right one for you," he says. "However, if I might point out, I want you to note that it's important for us to cry and to feel angry. There is no shame in it. Happiness, sadness, jealousy, anger, they are all discharges of our body. Is earwax better than snot?"

I lift up the corners of my mouth into a smile.

He looks at the wall behind me. "I'm afraid our session is about to finish. Now, Cliona, I want to ask you for one more thing. When you go back, can you write down what happened today? What you said to me, can you write it down? You don't have to show it to anyone. Just write, type it up on your computer, and delete everything afterwards if that feels easier. But write first."

"I'll try," I say.

I leave the institute and walk to the Costa next to Malahide Castle to meet my father. He is reading the *Independent* and puts down the paper when he sees me.

"How did it go?" he asks.

"Not bad," I say.

He folds up the newspaper, leaves it on the chair, and picks up his coat. We walk towards the exit. He places his hand on my shoulder briefly and says: "I'm very proud of you."

———

What is so significant about writing? Why is there this omni-present and ceaseless craving to write, as if it were a ritual? Let's go back to the notion of randomness and our species's hopeless struggle against it. Randomness is the fundamental law of the universe and it compels us to forget. It is our nature to forget and it's also in our nature to resist forgetting. Writing is the opposite of forgetting. It's the ultimate manifestation of remembering. To concretize it with language, to engrave it on stone, to encapsulate it in books, to pass it on and make it eternal.

It sounds incredibly appealing. But still, I find myself uneasy with any kind of order. Because it turns everything into signifiers and silences and obliterates all of us who are not in the center. All order is a system to rule. By whom? I don't know. I will stay vigi-lant and discover the answer.

I have trouble falling asleep, and when I finally do I have trou-ble staying asleep. As a result, I'm awake all the time. It prolongs the days and makes life more intolerable. In order to get myself going, I consume more victuals.

I go to the kitchen in the middle of the night and devour what-ever we have in the fridge before making myself throw up. One morning, my mother rises and finds no bread, no milk, no cereal— no nothing. She becomes extremely upset, especially since she usu-ally wakes up with low blood sugar.

"Can't you just leave a scrap for me, for Christ's sake," she bellows. "I need to eat right now! Jesus, I can't breathe!"

Her face turns pale, lips purple. She sags into an armchair and pants with her mouth open. "Anthony!" She calls my father. "Anthony! Anto!"

Nobody answers. It seems my father is not in the house.

"Let me find something for you. I'm sure we have food some-where." I open the cupboards and start searching. Finally, behind the gas meter, I find a half-finished Mars bar. I smell it.

"Here, have this first. I'll go to the shop now to get you some breakfast. But eat this now." I hand her the bar.

She examines it and gives in. The packaging rustles off like snakeskin.

"Do you want some water?" I ask her.

She nods. I give her some water before I grab the car keys to get groceries. Who hid the Mars bar behind the gas meter? I won-der as I start the engine.

The engine starts. I reverse my mother's silver Volvo slowly out of the driveway.

Later, I call my brother, Ian. He answers immediately.

"Hello, Jiejie, how's life?" His voice is bright and almost too loud. And he calls me Jiejie as always, Chinese for older sister.

"Not bad. And you?" I say.

"Excellent. Couldn't be better," he replies.

"Guess what I found behind the gas meter this morning."

"The gas meter?" He pauses for a few seconds before laughing out loud. "Don't tell me the Mars bar is still there!"

"Yep. And it saved Mam's life," I tell him.

"She's welcome. How are you doing?" he says.

"I am trying to write but it isn't working," I say. "They are sending me to a therapist."

"How generous. I'm sure it'll work out for all of you."

We change the subject. He tells me Sara is settling into her second trimester. They are making a trip to Naples next month.

"Come join us," he says. "It'd be lovely for you to meet Sara. And trust me, you'll feel so much better once you get out of that house."

"I'm afraid I can't," I say. "The situation is not great here with Mam and Dad. I think Dad is doing his thing again and that's why Mam wanted me to come back."

He doesn't speak for a while and sighs. "Why can't they just get a divorce?"

"You know what Mam is like," I say.

"I certainly do, the two of you."

"What do you mean?"

He laughs as if I'd told a joke. "I need to go now," he says. "It'd be nice to see you at some point."

"It would be," I say.

"Zaijian, Jiejie," he says.

My mother discusses my situation over dinner.

She asks my father: "I think Cliona is getting worse. Do you think the therapy really works? That place is very good, according to people from your work, no?"

"It's the best," my father says. "I think she enjoys the therapy."

"Do you?" She turns to me. "What do you think, Cliona, you think you're improving?"

"Maybe it needs to get worse before it gets better. That is often how it works." I pierce a rocket leaf with my fork.

"Do you hear that, Anto?" she asks my father again. "Is that how it works?"

"Could be." My father nods. "We should really leave this to the professionals."

"God bless us." She sighs. "She'd better get herself together before Christmas, when the O'Farrells come, otherwise I'm going to need more Valium."

"God bless," I echo as I halve a cherry tomato, skewer it with a piece of spinach, and then a slice of cucumber.

My mother is so lucky that she believes in God. I'm envious of her ability to find a place to rest, a corner to turn to. And my biggest problem, as far as I can see, is that I don't believe in anything. Our lives exist on the constant movement of atoms and subatomic particles. And our thoughts are trapped within the structures of language. I'm baffled both by the profundity of the former and the limitations of the latter. And the distance between them makes me feel sick every time I think about it. To a certain extent, everybody in my life, the ones I deeply love and the ones I pass by on the street, is the same. We are objects in this universe, confined by our epistemological limits. We brush against one another for an exceedingly short moment and drift apart. We will never be able to understand ourselves, let alone one another. I bow down to the sublimity of the impossible.

And this is exactly why I cannot write. I sit alone in my bedroom, staring at the screen of my laptop, hands on the keyboard, motionless. It occurs to me that the linear time concept is a lie and everything that happened in the past is with us forever, encircling us, enfolding us and asphyxiating us. In fact, if I turn my gaze away from my laptop and close my eyes, I am back in Shanghai, on one of those warm, damp summer nights when my mother would cry by herself like a beast and my brother, Ian, would sneak into my bedroom in his pajamas and say: "Wo haipa, Jiejie." I'd bring him into my bed and tell him we were simply privileged to be prepared, at such early ages, to embrace our designated solitude as humans.

From downstairs my mother is still wailing. She cries for so long that the rhythm of her crying begins to change, like the tide receding into the sea. Another day is over. And my father has left the house.

I realize that I'm looking forward to my appointment with Noel on Tuesday.

HOW I FELL IN LOVE WITH THE WELL-DOCUMENTED LIFE OF ALEX WHELAN

By the time Alex Whelan became part of my life he had already died. However, it was not until much later that I became aware of this fact.

I met Alex at a meeting of the Foreign Movies No Subtitles (FMNS) group. The date was March 2. The movie was *An Autumn Afternoon*. The meet-up place was Eoin's (the organizer's) studio off Meath Street. And the fee was five euros per person (with a glass of red/white wine).

When I arrived the movie had already started. I stooped and sneaked in, taking a seat at the back. Alex was sitting right beside me but we didn't talk for the duration of the movie. Only when it was over did he turn to me and ask for the time. I checked my phone and told him it was 9:15.

"I like the song they sang at the end," he then said. "What do you think this movie is about?"

"It seemed the old man was about to die so he arranged a marriage for his daughter," I said.

"I don't think so," he disagreed. "I think he liked that hostess woman and the daughter decided to get married so her dad could find his own happiness."

"Wouldn't that be too much of a twist?" I frowned.

"It wasn't straightforward anyway," he admitted. "But isn't that what Japanese culture is about? The forbearance and the elusive love."

"I don't know much about Japanese culture." I gave him a smile.

"I'm Alex." He grinned.

"Hello, Alex."

"What's your name?" he asked.

I told him my name and briefly coached him on the pronunciation. Then he asked me what it meant. I in turn elaborated on my factually tedious name. In response, he said it was unbelievably beautiful, and I nodded humbly to accept yet another round of applause for my culture and my smart-arsed ancestors.

It was all cliché. We then talked about the weather (wet and changeable), the place he came from (Kilkenny), and how long it took to drive there from Dublin (an hour and a half), among other things.

"How long have you been in Ireland?" he asked me at a certain point.

"Would you believe me if I told you I'm actually from Tipperary?" I said.

He laughed loudly. "You must be kidding me!"

He checked his phone, saying he needed to head to Vicar Street to join the lads, and he wondered if I had any plans.

"I need to go home now," I said. "It's too late."

"It's not ten yet."

"Long way to Tipperary, you know," I said, and picked up my satchel bag.

He wheezed.

"Add me on Facebook, will you?" he asked me before I left. "The name is Alexander Whelan."

"Sure." I nodded and walked out the door.

Apologies if I have challenged your attention span. I admit the dialogue above isn't particularly interesting. However, I had to relay it in full detail because it was the only time we spoke. I'll go through the crucial part of the story very quickly now. What happened was:

On my way back to the apartment I added Alex on Facebook; it was approximately 10:30 p.m.

When I got home, my roommate was in her bedroom, having left some tortilla chips and hummus on the coffee table. So I sat down, had some food, and lingered on Instagram for about half an hour before I went to the bathroom to pee. It was nearly midnight.

I had eaten too many tortilla chips and too much hummus to sleep. So I went back to my bedroom to work on my thesis/wait for the food to digest. I stared at the Word document for about twenty minutes and went to YouTube, where I watched some old Chinese TV series for about three hours.

Eventually I decided to get ready for bed. I went to the bathroom to wash up and got caught up in a test (Which *Game of Thrones* Character Are You?), and sat on the toilet for another thirty-five to forty-five minutes.

Then I lay on my bed, browsing through my phone to allow my day to sink in. It was 4:47 a.m. when I got the notification from

Facebook. Alexander Whelan accepted your friend request. Good man, I thought. I wanted to click into his page and maybe send a message but I was too tired, so I put my phone down and fell asleep.

The next day I woke up around 12 p.m. I was running around and doing whatnot for about five hours during which I routinely checked my phone every three to five minutes but there was no message from Alex.

I decided to PM him while I was preparing dinner, heating up a Tesco soup and buttering two slices of brown bread. So I went to his Facebook page and that was when I saw the posts coming up on his wall.

R.I.P. Alex. My heart was broken when I heard the news, one person posted. R.I.P. Bro.

Have a good one on the other side, another message read.

And many others.

It was 6:10 p.m., March 3. I learned from his Facebook that Alex had died that morning. There was an accident and he was sent to St. James's Hospital and died there at 6:15 a.m.

I almost dropped the phone into my soup.

It wasn't the first cyberdeath I'd experienced. But this one also took place in real life. Or did it? I spent the whole evening questioning the authenticity of this news. Could it be a prank played by Alex and his friends?

This was how I pictured the situation:

Alex: So I just met this girl. She is kind of cute.
Friend A: Oh yeah?

Alex: She is Chinese. Actually, I'm not sure. She said she's from Tipp. But she looks Chinese and her name sounds Chinese.

Friend A: Well, if it looks like a duck and swims like a duck . . .

Alex: Hey! . . . Wait, she just added me on Facebook.

Friend A: Cool. Show me her profile photo.

(Alex shows his friend my profile photo.)

Friend A: Hmmm . . . I don't know . . . You call this cute?

(Alex checks my profile photo.)

Alex: I don't know . . . Maybe? Ah, never mind.

(Alex puts away his phone. They go drinking and then the gig is on, so they enjoy the music until very late in the evening. Afterwards, they go to a friend's apartment to smoke some hash. It is around five in the morning when everybody is stoned and Alex cries out.)

Alex: Shit! I think I just accidently added her!

Friend B: Who?

Alex: This Chinese girl I met.

Friend B: You were in China? China has good food.

Friend C: The moon is coming to get us!

Alex: Shit. Shit. I can't undo this now. What do I do?

Friend A: What are we gonna do? It's the moon, man! Moon man is murdering the moon!

Friend B: Chill out. Watch me save your ass, loser!

(B takes out his phone and types.)

Friend B: Check your Facebook now, Alex.

(Alex takes his phone out and checks his Facebook. He laughs out loud hysterically.)

Friend A: What? Show us!

(A grabs Alex's phone and reads out: R.I.P. Alex. My heart was broken when I heard the news.)

Friend A: Epic! Wait!

(A takes out his phone and started to post on Alex's wall. Then friends C D E F join in.)

The more I thought about it, the more it felt plausible. In this case, Alex would still be alive. He might be a dick but he would be alive.

Here is the fundamental question: If you meet a guy who you sort of like and he turns out to be a dick, would you like him to remain, unapologetically, a dick and pretend he is dead, or would you prefer he is actually dead, but possibly a good guy?

It was not entirely rootless speculation. For a start, Alex had 1,257 Facebook friends. And just in the last month, he had checked in at Vicar Street twice (Feb. 10 and 17), Grogan's three times (Feb. 7, 8, and 20), the Lord Edward twice (Feb. 5 and 22), the Long Hall three times (Feb. 2, 14, and 25), and Bowes four times (I don't even bother to recheck the dates).

I understand you might say: But sure it's February, where can he go if not the pub? But still. Plus, how would you feel if I told you that among the fourteen visits to local pubs, Alex was *feeling crazy* for seven of them, and *excited* on five of these occasions. There were only two times where he was tagged, so I wouldn't be able to know exactly how he felt. But he certainly looked very well in the photos with his friends. And so did his friends.

So is it possible that he was a philanderer who played a prank on me via Facebook, because I was, according to Friend A, not cute?

On the other hand, there were things that suggested a slightly different lifestyle. For instance, he had read 572 books on Goodreads, rated 493 of them (3.73 avg.), and written 89 reviews. He volunteered for numerous (23) events at Insomnia Ireland, helping people who suffer from either coffee addiction and/or sleep deprivation. He was the guitarist in a band on Bandcamp, where they had uploaded three songs ("How to Murder the Moon," "Hippopotamus," and "The Telly Is On"). He also hosted a tour on Airbnb, which was called Phoenix Park Walk: learn about Irish trees and shrubs. He charged thirty euros per person and had three five-star reviews.

And so on and so forth.

I slouched in front of my laptop, searching through all the online statistics of Alex Whelan. My roommate came over to knock on my door and she said: "Would you stop watching Chinese soap operas? Work on your thesis."

"Did my mother tell you to say this?" I asked her without turning back.

"No!" she exclaimed. "She is only concerned about you, you know?"

"Relax. I am doing research for my thesis," I said, scrolling down Alex's friends' pages.

"I can see from here that's Facebook!" she bellowed and left.

Never mind the thesis. For now, I needed to get to the bottom of this. I needed to know what kind of person Alex Whelan was, whether he was really dead, and if so, whether he had added me on Facebook right before the moment of his death?

I looked into his 1,257 Facebook friends. There were 202 of them living in Dublin. So I clicked into the profiles of these 202 people and finally found a Micheál Hannigan who shared his timeline with the public.

It seemed there would be a Black Books night at the Bernard Shaw on Friday evening and Micheál was going. So I went and got a visual on him after a few minutes of scanning the crowd.

"Hi! Micheál!" I approached and tapped him on the shoulder.

He looked at me and was for a second visibly confused. "Hi?" he said.

"I'm a friend of Alex. We met at Vicar Street a couple of weeks ago, remember?" He was at Vicar Street with Alex on February 10.

"Oh!" He nodded. "I remember now. Hello, how are you?"

I relaxed and poised myself. "Good! I'm good, how are you?" I asked.

"Not bad. Not bad," he said.

"So sorry about Alex. I couldn't believe it!" I sighed and shook my head.

"I know! I was just thinking. Jesus!" He rubbed his eyebrows.

I wanted to proceed but he asked: "Sorry, can you remind me of your name again? I'm terrible with names."

"I'm Claire," I said.

"Oh," he said. "Claire?"

"Claire Collins," I assured him.

He seemed satisfied. If it came with a surname it must be real.

And then we conversed. He'd had a very busy week programming, fixing a new application that was basically unfixable.

"The QA keep sending it back to me! I said send it to the engineers but nobody listened. It just keeps coming back to me." My week wasn't great either. After three nights of toil I sent in my thesis before the deadline only to find out that the professor was on strike. "Would it kill him to let us know the week before so I could save myself a full tin of coffee." Another cold wave was coming from Russia. There was an amazing sauna place on South William Street. "Speaking of which, isn't it incredible, the emerging culinary scene in Dublin?" From there we slid into the friction-free zone of food talk, where I went on autopilot for about fifteen minutes before I seized a window to terminate the conversation.

"It was so nice talking to you. But I really need to run now," I said. "And, if you don't mind me asking, how did Alex, you know? I heard it was an accident. How did it happen?"

"Oh, you didn't hear? Right, they probably don't want to advertise it . . . He killed himself. Cut his wrist in the bathroom. Can you believe it?" he added, shaking his head.

I went numb and I heard him asking: "So are we friends on Facebook yet? Add me if we're not."

I learned this from my mother: if you want to ask something really important, leave it till the end. "Don't just go in and ask. It's impolite," she said. "You have to talk to people. You have to listen to them. You have to warm them up and show them you care. And then ask what you really want at the end of it. Ask casually."

My mother is the most capable woman I know. She is bright, hardworking, and unbelievably adaptable. She raised me all by herself after my father passed away when I was small (eighteen months, she told me). In 2005, she met a divorcee on the internet and they soon fell in love. He came to China to visit her in the summer and proposed at the airport before he left. They got engaged and tied the knot in the spring of 2007. Afterwards, my mother sold our apartment and we moved to Ireland with her new husband, Eugene Collins.

Mr. and Mrs. Collins still live happily in the picturesque town of Cahir, County Tipperary. She renamed herself Amy and introduced me as Claire. "Claire Collins." She tried to sell the name to me. "It sounds right, don't you think?"

"That is just not my name," I told her.

"But it'll be easier for everybody! Come on, Xiaohan. It'd be good for you!" she said.

My mother always knows what is best for me. In the end, I embraced the name and learned to take pleasure in watching people's faces change when I said I was Claire Collins. "Yes, that's me. It's a bit mixed up. Long story," I'd say. It was a great conversation starter.

I didn't do this when I met Alex, though. For some reason, I told him my real name and coached him on the pronunciation.

"Sh-aw, H-ung," I remembered him saying.

"That's perfect!" I laughed. I didn't let him know that I couldn't really remember the last time someone called me Xiaohan.

After talking to Micheál Hannigan, I felt light-headed and took a taxi home. My roommate and her boyfriend were watching TV in the sitting room. "Hi, Claire, how's your evening so far?" The boyfriend waved at me upon my entry. My roommate said: "Can you call Amy later? She said you haven't called for a week."

"I'll call her," I said, and closed my bedroom door.

Alex posted this on November 8, 2016:

Things we take for granted: A pint of Guinness. Packed and prewashed spinach. Eight bananas from Costa Rica for one fifty. Sparkling water. Electric sockets. Toilet paper in public bathrooms. Short stories of Franz Kafka. Free streaming music. Google Maps. 4G data. Facebook friends. Being white. European Union. A Democratic president of the United States. Solidarity. Globalization. Rationalism. Freedom. Life.

It got 210 likes and 3 comments.

Sitting on my bed, I read it about ten times, whispering the words through my lips, as if they were a spell.

I wanted to respond with something meaningful under the post. I tried and failed.

So I liked it.

Now 211 likes.

I didn't think I would have been moved by Alex's post had he not been dead. Death was a titanic LOMO lens, through which every word and paragraph, every line of code, and every algorithm looked solemn and prophetic.

In the early morning of March 3, after watching the Japanese movie *An Autumn Afternoon* (without subtitles), after a few drinks at Vicar Street, and after accepting my friend request, Alexander Whelan sentenced himself to death.

What he left behind was this post, which was written right after the American presidential election, along with other posts about news he heard, books he read, and music he enjoyed. There were also emojis, photos, video clips, events; in fact, his whole Facebook account, his Instagram, Twitter, Pinterest, Snapchat, Tumblr, PayPal . . . an entire world.

I believe I've made myself clear: This is a love story. This is a love story about boy meets girl. An Irish boy meets a Chinese girl in Dublin. They like each other instantly and decide to be friends on Facebook. It won't be long before they start seeing each other but the boy is dead. Except that in this case he leaves behind an enormous and self-proliferating online archive with which the Chinese girl will find no problem falling in love.

This is what our first date is going to look like:

> We are meeting for Thursday lunch at Mannings Bakery & Cafe on Thomas Street. Before I go, I check on TripAdvisor and learn that most customers recommend their carrot cake.
> **Me:** I'll have a slice of carrot cake, then. And a latte.
> **The waitress:** Good.
> (She repeats and writes down our orders and leaves.)
> **Alex:** So you're having cake for lunch.
> **Me:** Why not? It's Thursday.
> **Alex:** What's special about Thursday?
> **Me:** Its lack of identity.
> (Alex wheezes.)

Me: So what do you do?

Alex: I work at Maniac and Anarchist Co.

Me: That's not a real company.

Alex: This is what my Facebook says.

Me: And what do you say?

Alex: I say we should just trust my Facebook.

(I laugh. The waitress arrives with our orders. She lays out the cutlery, the cups, and the plates, and leaves. Alex takes a sip of his coffee. I cut a corner of my carrot cake with the fork.)

Me: If I could just read and trust your online profiles, why would we need to meet in person? Is there anything you can tell me in the flesh that your Facebook can't?

(Alex thinks for a while.)

Alex: Here's the thing: How do you define knowing a person? If we have spent, say, a month together, we share the space, we eat, we drink, we watch TV, and we have sex. But we don't talk—we talk about basic stuff but we don't have conversations. You don't know what I like and dislike, which college I went to, who my favorite writer is, etc. But we spend tons of time together. In these circumstances, can you say you know me? Or you've read my Facebook and other online archives, and we can trust all of them, okay? And you've learned all about me. I like the Cure and I hate Maroon Five. I went to UCD. My favorite writer is Kafka. You know all my thoughts and understand comprehensively what kind of a person I am but you have never actually spent much time with me—like, we just met really briefly. Then can you say you know me?

(I work on my carrot cake and finish it when Alex is talking. And I drink my coffee.)

Me: You are speaking hypothetically. But this is the reality: we are sitting here in your most visited café and I want to know something directly from you. Is that okay?

Alex: Shoot.

Me: Tell me, why did you kill yourself? And why did you add me right before you did it? If I had sent you a message there straightaway, would it have made a difference?

Alex looks at me. And he smiles.

He posted this a week before his death:

I'm thinking about moving to a foreign country. I'm not
talking about Canada, New Zealand, the UAE, or Spain.
I'm talking about REAL FOREIGN. Not any version of
little Ireland. No bacon and cabbage, fish and chips, or
any comfort food for that matter. No English. What I want
is to extract myself entirely from this life and to land in a
brand-new one, in which I have no language, no clue of
any cultural context, and can find no trace of my own kind.
People on Facebook, any recommendations?

Some suggested China. And one savvier and more cynical friend replied: "North Korea?"

I knew exactly what he was talking about. It was precisely how I felt the first year I came to Ireland and studied at the language school. And then the second year. And then the third. And the fourth the fifth the sixth.

"Claire." My roommate knocked on my door. "Stephen and I are going to Grogan's to meet friends. You want to come? It should be fun."

So I went with them to Grogan's. And there were their friends, sitting around two tables pulled together: beautiful blond women in their shining jewelry, tall men and their scented hair gel.

I was directed to sit next to a smallish guy with a friendly smile. "Alan," he introduced himself.

"I'm Claire." I smiled back.

"So how do you know Laura and Stephen?" Alan asked me.

"Laura and my mother are friends," I said.

"Oh?" He paused and took a look at Laura.

"I was joking. I'm her stepsister."

"I thought so. I've heard about you before." He laughed with relief.

Stephen brought me a beer. I took a deep gulp out of thirst.

"So you're from China," our conversation continued.

"Yep," I nodded.

"Tell me, what's China like? I've always wanted to go there."

"I can't really say. It's been almost ten years since I left. It is probably very different now." I drank another mouthful.

"Wow, ten years. And do you miss China?"

"Sometimes."

"And how do you find Ireland?"

"Good. Beautiful country. Nice people," I said, and finished my beer.

"You're drinking fast!" he finally noticed. "Can I get you another one?"

"Nope." I put down my glass and sat back. "I'm good now. Let's talk."

After taking a moderate amount of alcohol I became interested in the conversation. We talked and laughed. And then we got up to go to the bar/toilet and switched seats subtly. New drink. New friend. Shake hand and smile. I'm Claire. I came from China. No, my English is not really good but thank you very much. Yes, I do like Ireland. Beautiful country. Nice people.

Later, in the cab home, Laura said: "I'm glad you came. It looked like you were enjoying yourself."

"Yes. I had a good time," I said.

"So, how's Alan?" Stephen turned from the front seat and asked.

"How's Alan?" I asked back.

"What do you think? Any craic?" he pursued.

"I don't know. I only talked to him for, like, ten minutes."

"So no craic?" Laura said.

"No craic," I said firmly, making sure she'd include this in her report to my mother.

I put "Hippopotamus" on repeat, the song from Alex's band, and went on working on my thesis. It was a light song with subtle and intricate melodies, a sort of Scandinavian indie type.

Once upon a time I was about to die
Fired from my job and kicked out by my girlfriend

She said, Go to hell, you asshole

She said, Don't come back unless you buy me the Ferragamo

Once upon a time I was about to die

I sat outside Heuston Station, begging for change

I said, I'm starved, please, I am starved

I said, I want to have a spring roll or I am gonna die

Eventually my way walked a man from Sligo

He said, Here you go, son, a ticket for Dublin Zoo

He said, Trust me, you just need to see the animals

You need to see the animals and you will never die

Once upon a time I almost died

I went to Dublin Zoo to see the animals

I saw giraffes, elephants, and monkeys

Sea lions, zebras, and flamingos

And I didn't even forget the hippopotamus

Giraffes, elephants, and monkeys

Sea lions, zebras, and flamingos

And oh, don't forget the hippopotamus

Hippopotamus, hippopotamus, hippo, hippopotamus

It was not specified on the website but I believed it was Alex who wrote the lyrics. He seemed like the kind of guy who would not forget to see the hippopotamus when visiting the zoo.

I found myself roaming the internet again, tracing Alex's footsteps. It had been two weeks since he'd died. On his Facebook page, there used to be post after post of tributes, washing onto his wall like the most ferocious tide. And now his wall had gone quiet. Only once or twice a day, a casual R.I.P. would pop up, or a red candle emoji with praying hands.

Naturally, I decided to read all of these 203 posts, studying people's thoughts about Alex and their memories of him. He was described by lots of friends as generous. The word passionate came up fifty-two times. And then there were adventurous (thirty-one), affectionate (twenty-eight), intuitive (seventeen), original (fourteen), and artistic (ten). One said he missed his whimsy. Another called him scintillating. And a Susie Burns wrote that he was the most charismatic character in Dublin.

We've lost the most charismatic character in Dublin. I don't know what you are gonna do, people, but I'm getting DRUNK tonight, she posted.

The most surprising post came in three days ago. It said: So I quit my job, ended my lease, and bought a ticket to Bangkok. You were right, my brother. Our life here has turned into a monster and it's time to run. Get out before it eats you alive.

It was from Micheál Hannigan. I clicked into his page and there he was, already checked in at Brown Sugar, Bangkok, wearing a salmon-pink short-sleeve and a pair of sunglasses, holding a tropical-looking cocktail, grinning at the camera.

I laughed out loud. I laughed so hard that I started coughing. Struggling, I pushed myself up from the desk and closed my laptop.

It was late in the afternoon and I hadn't eaten. I went to the kitchen, scavenging for food. There was a half-eaten cheesecake in the fridge and the expiration date was today.

As I sat by the kitchen table, saving the cheesecake from decay, I thought of the monster of life. I thought it might be hiding, actually, in my bathroom. It was dark. It was heavy. Its skin hairless. Its breath foul. Its eyes small and vicious. Its mouth enormous and greedy. It was this monster that had devoured Alex's life and it was now hiding in my bathroom, watching me.

"Claire!" Laura called behind my back. I shivered.

"What? You scared me!" I turned around.

"It's not me." She passed me her phone. "Amy is on the phone. She wants to talk to you."

"Hello, Claire." My mother had the voice of the English listening test.

"Hi, Mum," I said.

"Where have you been? You didn't call me last week. I asked Laura to tell you to call me," she said.

"Yes, you did. And she told me," I said. "I was just busy."

"Everybody is busy. We all have different things going on. But I call you. I call you because I think it's important. I prioritize." She laid out the principles.

"A friend of mine died," I said.

"Oh," she exclaimed lightly. "Well, I'm sorry to hear that."

I didn't know what to say and she continued: "You know what we say in Chinese, *the one who stays near vermilion gets stained red, and the one who stays near ink gets stained black*. You should be careful about whom to be friends with. Dublin is a very mixed city."

Knowing my mother, I really shouldn't have been surprised, but I was still stunned. I took a breath and said: "It's not what you think. He was a good person."

"I'm sure he was," she agreed. "Anyhow, I just heard from Laura that you didn't like her friend. She said you think he is not very interesting? Claire, I cannot believe I'm repeating this to you:

166

before you make any decisions, can you evaluate yourself first? You are not a very attractive woman. You are a foreigner in this country. You are already twenty-seven and you're still in college, studying journalism." She stressed *journalism*. "So don't be silly, daydreaming about some Prince Charming—that's not going to happen for you. Be realistic and efficient. We've wasted time already. When we came to Ireland, you had to go to the language school and then back to secondary school for two more years. So now you must act. Listen, there are reasons I arranged for you to live with Laura . . ."

She went on and on. My understanding was she'd probably had a bad day and she missed me. Since I moved to Dublin for college, she had become more and more neurotic and then aggressive every time she called. Or it might just have been that Chinese, our native tongue, reduced us to the primitive form, made us incredibly susceptible and vulnerable. I felt a burning sensation in my throat. It was graphic.

The last time she'd called had been two weeks ago. It was the night of the FMNS meeting and I was running late but she wouldn't stop talking until after seven.

When I arrived at Eoin's I texted him and he came down to let me in. The movie had already started. There were six or seven people sitting in the room. Only silhouettes. On the big pull-down screen, a pale Japanese woman was staring blankly and uncannily. The buzzing sound of the projector rendered the space eerie and still.

It wasn't long before I realized the movie was about a father and a daughter, a widowed father and an unmarried daughter, living together in their old and run-down house. They sat by a small table and ate together; in front of each was a dish of vegetables and a bowl of rice. I started to cry. The movie was extremely quiet so I bit my lips and clenched my fists.

And that was when the strangest thing happened. There was this guy who was sitting beside me. I noticed his shoulder begin to tremble and his nose sniffing from time to time.

He was crying too. And tears were pouring out from my eyes. It was Alex and me, our silhouettes trembling, crying quietly while the Japanese father and daughter spoke, in a strange language, in black and white, without subtitles.

MOTHER TONGUE

何處是歸程 長亭更短亭。

李白 《菩薩蠻》

But where is the way home, post after post—
some far apart, some so near.

—Li Bai, *To the Tune of Dancing Buddha*

One autumn afternoon, an old friend contacted me during his brief stay in London and wondered if I wanted to meet for coffee. It was from this friend I learned that, seven years ago, Vertical and Chilly had finally got married and had a child. More astounding, the couple had, from the beginning, instituted an unorthodox parenting plan. When they'd found out about Vertical's pregnancy, they hadn't, like other prospective parents in China, stocked up on baby essentials like bibs, diapers, and imported formula. Rather, they had hoarded pile upon pile of English learning materials: textbooks, flashcards, electronic dictionaries, audio stories, CD players with hi-fi stereo speakers, etc. They had even booked a thirty-seven-week online oral English course.

What the couple had planned, according to the mutual friend, was that as soon as the child was born, they were going to interact with her only in English. They wanted their child, quote/unquote, to grow up in a one hundred percent English-speaking household and to consider English as her native language.

"Did it work out?" I asked.

The friend said he had no idea. The last time he'd met them, the child had been six months old and had only managed to emit strings of *aahs* and *oohs*.

"It was impossible to tell if they were Chinese or English, prose or verse," said the mutual friend.

Vertical and Chilly were both poets I had met in Chengdu in the summer of 2008, when I was going to pubs a lot. Vertical was small and plump, Chilly was lean and tall; Vertical tended to seclude herself in a cozy chair, imbibing bottle after bottle of beer until the bar closed, whereas Chilly always got pissed on shots and provoked arguments with strangers in the small hours. The arguments were often about politics, sometimes about poetry. Once, Chilly got into a fistfight with two undergraduates because the latter insisted that the greatest poet in Chinese history was Li Bai.

"You ignorant green-assed kids!" Chilly shouted. "You just fucking walk around with the one hundred words you picked up from kindergarten, and you great this and great that. What do you know about Li Bai except that your teacher told you he's great? Try a different adjective, would you? Find some thoughts of your own in your dumbass heads!"

With a bruise on his cheek and a bump on his forehead, he came back to our table and slumped in his chair. Patient and I gaped at him while Vertical shook with laughter. Chilly grabbed a Beer Lao from the table and took a long pull.

"So, how would *you* describe Li Bai?" I asked him.

Chilly swallowed the beer and pulled up his shirt to wipe the sweat off his face. Then he said: "The fucking greatest poet in Chinese history."

Vertical laughed louder, clapping as if she was getting out of breath.

Patient lifted his beer bottle by its neck and drank. "I hear you, Chilly," he said. "Just like the old Zen aphorism: *when you look at the water, you see the water.*"

Finally managing to contain herself, Vertical stood up. "We need some shots." She turned to me. "Pigeon, you coming?"

She pulled me up from the sofa. Her hand was fat and soft like cotton candy. She wore a tight slip dress and, as we walked to the bar, I heard her flesh rubbing against the thin fabric, generating a tense hissing as if her clothes were about to split with her next movement.

She lifted her arm and waved to the bartender. "Paul, can I get six shots of tequila?"

Paul was staring at the TV on which the women's 400-meter freestyle final was playing. He seemed preoccupied, eyes bulging, nostrils flaring, slurring streams of unrecognizable words. Vertical and I turned to the TV and watched the blue water splashing.

The next second Paul jumped up, crying out in English, his face scrunching with either excitement or pain.

"You understand English. What's he saying?" Vertical asked me.

"I guess the UK won?" I said, studying the screen.

"We won! We won!" Paul exclaimed, finally remembering

to speak Chinese. "Drinks on the house, tequila shots for everybody!"

That day—August 11, 2008—we all got hammered at Paul's pub. Later I heard that it was the night that Chilly proposed to Vertical and Vertical said yes.

Two thousand and eight had been a special year. In May, an unprecedented earthquake hit Sichuan Province, causing more than eighty-seven thousand casualties. Less than three months later, equally unprecedentedly, Beijing held the Summer Olympics at which China finally topped the medals table.

By the middle of August, when China's gold medal number exceeded that of the USA by double digits, the city I resided in had been taken over by an eternal carnival. Every day, after dinner, people took their evening strolls, parading in the street in athletics uniforms, waving scarlet national flags, singing the national anthem while fireworks exploded in the sky like tropical flowers.

The night after the big hangover, we sat outside Paul's pub. Occupying four roomy outdoor cane chairs, we stretched our limbs like old lizards, sipping beers while Vertical read us a new poem she had just finished. It was a sonnet on pork.

Across the street, a barbecue stall was in business. The owner squatted by a big plastic basin, piercing meats with skewers while his wife, stationed beside the stand, bawled obscenities at him in dialect.

Vertical's reading came to an end and Chilly said: "Now I have some really important news. Vertical and I are thinking about popping over to the Civil Affairs Bureau next week."

A monstrous red lantern blew up in the indigo sky above us, flushing our faces, its sound deafening.

Patient put down his beer. "For what?"

"To get the marriage certificate." Chilly grinned.

Vertical gave me a nod, vouching for her boyfriend.

Patient clapped. "Congratulations!"

The two men clinked their beer bottles and drank.

"May I ask why?" I said to Vertical.

She scrunched her face. "That's a very good question," she said. "I suppose the immediate cause is we found out that once you're married you can claim unlimited free condoms from the Neighborhood Committee."

I looked at Chilly, who gave me a thumbs-up.

A giant sliver dragon leaped towards the north, followed by a golden carp.

"Isn't that weird?" Patient said. "We'd all assume that the ethical purpose of marriage was reproduction—I mean the Neighborhood Committee is weird."

"In exercising my free will, I refuse to succumb to the reproductive cycle," Chilly said. "Because I'm not an animal."

"I hear you," said Patient. "And what a magnificent plan the two of you have brought forward! I'll get another round now. We must celebrate!" He stood up and walked into the pub.

Lotuses came to light and scattered overhead.

After the sky dimmed, Vertical said: "Why haven't you and Patient slept with each other yet?"

"What?" I said, suddenly feeling an emptiness in my stomach.

"There's tension," she explained to me. "And I'm always troubled by the restless vibe between two people who want to fuck and

haven't quite managed to—every time, it irritates my skin to hell."
She scratched her shoulder.

My ears sizzled with the vibration of the fireworks.

"Easy, woman," Chilly said. "Pigeon's still a child."

"Whose surging libido is giving me hives." Vertical grunted,
pinning her fingernails into her rounded arm.

"Maybe you're just nervous because of the gig tomorrow?"
Chilly said. He turned to me. "We have a big gig, going to perform
at the Municipal Agricultural Bureau director's daughter's wedding."

"Wow," I said. "How did this come about?"

A cluster of golden and silver fireworks burst in the sky, con-
figured into a giant panda.

"Connections," Chilly said in an unhurried manner.

Patient reemerged from the pub, holding bottles of Beer Lao in
his arms like a litter of cubs. Behind him was Paul, carrying a slim
tray on which a row of shots stood.

"I told Paul your good news, my soon-to-be-united friends,"
Patient said, releasing the beers to the table. "And he wants to join
us for the celebration."

Paul put down the tray, dragged a cane chair over, and sat
down. "All on the house," he said. "Tequila shots for everybody!"

Chilly's mother, whom I'd never met, used to be a celebrated magician and the vice chairperson of the Sichuan Acrobats and Magicians
Association. After she died in a car accident, her old colleagues and
apprentices at SAMA, in gratitude to her kindness, would occasionally pass Chilly performance opportunities for private celebra-
tions, such as birthdays, weddings, and funerals.

According to Patient, although Chilly had done a year's training with his mother and, through her influence, gained SAMA membership, he was not able to perform magic routines. On the other hand, Chilly simply couldn't turn down the offers, which often came with sizable honoraria. So he partnered with Vertical, who had majored in applied chemistry in college, and developed a hybrid performance style that involved acrobatics, magic, and poetry. This new approach had gradually gained an unexpected popularity among newlyweds, and Chilly and Vertical had been receiving invitations regularly.

"Might be slightly undignified but not a bad way to make money," Patient said, sitting on my bed cross-legged and peeling a tangerine. "I wouldn't mind burning some firecrackers if I'm paid."

While Patient narrated the story of Chilly's mother, I was sitting at my desk, thinking about the crimson rash on Vertical's arm the night before. When he finally paused, I handed him a piece of tissue and motioned for him to lay it underneath the peel. "What is undignified about their performance?"

"Well, it really is a con, no?" Patient said, pushing one segment of tangerine into his mouth, chewing. A revolting acid smell permeated the room. "Neither of them is a magician, but just because Chilly has the connections, they get in." He swallowed. "Think about those people in the audience. They go to a wedding, expecting to see some extraordinary tricks but instead they get a poetry slam."

"I wouldn't mind if I were in the audience," I said, repressing an urge to sneeze.

"I know you wouldn't mind, and neither would I, because

we're literary people—but think about other people, the ordinary people."

I pulled another tissue and blew my nose. I wondered how much one needed to pay for the performance.

"Want some?" Patient broke off a few segments and handed them to me.

"Uh no, thanks."

He fed the fruit into his mouth.

I watched him eat. His Adam's apple moved rhythmically while I considered possible prompts to get him horizontal on my bed and have sex with me. The tangerine peel would need to be removed first.

"I've been thinking a lot recently," Patient said, "about what I'll be like when I'm thirty."

"I don't think I'll be able to live that long."

He laughed. "Of course you will. It's actually difficult to die in this day and age."

"You never know," I said. "Just before International Labour Day, the school my mum worked in arranged full checkups for the teachers as their festival gift. So my mum went for it since it was free. During the ultrasound scan, they found out there were shadows in her left lung. She was then referred to the specialists, did a CAT scan and everything. Now she's in the cancer ward and they say she has no more than a month to live."

Patient looked at me, his hands fallen on the half-eaten tangerine and its peel. "I'm so sorry to hear this, Pigeon."

"It's okay. We're all going to die at some point," I said.

"Fuck," said Patient. "Fuck this world."

"It's okay," I repeated.

We sat in awkward silence. Had I not brought up my mother's condition, Patient could have finished the tangerine and begun talking about Gogol or Chekhov; I could have slipped to sit beside him on my bed, wrapped the tangerine peel in another tissue and thrown it into the bin; we might have been kissing each other by now.

I wondered if it would help if I cried. My plan had been to tell him about my mother's dying and then everything that had happened between me and her. I would in particular mention that my mother had always wanted me to save my virginity for my future husband and I'd always done my best to make her proud. Then I would propose to him, asking if he wanted to screw me on this bed.

I could not manage either to cry or to carry through with my proposal. Glued to the chair beside my desk, I eyed the golden yellow peel on my beige duvet cover and thought of the day when my mother had purchased the cover for me, before I came to the city for college.

"It just occurred to me," Patient said, breaking the silence. "I have this book you should totally read."

Later that day, at Paul's pub, Patient and I met with Chilly and Vertical, who had just returned from the director's daughter's wedding. The pair slouched on a sofa next to the innermost wall, their faces flake-white, bearing a faint residue of makeup.

"Look at the two of you!" Patient said as he marched towards them. "Don't you look stunning."

"I'll buy you a beer now, if you shut up," Chilly said.

"Come and sit beside me, Pigeon," Vertical called.

I crammed myself down between her and the armrest. She smelled of sulfur. "How was the performance?" I asked. In her gelled hair, red and green glitter flickered.

"It was extraordinary," Chilly said. "They all went crazy for us. We were hailed with thundering applause for ages." He raised his arms dramatically and spread them wide.

Vertical slapped down the limb thrusted in front of her. "Except," she said, "except we accidentally strangled one of the pigeons during the last act, but we haven't yet received any complaints from the audience."

"Would you get over that fucking bird, woman?" Chilly said. "No one remembers it now."

"Interestingly," Patient said, "in the mountain area, it's customary to kill a rooster at a wedding, so its blood boosts the groom's masculinity—let's hope it was a cock you executed."

Nobody uttered a word until Vertical burst out laughing.

"This man *here* needs a boost." She turned to Chilly. "Why don't you go get him a drink?"

Behind the bar, Paul was talking to two skinny white women. One was small, the other tall. The small woman blasted out in English: "Are you kidding me? How do you define an emperor or a baby? You're delicious!"

Chilly looked at them distantly.

"These foreigners!" Patient sighed, falling back into his armchair. "Their bird's tongue gives me a headache."

"Pigeon, you should go talk to them," Chilly said. "Don't you major in English?"

I hesitated, still trying to make out what exactly the small woman had said.

178

"Would you leave Pigeon alone? Just go get your drinks. It's not like Paul doesn't speak Chinese." Vertical pushed her fiancé on his back.

"Easy, woman." Chilly recoiled sideways.

"I'll go," I said, standing up from the sofa. "Four Beer Lao?"

"A Seven-Up for me please," Vertical said.

We all stared at her. Patient leaned forward, clasping his hands. "Is there any news you'd like to share?" he asked the couple pointedly.

Vertical glanced at me. A soft light rippled in her eyes.

"You prawn!" Chilly snorted. "Clean up your filthy mind. Don't bring your old man bad luck."

"I'm still feeling sick because of the dead bird. Do I need to make a special statement every time I drink soda?"

I left the trio with their farce and proceeded towards the bar.

The foreigners were talking in low, rapid voices. The tall woman frowned severely. With hands gesturing like sails in a storm, she spewed out a whirlpool of words—I couldn't tell them apart, let alone understand them. Perching my elbows on the bar, I listened carefully. She repeated a strange word a number of times, which sounded like it had something to do with petrol.

"Hello, Pigeon," Paul greeted me in Chinese. "What can I get for you?"

"Hmm, Can I . . ." My heart pounded as I realized English was coming out of my mouth. "Can I get three Beer Lao and a Seven-Up please?"

"Sure. Coming right up." Paul switched to his native language and turned back to open the fridge.

"Hi." The tall woman smiled at me. "Your English is good."

"I am studying English as my major in college," I said, wishing I were able to say something profound.

"Awesome," the short woman said, leaning over on the bar to make eye contact with me. "Tell me, what are your thoughts on womanhood? How does it feel to be a Chinese woman?"

I looked at her emerald irises and her freckled cheekbones, feeling as if the bottom of my stomach were being scraped by a chipped spatula.

Paul returned and placed three bottles and a can on the bar. "We were just talking about this sort of stuff," he said. "Abortion rights, being a woman, women and men, and . . ." The same word came out, petrol something.

Blood rushed to my throat. Carefully, I produced: "Women and men are different. Just like pigeon and chicken. Pigeon is small. Chicken is big. But pigeon can fly and chicken can't. However, in the end, they all get killed at people's weddings—in this way, they are the same."

They processed what I had said. "It's interesting," the tall woman commented. "I've traveled to lots of places in China and I never knew they killed pigeons and chickens at wedding ceremonies."

I wanted to explain that it was meant to be a figure of speech but I had no idea how to say a figure of speech in English. I smiled.

"Pigeon!" called Chilly. "Time to return to your own people!"

"That's my friend," I said to the foreigners, relieved. "It was nice talking to you."

I took the drinks and walked back.

"What were you chatting about?" Vertical asked as I sat.

"They asked me how it feels to be a Chinese woman," I said.

Patient gulped down a mouthful of beer before cracking up.

"What did you say?" Vertical said, reaching over for her Seven-Up.

"I didn't answer," I said. "I don't know how I feel."

"I'll tell you how you feel," Chilly said, taking another pull. "You should tell them it's a great privilege to be fucked by Chinese men—that's how it feels to be a Chinese woman."

Two thousand and eight was a significant year. I was a sophomore at Sichuan Foreign Studies University and my mother was dying in hospital because she had cancer. I refused to turn up for classes because the idea of acquiring knowledge while my mother was suffering irritated me. But whenever my father called, asking if I'd visit my mother soon, I said I was very busy with my studies. I was not able to see my mother in the hospital because I was so madly enraged by the notion of her impending death.

Instead, I sought solace in poetry. I drank with my poet friends in the pub until the small hours and woke up around midday in a rented apartment that I shared with two filthy graduates. I had plenty of time to kill before nightfall when the pub opened, so I read books.

The book Patient gave me was *The Temple of the Golden Pavilion* by Yukio Mishima. I had heard about it for as long as I could remember but had never actually seen the book. *Ever since my childhood, Father had often spoken to me about the Golden Temple*, it began.

I sat cross-legged on my bed and read. It was an old book, once belonging to Sichuan Provincial Library. Its cover had been torn and then taped back and laminated. Its pages were yellowish white, crumbling like butterfly wings as I leafed through. After finishing a number of pages, I was overcome by the serenity of my afternoon and called to find out what my mother was doing.

"I just ate some pomegranate," she said. "It was delicious. Would you like to have some? I'll ask them to save one piece for you."

I said I didn't like pomegranates, they were too much trouble to enjoy.

She chuckled. "Your aunt broke the seeds off for me. I wouldn't want to do it myself."

I asked her if my aunt was still around and she said everybody had gone somewhere and that she was in the room by herself.

"It's nice you called," she said. "I was just thinking about you."

"Me too," I said.

We talked on the phone peacefully. The lack of a visual and corporeal substance reduced my mother to a concept that, for reasons unknown to me, eased my apprehension.

I told her the question the white woman had asked me and wondered if she had any personal interpretation.

"Hmm, that's interesting," she said. "I suppose I never see myself as a *Chinese* woman. I can only tell you how I feel about being a woman." And then she stopped.

The phone went silent. The electric current hummed, throbbing into my ear.

"Mum?" I called. "Mum?"

"Yes, yes. I'm here," she said. "Sorry, I suddenly felt really drowsy."

She said she needed to have some shut-eye and I said goodbye.

'Don't worry about me. Focus on your studies. Everything is fine," my mother said before hanging up.

Afterwards, my bedroom became unbearably hot and stuffy. So I went to take a shower. As the steaming water fell, I applied soap, rubbed scum off my body, and watched the dirt and dead skin being carried away, swirling before flowing down the drain.

I remembered that Vertical had once asked me if I'd ever peed in the shower. She had said she loved peeing in the shower. When the urine became invisible, vanishing into the water, the prickling sensation in her lower abdomen always sharpened. It thrilled her to think that, in this scenario, the only evidence of her urination was this sensation, which would stay with her for a long time.

A few days later, we gathered at Paul's pub in the evening to watch the women's 3-meter springboard diving final. Vertical arrived late. She dashed in and sat down beside me, panting heavily, gripping a sparkly handbag embroidered with bright red sequins. I had never seen this bag before.

"Don't tell me you just robbed that bag from a drag queen," Patient said.

Chilly wheezed.

"Fuck off," Vertical said.

The two men shrugged and soon made their way to the bar, above which a large flat TV hung. The competition wouldn't start for a while. Vertical said she needed to use the bathroom and asked me to go with her. I went and waited outside the toilet stall with her handbag, trying to ignore the trickling sound coming through the door. When the noise finally stopped, Vertical cursed loudly.

"Are you okay?" I asked.

"There are pads in my bag. Give me one," she said. Her hand appeared underneath the door.

I unzipped the red sequin bag, reached in, and retrieved a plump sanitary pad in a pink package. I gave it to the hand, which snatched the pad like a fox.

When Vertical reemerged, she looked pale. I noticed she hadn't fully pulled down her dress and I could see either the very top of her thighs or the lower rim of her buttocks.

"Are you okay?" I asked again.

She groaned, turning on the tap in the basin—there was oozy blood on her hands.

"Periods are the worst," I said. "Do you need a painkiller? I have some."

She cleaned her hands and dried them with the towel. "I'm okay," she said. "Everything is fine."

"Are you sure?" I stepped forward, tapping her back.

She flinched. Before I realized, she had turned around and gripped my shoulders, inhaling deeply. "Relax, Pigeon," she said, letting out her breath. "Nothing's wrong—my vagina bled a bit. And that's absolutely normal, according to the instructions. So all good. Okay?"

"What?" I said. "What instructions?"

"It's just a tiny teeny bit of blood," she said. "And it's gone now. It's nothing."

Failing to fully comprehend what she was saying, I watched her turn around and arrange herself in front of the mirror. She smoothed her hair and straightened the hem of her dress.

"Vertical, what did you . . ."

"No," she said. "I don't want to talk about it. Now let's go back to the table and have a drink—God, I've been thirsty like mad the whole day."

She gulped down half of her bottle as soon as we returned to our table. Chilly and Patient were standing in front of the bar, now surrounded by the other customers, looking up like a group of geese, while on the flat television screen, the lithe divers walked out in their bathing suits. Among these women, there would be Guo Jingjing, the diving queen and the girlfriend of the fourth grandson of Fok Ying Tung, the seventh-richest man in Hong Kong. The rumor was that the diving queen would soon announce her retirement and start a family with the grandson. If that was the case, this would be her farewell competition.

The crowd clapped when a close-up of the diving queen emerged on the screen. "Jingjing! Jingjing!" Chilly shouted wildly.

"Do you want to go and watch?" I asked Vertical.

"Nah." She grabbed another bottle, settling into the armchair. "I'd rather stay here and enjoy my beer. You go."

I sat reluctantly as another clamor rose from the bar. It appeared that a few Foks were sitting in the stand, including the boyfriend. "I'll go have a look," I said. "But give me a shout if you need anything."

She waved at me with a smile. "Will do," she said.

Not knowing it would be the last word I heard from Vertical, I promptly made my way to the bar. The competition had already started. On the screen, a diver rose from the springboard, twisted and turned in the air before plunging into the water. Her moment of suspense was extremely short-lived and could only be captured by cameras before being replayed in slow motion for our appreciation.

The audience in front of the bar sighed in awe. I inserted myself into the crowd and watched with them.

"You look incredibly sad," a man next to me commented in English.

It was Paul. He stood with his arms crossed, one hand holding a Beer Lao, smiling at me. "You look incredibly sad," he repeated, this time in Chinese.

All of a sudden, I was infuriated. "Don't talk to me in Chinese," I said in English.

He glanced at the television briefly before turning back to me. "Why?" he asked in English.

"Because that's *my* language," I said.

He frowned a little and laughed. "Well, you're speaking mine."

I sank my teeth into my lip and turned towards the television, where the diving queen was ascending the platform.

Guo Jingjing walked to the edge of the springboard and made an impeccable jump. When she shot into the swimming pool, the water split only faintly before returning to its undisturbed state.

We all cheered. I heard Chilly crying the diving queen's name.

Without averting his eyes from the screen, Paul said: "But seriously, why do you look sad all the time?"

The competition continued. A Russian diver finished her routine beautifully, getting a high mark of 80.60. The crowd booed.

"My mother is going to die soon because of cancer," I said in English, the unfamiliar consonants erupting on my tongue. "But I don't feel anything. All I can think of is getting laid with this guy Patient."

Paul didn't make a move or utter a word. We stared at the Russian, who was pulling her drenched body up from the pool.

"I'm sorry to hear that," he said eventually. "It must be very difficult to you."

"I just told you I don't feel anything."

"Don't be so hard on yourself." He tilted his beer slightly. The bottle rested coldly against my arm.

We gazed at the screen in silence. One by one, the divers got in and out of the water. A hot sensation permeated my eyes. I blinked.

Guo Jingjing finished her last dive, leading with nearly one hundred points more than the runner up. We didn't need to wait for the competition to finish to know the queen had won another gold medal. The applause thundered.

"Jingjing! Jingjing! Jingjing!" the viewers in front of the bar chanted together. Some started a Guozhuang dance, spinning in a circle hand in hand. A pissed man climbed on a table and grasped the blades of the ceiling fan, trying to pull himself up.

Paul cursed and darted over.

It was not until I laughed in a strange exultation that I thought of Vertical. I turned back to our table and saw she was swaying in the armchair. Raising her arms in the air, rocking from side to side, she beamed like a child.

I ran to her and took her hands. "Come," I said. "Get up and dance with me."

She smiled and said something. Behind us, people were screaming. "Get off!" It was Paul shouting loudly in English. "Get the fuck off, you fucking buckwheat!"

"Say it again?" I bent towards her. Her skin glowed a green-blue hue under the light.

She spoke. Her lips parted and closed a few times, her pink tongue on the tip of her teeth. But there was no sound coming out.

Instead, I heard a savage thump, and then the clashing of tables and chairs. A woman shrieked.

It was the evening of August 17, shortly after Guo Jingjing claimed her fourth Olympic gold medal in diving, that a drunk man fell from the ceiling fan at Paul's pub and, at the same moment, Vertical and I realized that she had lost her ability to speak.

Before the night ended, the three of us and Vertical went, along with the drunk man and his friends, to the West China Hospital. The two patients were quickly assessed at the emergency department and transferred to specialists—the drunk man to an orthopedist, Vertical to a psychologist. Before dawn, thanks to the doctors' extraordinary efficiency, they were both discharged with their respective diagnoses, the drunk man contusions and an ulna fracture, Vertical temporary aphasia.

"Aphasia? What does it mean?" Patient scooped a dollop of fat pig skin from the bowl and sucked it into his mouth. "And they didn't give you any medicine?"

The four of us were sitting at a pig's feet stew shop beside the People's Park, a famous breakfast spot for overnight drinkers. It was around six in the morning. Through the smudgy air, the first sunlight was shining. On the road, the yellow-vested street cleaners had just started sweeping last night's litter: newspapers, scattered firecrackers, crisp packets, cigarette butts, and the business cards of prostitutes. In the stew shop, drunks clustered around tables, munching pig feet, drinking beer, smoking and chatting loudly.

Chilly took a swig of his beer before answering: "Apparently she underwent some kind of shock and that messed up a certain nerve in her brain, which impaired her speech. But it's temporary, the doc assured us. He said there was nothing to worry about— also nothing much we can do. They scanned her brain and everything. All good." He tapped Vertical's head.

Vertical smiled.

"Nothing to worry about?" I stared at the couple.

"Relax, Pigeon," Chilly said. "Everything is fine." He went on eating his pig's feet stew.

I looked at Vertical. She smiled again and gestured towards my bowl.

"I'm not hungry," I said, my voice shivering.

"Ah, poor Pigeon." Patient squeezed my shoulder. He picked up my spoon from the table and handed it to me. "Come on, you need to eat. Breakfast is the most important meal of the day. People say you should eat like a king at breakfast."

I gripped the spoon. "Who cares about breakfast. Vertical has aphasia!"

Chilly winced. "Jesus, woman."

"Don't worry, Pigeon," said Patient. "You heard what Chilly said: it's only temporary. The doctors have checked her. Everything is fine."

"Stop telling me everything is fine!" I said, throwing the spoon into my pig's feet stew, the soup splattering on the table. "What does it even mean? She is obviously not fine, we are not fine— nothing is fine!"

Chilly pounded the table with his beer bottle. "Stop making a scene, Pigeon. She is *my* fiancée, and I'm telling you: she is fine. So now shut the fuck up and eat your breakfast."

I turned to Vertical and saw she was looking outside. I searched her face, desperately, trying to find the faintest sign of loss, annoyance, or disappointment. But she looked insanely undisturbed. The morning light slanted across her, illuminating an otherworldly stillness.

I clutched my hands to stop them from quivering. Still, a formidable fury surged from my stomach. "Damn you." I pushed myself up and grabbed my bag from the floor. "Damn all of you. I'm not buying any of this bullshit. Go fuck yourself and your breakfast."

I walked out of the pig's feet stew shop without looking back, and I heard Patient calling my name, or maybe it was Chilly.

Marching along the spotless road, I noticed all the yellow-vested cleaners had vanished. The city looked refreshed and expectant. Ahead, a massive rectangular backlit PVC poster hung horizontally on the side of a footbridge, watching me like a god as I passed underneath. It was an advertisement with the Beijing Olympics slogan, the kind that had been overgrowing in the city since July.

In bright white characters against a golden red backdrop, it said: *One world, one dream.*

For days, I didn't hear from Vertical and refused to make contact with any of them. All the sound in my world had vanished. I stayed in my apartment, savored instant noodles, and slumbered through long naps. I called my mother in the afternoon when my flatmates had gone to campus and took quick showers afterwards. Most of the time, I sat on my bed and read *The Temple of the Golden Pavilion.*

I sat cross-legged, unfolded the novel in front of me on the sheet, and looked at the pages. I fixed my gaze on the black characters against the yellow-white paper, the void of indentations and the narrow, elongated line spacings—I stared as if I were watching a dewdrop, a cicada, a mayfly. I sat until my neck was stiff and my legs had turned dead, until the outside world had ceased to exist, and I began to imagine the Golden Temple, its insurmountable beauty with which nothing else in the world could compare. Except its own shadow in the Kyoto pond—when the boy was finally taken to visit the temple by his critically ill father, he realized that the temple's perfect shadow on the surface of the pond was more beautiful than the building itself.

One rainy afternoon, when a summer shower was thrashing against my window like a demented swan, Patient visited with a bag of tangerines. He sat down on my bed and started peeling the fruit while informing me that Chilly had purchased Vertical a Motorola smartphone with an impressive slide-out keyboard. He reclined against my bedhead, spitting pips into his palm while claiming that the couple was doing exceptionally well. They had received, thanks to the nationwide celebratory atmosphere, quite a number of invitations to perform at weddings. Due to Vertical's condition, they had to reconfigure the composition of their routines, lessening the literary element and enhancing the visual stimulation—which, to their surprise, had won the audience's ferocious approval.

A couple of days later, when the sun blazed in the reflectively white sky and I was sweating like a toad in my bedroom, Patient came to share with me the pair's career breakthrough—at the SAMA summer symposium, Chilly and Vertical had performed and won the best creativity award. Chilly had then delivered an emotional and powerful acceptance speech that floored not just his mother's old subordinates but also her enemies. Significantly, this award and the speech would instigate Chilly's appointment to the SAMA committee, and henceforth the rehabilitation of his mother's clique. When I asked Patient how he had got hold of such information, especially as he wasn't present at the symposium, he pulled out, from the back pocket of his jeans, his cell phone and showed me a lengthy text message from Vertical, which read exactly as the retelling above.

On the day of the closing ceremony of the Beijing Olympics, after I had finished the last sentence of *The Temple of Golden Pavilion*, an unexpected hailstorm lashed down, accompanied by thunder. Patient strode in, sullen faced, with no fruit in his hands. He asked if I could come up with any justifiable reason for my nonresponse to Vertical's messages, which contained my invitation to the couple's marriage registration. Before I could reply, he carried on expressing his disappointment when, this morning, he couldn't find me at the Civil Affairs Bureau, attending our friends' impassioned union—which, as it turned out, hadn't happened. The registration officer had deemed the couple's application materials insufficient. Satisfied with neither the inexplicable silence of the bride-to-be nor a letter of representation written by Vertical, the officer had required a doctor's note to relay Vertical's medical condition and, in addition, a stamp on the note by a public notary— Patient paused for a long second and urged me to cogitate on this bureaucratic absurdity. I thought about what he said before asking him if he needed a towel to dry his hair.

The dreadful rainy season ended with the arrival of September. A clear sunlight toasted the wet and dull sky, day after day, transforming it bluer and lighter. On a beautiful early autumn afternoon, Patient knocked on my door with a bag of navel oranges and asked for a knife. He sat beside my desk and carefully skinned the orange, picking off its pith bit by bit. He was totally absorbed in this handiwork and was startled when I asked him if he'd recommend another book for me to read. He laid the knife and the orange aside and told me that the situation between Chilly and Vertical had gotten out of control. After the failed registration, the couple had grown increasingly hostile towards each other. First, they would sit across the table in the pub, eyes on their cell phones, thumbs on the keyboards, hitting the little buttons as if they were firing machine guns at each other. After a few nights, when the arguments via text had gradually drawn to an end, a cold war began. Now the couple would sit and drink beer until the small hours without saying a word—the tension had become so unbearable that Patient worried it would eventually burst his head as if it were a watermelon. Then he said to me, urgently, that I must break my irrational silence and reconnect with our friends.

Before I managed to reply, my phone rang. Its bright tune ruptured the space. I retrieved it from underneath my pillow. It was my father.

"Hello, Dad, is everything all right?" I said to the speaker.

My father's voice droned from the other end, and I nodded and said yes.

I put down my phone and pushed myself up from the bed. Fetching my satchel, I began to throw into the bag my glasses, my contact lens case and solution, a travel-size moisturizer, a pack of tissues, a notebook, a lipstick, a scarf, a sleeping mask, and a pair of earplugs.

Patient stared at me as I trotted around the room and fumbled through my drawers and closet. "What's going on?" he asked when I reached over him to grab the book from the desk.

"It seems my mum is in a critical condition, probably not going to last more than twenty-four hours. So I need to go to the hospital now." I slipped the Mishima novel into my satchel and clipped the buckle.

Patient sprang up. "Shall I go with you? Is there anything I can do?"

"Just throw away the peels and the oranges when you leave," I said before walking out from my room.

My mother was asleep when I stepped into the hospital ward. My father told me the doctor had just drained another 400 milliliters of fluid from her chest and that she must be exhausted. I sat down beside her, held her hand, and watched her breathing through a clear tube. Oxygen was flowing into her nostrils, her rib cage rising and falling. I tried to say something to her and found my throat blocked. A while later, I noticed the color of her skin beginning to change, from a pale ivory to a thick sallowness, from the tip of her ring finger to her palm—gently, it extended to her wrist, ascended along her arm, brushed across her bosom, and covered her whole body.

My mother died before nightfall, as the evening sun turned the room into a golden chamber. September 6, 2008.

The moment of her death turned out to be our last moment of serenity. Afterwards, the staff from the funeral home dashed in and began to dress her in the preselected grave clothes before her limbs hardened. They soon found out the shoes they'd brought wouldn't fit because of the edema in her feet. So I was sent downstairs to buy a pair of black shoes while my father, guided by a nurse, stamped his thumbprint on page after page of forms.

As I stood in the shop, browsing through stylish leather shoes in vivid colors, my phone rang. It was Vertical.

"Hi, Pigeon." I heard Chilly's voice instead. "Patient told us what happened. How is your mum doing now? Which hospital are you in?"

I hung up.

After I purchased the shoes and returned upstairs, the hospital room was crowded with people: my mother's co-workers, the headmaster of her school, our relatives, other patients from the same floor, and a couple of cleaning ladies stripping off the bedsheet—my mother had disappeared and so had the funeral home staff.

"Where is she?" I asked my father. "I've got the shoes."

"There's a parking issue with the hearse, so they had to leave," he said. "Now, can you go and pack all your mum's stuff? The hospital wants this room back as soon as possible."

I attended to my mission and then the next mission and then the one after. The world was extremely quiet and I moved effortlessly upstream like a fish. Except, from time to time, I thought of Vertical. I wondered where she was, what she was doing, and how she was feeling. I remembered her round, occasionally innocent-looking face, her soft and moist hands, her thick and curly hair, and, underneath the hem of her dress, either the top of her thighs or the lower rim of her buttocks.

A few days later, when I saw Patient in front of the reception desk at my mother's funeral, I couldn't decide if I was hallucinating until he walked over and gave me a firm squeeze.

"How did you find out about this?" I asked in shock.

"I have my connections," he said.

I ushered him into the banquet hall, wound through more than a dozen big round dining tables, and sat him at the table where I would sit, right next to the rectangular stage at the top of the hall. The guests were arriving in groups, checking the seating board at the reception desk before going to their respective tables. A soothing melody was playing in the background while a sympathetic male voice announced that the funeral and the lunch would start at 12 p.m. sharp.

"Shall I save two seats for Chilly and Vertical?" I said.

"Ah." Patient thought for a second. "No, that won't be necessary."

I went back to my post at the reception desk and only returned when it was noon. At our table, Patient had made friends with my relatives, who had finished inquiring into his educational background and his occupation and were now asking how much he made in a year.

When I sat down, everybody stopped talking and the host in his black suit walked up to the stage.

"Welcome to the funeral of Zhang Qiufang, a respected senior teacher at Number Six Middle School and the academic leader of English teaching in Qingyang District. First, let's welcome the headmaster of Number Six Middle School, Mr. Xu, to give a speech."

The appetizers were served as the headmaster orated. The guests sampled the dishes while sipping wine. Patient put a few honey-coated walnuts into my bowl and gestured for me to eat but I didn't move. When the headmaster's speech ended in applause, the next speaker, a section chief at the district education bureau, commenced his speech and the hot dishes were put on the table. During all of this, I held my hands in my lap, kneading my thumbs into my kneecaps and wondering where Vertical was. I thought about her voice, her laughs, the touch of her naked shoulder, the multicolored glitter shining in her gelled hair. A familiar smell of sulfur cocooned me.

"Pigeon." Patient nudged me with his elbow. "Look."

I looked up and saw that the host had finished announcing the next slot in the program and stepped down. A long belt of thick dry ice meandered across the empty stage, and a man's voice sounded sonorously in the distance:

"*A boat I have boarded, Li Bai am I, and I'm all set to go; when suddenly from on the shore I hear, of footsteps and singing I know . . .*" From the far end of the stage walked a striking young man in a long white robe. Holding his hands in the wide sleeves in front of him, he chanted the poem while bowing to the audience. It was Chilly in a traditional Tang costume. He stopped at the center of the stage and smiled at our table as he continued, "*. . . the water in the Pool of Peach Blossoms is a thousand feet deep; but not as deep as the parting love, to me, from you, Wang Lun, my friend.*"

Tears leaped out of my eyes; my ears drummed. Through my blurred vision I saw a thick brown pillar, which roughly resembled a tree trunk, walking onto the stage—in the middle section of the pillar was Vertical's face. She waved her arms, disguised as bare branches, and lumbered towards her partner. The audience burst out laughing.

Vertical stood still at the center of the stage, her face disappearing behind the brown cover. Again, Chilly sang the famous farewell poem of Li Bai while circling around the trunk. As the singing continued, the artificial brown cover on the make-believe trunk became thick and wooden and eventually turned into authentic bark, and the fake pillar a real tree. Then we all saw that the tree had started to grow: its trunk extended upwards, its branches multiplied and unfurled above the stage and along the ceiling and veiled the entrance.

We sat with eyes wide open, watching Chilly retrieve from his chest pocket a bamboo flute. He perched the flute on his lips and an incredibly beautiful tune emerged. Pink buds began to appear on the branches one by one, and before we realized it, they had swirled open like birds. These flowers were peach blossoms, tens of thousands of them, blooming in the banquet hall at my mother's funeral, light as cloud, bright as stars.

The moment the music halted, the flowers exploded, flaring and burning above us before finally vanishing, along with the branches and the trunk—then the whole peach tree evaporated, leaving only Chilly standing on the stage in his white robe. In the deafening applause, he saluted the audience with a deep bow.

That night, when my relatives gathered at my mother's wake, playing overnight mahjong, I went with Vertical, Chilly, and Patient to the pub. Paul brought out free tequila shots, Chilly ordered endless rounds of Beer Lao, Patient told imperceptible jokes, and Vertical, still unable to speak, sprawled on the sofa like an octopus, relentlessly knocking back shots. And it was on this night that I finally had sex for the first time.

●

Many years later, when I met with Patient at the café in the British Museum and tried to picture Chilly and Vertical as parents, I was suddenly struck by acute vertigo. Through a psychedelic swirl, I saw myself back in Chengdu, sitting at my mother's funeral, underneath the inexhaustible fireworks of peach blossoms, with tears streaming down my face.

Having suddenly lost my strength to climb upstairs and show Patient around the exhibitions, I sat with him in the café until his wife, who had just finished her talk at a symposium at SOAS, summoned him, via a text message, to go shopping with her. Patient said goodbye to me and apologized for the rushed reunion. He promised that if they came to London again, or if my husband and I ever visited Berlin, the four of us could perhaps have dinner together.

Later that evening, when my husband returned from work, I told him, without mentioning the meeting with Patient, the latest news about Chilly and Vertical.

"Hold on," Paul said, fetching a lager from the fridge and pulling the cap off. "So Vertical is talking again? And she's still with that flimsy guy, and married?"

"And they have a child who they've allegedly brought up solely speaking English," I said.

He drank the beer. "God, what are they thinking? This is typical ba miao zhu zhang," he commented.

"Please, no Chinese, especially idioms."

He laughed his way out of the kitchen. I heard him flump down on the sofa and turn the TV on.

That night, around 2 or 3 a.m., I woke up in a sweat. Possessed by an impulse, I hauled out my suitcase from underneath the bed and unearthed my Chinese phone, which I gripped in my hand while going to the sitting room and starting to look for a charger. As I rummaged through shelves, my chest burned with an irrational craving and I eventually saw, in a mixed state of delirium and lucidity, the phone switching itself on and dialing Vertical's number automatically. Right away, I heard her familiar voice on the other side of the phone, speaking to me in perfect English. "I have some very important things to tell you," the voice said. "Find some paper and write them down."

I was woken up by my husband in the fresh morning light, lying on the sofa with a sore back and a notebook half-filled with fragmented and incomplete sentences. On the floor was the chargerless Nokia, long dead.

"Hurry up or you'll be late for work," Paul said.

I walked to the yoga center and found myself preoccupied behind the reception desk. My nocturnal mania had carried on into the daytime as the sentences, read out quietly in Vertical's voice, continued to sound in my head. In between guiding customers and answering phone calls, I took out my notebook and recorded them on the page. By the end of the week, my words had filled up a whole notebook and my boss told me he'd received five complaints.

"Whatever it is, Pigeon, do something about it, okay?" my boss said.

Paul was still at work when I returned home. And I went online to look for possible solutions. Typing in *poetry class london*, I typed and clicked SEARCH.

At dinner, I told Paul: "I signed up for a baking class."

"What for?" he said, holding his fork in midair.

"I thought it might be nice to learn how to make cakes and stuff," I said. "Plus, this one takes place at the weekend, so it doesn't affect work."

"All right. In any case, I'd be happy to eat your homework," he said.

The two-month poetry course was at a writing center near Covent Garden. During the first class, the teacher, a kind-looking woman from Hong Kong, asked us to introduce ourselves. When it was my turn, I opened my mouth and bubbled out a bunch of incompatible syllables—I heard myself saying in a shrill and comic voice: "Hi, my name is Vertical."

"Cool name!" said a young blond guy with a crew cut to my left.

"Thanks," I said.

From that moment on, each Saturday, I attended the poetry workshop as Vertical and went home after each class with some pastry I'd purchased in a shop on Rose Street. While my classmates kindly applauded my incremental progress, my husband generously praised my talent in baking. We would have the dessert after dinner and go to sleep together in a giddy sugar rush. And I would open my eyes, while he was sleeping soundly, and go to the sitting room and write.

After the fifth week's class, the teacher came to me. "Vertical, can I just say: you're incredible."

I suspended my hands above my bag. "You're too kind."

"Ah no, you're too modest," the teacher said, smiling. "I just realized: I actually came across your poems in Chinese a while back and I loved them." She showed me the book in her hands. The Chinese title on the cover read: *Today: A Poetry Journal*.

I froze, watching her leaf through the magazine, the black Chinese characters flickering like lightless windows. I listened to her remarking on how much she admired, in both my English and Chinese poems, the unsettling acuity and the uncompromising ferocity. She stopped at a page and handed me the book, on which I saw Vertical's name and the congested lines.

I flinched and withdrew my hands as if the book were burning. Grasping my bag, I walked quickly out of the building, the Hong Kong woman's voice echoing after me.

Later that evening, when Paul came home, he was surprised to see me in the sitting room.

"Did you not bring back what you baked in the class today?" He put down his briefcase, took off his coat, and walked towards me in a navy-colored suit.

I glanced at him before turning back to the coffee table, on which my bag, my notebooks, pens, and other personal belongings lay in a mess.

"I burned the tart," I said.

My husband didn't seem convinced. He examined the coffee table before reaching out his hand to hold mine. "Pigeon," he said in a gentle voice, switching to Chinese. "Is everything all right?"

I shivered. The Mandarin words sank into my stomach with their heavy vowels.

"Please, Paul," I burst out. "How many times do I need to say this: Can we just speak English?"

Luckily for me, years of bartending had familiarized my husband with the complexity of the human condition. Without a word, he stood up, went to the kitchen, and took out two pizzas from the freezer.

That night, I woke again in the small hours, in a cold sweat, my heart thumping like a propeller. I tiptoed to the sitting room and saw an unusually large full moon gleaming, as if it were being superimposed on the night sky. The moon made me think of a certain poem, a line so familiar, yet it kept slipping through my fingers like a ghost. Finally subsumed by an irrepressible yearning, I turned on my laptop.

I watched myself switch the input system to Chinese, punch Vertical's name into the search engine, and press ENTER.

As December approached, Paul booked tickets for *The Phantom of the Opera*, ordered the Christmas presents, and planned our trip to my in-laws in Cotswolds. I had purchased *Today* from the publisher's website and read, in one restless night after another, Vertical's poems from magazines and online forums—some quirky, some cynical, some making me weep in the dark. I had also learned through a newspaper report on the 2014 New Year's Gala of Sichuan Federation of Literature and Art that Chilly had been elected the chairman of SAMA. I presumed it was through Chilly's influence and the money he'd amassed in the position that Vertical opened an early learning center in 2017, featuring all native English-speaking staff—the launch of the school took up a whole page of the *Chengdu Evening News*.

My husband had noticed that something was off, having repeatedly found me on the sofa in the morning and having received a phone call from my boss at the yoga center. "Have you trouble sleeping these days? Have you been taking your vitamin D supplements? Perhaps top them up with some magnesium," he said.

"Or maybe tequila shots," I said.

He laughed and left the kitchen.

One night in early December, on the website of the early learning center, I came across a photo of Vertical's daughter. According to the caption, the picture was taken during the play *A Midsummer Night's Dream*. In the photo, a group of kids had been dressed up as fairies and flowers, clustering on a stage. Among them was a round-faced little girl, standing still in a thick brown pillar, reaching up her green arms, pretending to be a tree.

Gazing at the girl's face, my hands finally stopped jittering and a gentle drowsiness folded over me. I thought of the little girl playing in the English drama, and when she finished her part and got off the stage, Vertical would be there, waiting for her, and then the girl would call her—I was certain of this—Mama.

I returned to the bed beside my husband and sank into a dream: I was traveling alone across a mountain, thirsty, hungry, and exhausted. I climbed up the steps, turned onto different paths, and eventually I reached the top, where a golden light shone in front of me, and a voice in the light asked if I wanted to see my mother. I said yes, and followed the light to an old pavilion in which a verdant and fruitful pomegranate tree stood. I saw a bird perching on a branch, its body illuminatingly pearl, its beak scarlet, and its eyes ebony. A white pigeon. She looked at me and I recognized her.

"*He chu shi gui cheng,*" I said to my mother. "*Chang ting geng duan ting.*"

HAI

醢

When Zixia arrives back in Qufu, the symposium has already begun. There are only two guards at the city gate and nobody on the street. All the stores are shut, wooden boards sealing their fronts. The town square is thronged with carriages and trailers from counties all over the warring states and reeks of horse piss and donkey manure. The street sweepers, like everyone else in the city, have gone to the Rostrum of Apricots.

"Ah, for fuck's sake," Zixia murmurs, running past the square. The Master expects his disciples to be punctilious, and Zixia has never been late before.

He holds the earthen jar tightly and races along the avenue. The jar is hard and coarse, grating against his chest. As he gets closer to the Rostrum, he can hear the voices of the heralds rippling through the air.

"The Master says . . . the Master says . . . Zigong replies . . . Zigong replies . . ."

It enrages Zixia to imagine Zigong's gloating face once he finds out what the jar contains. And then he thinks of Yanyan, and all the other seniors who are sitting on the stage now, surrounding the Master.

"For fuck's sake." He sighs.

The vermilion gate that leads to the Rostrum comes into sight at the end of the road. There is a large mass of people assembled: the lords from County Jin and Qi, the scholars from County Wey and Cai, the merchants of Wu and Chu, and, locally from Lu, the solicitors, guards, agents, matchmakers, fortune-tellers, peddlers, thieves, prostitutes, and beggars. Stretching out their necks, the audience buzzes like cicadas in midsummer. Their noise is punctuated by proclamations from the heralds, who stand in their white robes, one hundred steps apart from one another, parroting the conversations on the stage out to the periphery of the gathering.

"Zigong asks: Master, teach me one thing that will guide me through my life . . . Zigong asks: Master . . ."

Zixia adjusts his breath and slows down. He grips the jar and walks towards the gate, where a group of young men in light brown robes stop him.

"Hey! You! Where's your ticket?"

It takes Zixia a second to realize what is happening. These damn juniors must have had their eyes eaten by dogs. He glares at them. "Do you not know who I am?"

A young disciple examines him. Zixia is wearing an old gray cloak, smeared by dust and sludge from his journey. He hasn't really rested or washed himself for days and has long exhausted his last coin.

"I don't care if you're a ghost from the graveyard or a demon from hell," the junior says. "Give us ten coins or get lost immediately."

From behind the gate the audience bursts out cheering as the heralds announce: "The Master answers: What you do not wish for yourself, do not impose on others . . . do not impose . . ."

"Shoo!" The junior waves at Zixia. "No eavesdropping. Shoo!"

It has been many years since Zixia tried to enter the Rostrum from this side of the gate and he has forgotten how insurmountable the task could be. The juniors scowl at him as if he were a stray dog.

I'm sorry, Zilu, Zixia thinks, feeling the weight of the jar in his arms. It seems we are out of options.

Carefully, he puts the jar down on the ground and removes his gray cloak. The young men encircling him freeze. In shock, they watch Zixia, like a herd of lambs witnessing one of their own kind being skinned, and see that underneath the pale covering is a gown the color of dark red.

"Please forgive our irreverence!" The juniors bow keenly at Zixia, as his cardinal gown gleams in the late morning sun. "Master Zixia, we must have been blinded, and failed to recognize you. We beg for our punishments!"

"Never mind," Zixia says, wrapping his cloak around the jar and picking it up. "Just let me pass."

He walks through the giant red gate named Great Feat. His gown wavers as he proceeds towards the crowd, the loose threads on the sleeves brushing his wrists. This old cardinal gown used to belong to Zilu, who had gifted it to Zixia the year he was appointed to his current position.

"Here arrives Zixia, the senior disciple of Confucius, the master of literature, the practitioner of the *Book of Poetry*!" the group of juniors bellow in unison behind him.

Who the hell admitted these idiots? Zixia flinches as the audience turns and, like billows of locusts, rushes towards him, screaming.

"Zixia! The youngest senior disciple of Confucius!"

"He's not even thirty and he's already authored the *Great Preface of Poetry*."

"Zixia, where did you go to collect poems this time?"

"Zixia, please enlighten me. How shall I interpret *the tones of a ruined state*?"

"Here's my daughter, Zixia, look how plump and fecund her bottom is. Would you accept her as your concubine?"

Zixia bends his neck and hides his face behind the jar. As his forehead knocks the lid, a revolting stench surges into his nose. His eyes sting. He blinks forcefully and squeezes forward. His leg is dragged back and he kicks out with all his strength. His sleeve is tugged at and he hauls it away.

"Move! I have important messages for the Master! Move!" he yells. In spite of his cries, more and more people swirl towards him, like fat carp fighting over feed.

"Zixia! Zixia! Zixia!"

Zixia doesn't need to see to know that the Master is sitting on the stage, his face hidden beneath his black hat of prestige, watching him in disapproval. So are all the other seniors: Zigong, Ziwo, Ranyong, Yanyan.

Zixia is dead sure that Yanyan is frowning at this havoc. *Yanyan would have handled the matter more prudently*—he can almost hear the words Zilu would've uttered had he been present.

Damn it, Zixia thinks, fighting his way towards the Rostrum. Like it or not, this is how the show begins.

Zixia will never forget the first time he saw a stage play. When he was eleven years old, he watched *Confucius Defeats Three High Ministers of Lu*, in the ancestral temple of the village where he was born.

It was year fourteen of Duke Solidity of Lu. County Chu had just annihilated County Dun, and County Wu was charging its army into Yue while Jin besieged the capital of Wey. Across the warring states, Confucius, as one of the most erudite scholars, had already become a household name, to which Zixia was no stranger. And he was sent into feverish ecstasy, along with all the other villagers, when he heard the news that the great man, having been deposed from his position as the minister of justice in Lu, was traveling to Wey under the invitation of Duke Derangement of Wey.

The townsfolk held a lavish celebration in the temple, where buns and millet wine were served and plays that glorified the sagacity of the Master were performed.

Zixia still remembers standing in front of that dilapidated stage, and while his pissed brothers chased one another around, he gazed up at the actors. Despite their worn gowns and fake swords, their ceremonial manners and eloquent debate were mesmerizing.

"One day I'm going to follow Confucius," he told his father. "I will be his disciple and a noble scholar."

His father laughed. "You will in your hole. Now, when you come back down to earth you can help me bring in the millet."

Zixia didn't respond. He was convinced that he had in him something extraordinary, a gift too great to be perceived by his peasant father. Each day, after finishing the farmwork he was assigned, Zixia would sneak to the local scholar's house and eavesdrop on his lectures to the noble children from outside the window. By trading out his lunches with the landowner's son, he had got hold of the latest edition of the *Analects* and devoured, in a pressing hunger, every line and every character.

Three years later, when Confucius fell out with the duke and left County Wey, Zixia bowed farewell to his parents and traveled to County Cao, where the great scholar and his disciples were heading. For another three years, he chased their caravan, trailed through Cao, Song, Zhen, Chen, and finally arrived at County Ye, where a debate was to be held between Confucius and the Hermit of Ye.

Zixia couldn't afford a ticket and went, instead, to the hermit's estate and lingered outside the back door.

Afraid of being dispelled by the heralds who would be on patrol, Zixia had hidden by an elm tree across the street. While waiting, he flayed a piece of bark from the trunk and sent it into his mouth. Having not eaten in days, he chewed assiduously, turning the sugary bark over in his saliva so it would soften and he could swallow it. Just as he was about to accomplish this mission, a call came from behind him.

"Bog off, beggar!"

Zixia nearly chocked. He turned around and saw a group of men walking his way. His heart stopped. Among the company of light brown robes fluttered a piece of bright cardinal.

Zixia stepped aside, palms sweating. He bowed. "M-masters."

Taking no heed of his greeting, the group walked by, chatting with one another.

"Masters!" Zixia called again. "Please, may you spare me one of your precious moments?"

The men halted. "Poor beggar," one of them said. "Here, take this coin and be gone from our sight." The disciple who handed him the money was Zixia's age, his face exquisite, white as porcelain. He wore a golden necklace outside his brown gown, its pendant the shape of a turtle, the symbol of County Wu.

Zixia recalled the astounding news from last year that the son of Marquis Yan of Changshu had departed from his clan in Wu, traveled northward thousands of miles across the Yangtze River, and joined the house of Confucius as his only disciple from the south.

"I thank you for your generosity, Master Yanyan," Zixia said. "But it is not money that I'm after."

"Huh." The junior disciple retrieved his hand. "This beggar knows who I am."

"An interesting lad." Zixia's heart twitched as the older man in the cardinal gown finally spoke. "Can you tell who I am?"

Zixia looked at him. No doubt he was one of the six seniors. But which one? He recounted the names in his head, shivering involuntarily: Ziyüan, Zigong, Zilu, Ranyong, Ziwo, Ziyou. The man in front of him had a grizzly beard. His gown was thick and fine-woven. His collar was embroidered with golden thread, resembling a bear, the symbol of County Lu.

"You're Zilu, the most valorous senior disciple of Confucius, the practitioner of the *Annual of Spring and Autumn*, and you're from Bian Town in County Lu," Zixia answered in one breath. He felt his stomach turning until he heard a chuckle.

"I'm impressed," Zilu said, nodding. "Now tell me, young man, if you don't want money, what is it you desire?"

"I want to follow you and to study under your guidance," said Zixia. "For this reason, I've renamed myself Zixia because I know most of Confucius's disciples have names that start with Zi."

The juniors burst out laughing. "The kid has lost his mind!"

"Did you hear what he said, this beggar dared to call himself what? Zixia?"

Zilu didn't laugh. "I can see you're smart," he said. "But mere nimble wits will not make you a scholar. Now, try to persuade me: Why should I take you, a beggar, into the House of Confucius?"

His question was fierce but when Zixia looked up, he saw in the senior disciple's eyes the rippling of gentle light.

Clenching his fists, Zixia recited: "The Master said: *My teaching is for everyone, irrespective of their background.* The *Analects* 15:39."

●

Zixia's gown is torn when he finally climbs onto the stage. He kicks aside a long shred of cloth dangling from its frayed hem and, holding the earthen jar to his chest, stands up straight.

The audience claps.

Zixia feels the stage trembling. Ravaged for years by sunlight and rain, the Rostrum is in decay. The dark paint is peeling off like scales, unveiling blotches of rotten wood underneath.

At the center of the stage sits the Master, his face obscured by the brim of his tall black hat. He is wearing a sable gown, its color faded after much washing, his bamboo mat worn as well. Around him, six other mats are spread in a circle, fine and glossy. These are occupied by the seniors, except two of them, assigned to Zilu and Zixia, which are now empty.

"Welcome back, Zixia. What a grand entrance," Zigong says, folding his hands together before raising them in salute. The red garnets on his cardinal sleeves glint. Beneath his gray and meager brows, his narrow eyes glower.

"Back, Zixia . . . What . . ." the heralds repeat, ". . . a grand entrance."

Some of the audience cheers. Others boo.

Zixia waits until the clamor settles before walking over to the Master. He kneels down and kowtows. "Please forgive me for my late return, Master."

"Zixia says: Forgive me . . . forgive . . . Master."

The Master speaks: "I trust you have good reasons. Rise and tell us what happened during your and Zilu's trip to Wey. I heard there was a coup in the palace in Chaoge. And I surmised that Zilu must have got himself involved."

Zixia waits again. One after another, the heralds repeat the Master's words while he presses his forehead on the cold wood until the last note from the farthest herald sounds. Then, in a measured pace, he answers: "It is said, *the one who understands a student best is his teacher*—and the proverb is indeed true. When Prince Kuaikui, the father of Duke Exile of Wey, led a coup to overthrow his son, Zilu could not bear to ignore this injustice and went to the palace to aid the duke. Then, unfortunately, he was captured by Kuaikui and sentenced to death"—Zixia pauses—"by the method of hai."

A high-pitched gasp emanates beside him. Zixia glances over and sees Yanyan covering his face with his sleeves, trembling like a willow tree in a storm. Easy, easy. Ignore him, he tells himself, pushing his nails into his palms.

The heralds deliver the news: ". . . sentenced to death . . . by the method of . . . method of . . . hai . . . hai . . . hai . . ."

The audience explodes into shrieks and wails. Rows of people pass out on top of one another and are removed from the site. In the tumult, the herald next to the stage hits the bronze gong.

"Silence!" he shouts. "Silence!"

Zixia's ears ring. He fixes his gaze on the Master, who begins to speak solemnly once the audience has settled. "Thank you for relating to us this story, Zixia," he says. "I gather that they are Zilu's remains in the jar you carry?"

Zixia can feel his blood rushing. He knows assuredly that this is the moment, one of a few rare occasions in a disciple's life, when his next words will be recorded in the *Analects*. The ecstasy of immortality, Yanyan once called it.

He lifts the earthen jar high above his head, hearing the audience's sweet exclamation at the sight of it. "Yes," Zixia answers loudly. "What I have here is the minced flesh of Zilu."

"Let me see," the Master says.

Zixia places the jar in front of him and removes the lid. A sharp reek rushes out. Inside is Zilu's mushed red flesh, putrefied, oozing liquid.

The Master produces a long and sonorous sigh. He throws his tall hat down onto the mat. Under the harsh midday sun, his hair is lead white, his face pallid, wrinkled like a piece of dried citrus. Tears flow down along the crevices of his blotched skin. "Dispose of all the meat in the house," the Master announces. "I shall never eat meat again."

The heralds chant: "Never . . . never . . . eat meat . . . meat . . ."

Gasps rise from the audience, followed by an ardent ovation.

No one on the stage is applauding. Zixia looks at Yanyan, whose eyes are flamingly red, his face distorted and, for a moment, almost demonic.

With a flinch, Zixia turns back to the jar. For one last time, he examines its coarse surface mottled by dried blood. Then he hands it to the herald who has stepped up to the Rostrum to take it away.

The Master gestures to Zixia to return to his mat, fetches the teacup from the floor, and takes a swig. "Now, my disciples," he says. "I encourage you to overcome your grief and instead to think about Prince Kuaikui, now the new duke of Wey. How shall we view him and his character?"

While the heralds parrot the next topic of discussion, Zixia settles in his seat and takes out a roll of silk, a brush, and an inkstone from the bamboo case in front of the mat. To his right, Yanyan is still frozen like a trunk, staring at the empty mat to Zixia's left.

"I understand you are upset," Zixia says to him, in muted tones. "But Zilu is gone and we must restrain our sorrow and gather ourselves."

Yanyan blinks and, as if having just being woken up, turns to Zixia, his pale face glowing with an ethereal beauty. "I am in shock," he says softly. "Why didn't you send me a message and wait at the post house? Do you have to dash in, in the middle of the symposium, and stir up such a hideous scene?" He frowns. "Are you stupid? Or can't you help your addiction to attention and fame?"

Zixia is not entirely surprised by Yanyan's comments. But still, his hand quivers as he grazes the brush on the inkstone. "Aren't we all?" he mutters, and turns to the white silk spread out before him.

Across the stage, Zigong is talking: ". . . Therefore I cannot agree with you, Ranyong. I don't think Prince Kuaikui's claim to the throne is unjust. We all know he was haplessly driven out of the county by a concubine and has as much right to be the duke of Wey as his son. In my view, Kuaikui taking back his title shows him serving his rightful self-interest and is hence a justified act. And I would add that Zilu's actions were rather impetuous and reckless."

Zixia grips his brush. Why don't you shut your hole. He is just working out a reprimand in his head when Yanyan lets out an immoderate laugh.

"I apologize," Yanyan says, and pauses while the heralds pass on the message.

"Yanyan says sorry . . . sorry . . . sorry . . . to Zigong."

From the audience, sighs and laments resound.

"Ah, come on Yanyan, not to him!"

"Why apologizing!"

Yanyan smiles. "I couldn't restrain myself at the absurdity of your argument, Zigong. So forgive the laughter that escaped me. I respect you for all the extra years you've spent studying under the Master, but I am compelled to deplore your ignorance for misinterpreting one of the most crucial notions of Confucianism, namely yì—justice. In the *Book of Changes*, in the chapter 'The Text of Heaven,' the Master said: *Justice is but the harmony of interests*. Therefore, what we should be concerned with, in this scenario, is not whether Kuaikui's act served his own interests, but rather if he managed to balance the interests of different parties. I agree with you that he has the right to reclaim his title, but the means to achieve such a goal must never be a coup, an interruptive move that has thrown County Wey and its royal palace into chaos. Contrary to your conjecture, I believe that Zilu's judgment on Kuaikui was completely appropriate and by availing Kuaikui's opponent and therefore rebalancing the interests of different parties, Zilu was serving justice."

This smartass, Zixia thinks, writing the character *yì* on the silk. 義. He knows well that Yanyan's also chiding him for the mayhem he caused earlier, but he can't say he doesn't take pleasure in watching the color of Zigong's face change.

"You sophistic and disrespectful parvenu, you—" Zigong roars, his face red as pig's liver.

"Please allow me to finish," Yanyan cuts him off. "In my view, Kuaikui is worth nothing but our condemnation, for not only was he unjust in leading the coup, betraying the virtue of yì, but also in failing to enact the notion of rén when he murdered Zilu, exerting the brutal method of hai and showing no sign of benevolence. In conclusion, I would propose that Kuaikui is devoid of both yì and rén."

"Yì . . . yì . . . yì . . . Rén . . . rén . . . rén . . ." The heralds' voices move across the audience like a stone skimming water.

The audience hurrahs.

"Well said, Yanyan!"

"Marvelous!"

The Master nods. "Not bad," he says, lifting up his hands to silence the crowd. "I take your point on yì, Yanyan. But I would like to explore the notion of rén here and advise us to consider Kuaikui's killing of Zilu again. Is it an act of rén or not?"

"Of course not," Yanyan retorts. "As we all know, Master, *rén* means 'benevolence,' to be merciful, to love, to forgive, and to trust—and Kuaikui's killing of Zilu stands in opposition to all of these notions. Now, in the *Book of Rites* . . ."

While Yanyan talks urgently, Zixia stares at the character he has just written. 仁. *Rén*. He thinks. It was Zilu who told him that he should never listen to the words people say. Because phonetics are merely garments to conceal what's beneath. Only the characters, carrying the wisdom of our ancestors, were created to reveal.

仁. Zixia gazes at it. He breaks the character down and writes: 人, 二. People and two. It says: you and the other. It says you need to treat the other according to the correlation between the two of you: be respectful to your king and be fair to you servants; be kind to the kind and be cruel to the cruel; love your allies but when it comes to your enemies, you must be ferocious and merciless. In this sense, Kuaikui sentencing Zilu to die by the method of hai was in fact an act of rén.

Zixia doesn't realize he has said anything out loud until he sees others on the stage gaping at him as if he were a ghost.

The heralds chant: "Zixia says . . . Zixia says, you must be ferocious and merciless . . . ferocious . . . merciless . . . is an act of rén . . ."

Zixia's stomach turns at the reverberations. He swallows, a faint taste of bile.

"I'm afraid I can't agree, Zixia," Zigong says, his voice theatrically sharp. "Frankly, I find it quite disheartening to hear you make such a judgment on the murder of Zilu, who had selflessly looked after you and mentored you for so many years." He shakes his head.

"Perhaps this kid is delirious," Ziwo says, echoing Zigong's point as always. "I'd lose my mind if I had had to carry that jar of spoiled meat all this way."

"Delirious . . . delirious . . . delirious . . ."

Nobody on the stage makes a sound. The audience whispers.

Zixia stares straight ahead, his neck stiff as stone. He doesn't dare to check the look on Yanyan's face.

The Master bursts out laughing. "I'm impressed, Zixia," he says. "You're right that the true meaning of rén is beyond benevolence. To be merciful is practicing the notion of rén only in a narrow sense. One of the great approaches to rén is, precisely, cruelty. Rén is indifferent and adaptable and therefore we must view Kuaikui's killing of Zilu as an act of rén. And I'm delighted to announce that Zixia has mastered the idea of rén."

The Master's elucidation is passed on by the heralds. And the audience, after a short delay, thunders in acclamation.

"Zixia! The Master of Rén! Zixia! The Master of Rén!"

Zixia sits in a daze, his stomach knotted. Would you be proud of me now, Zilu?

○

It has evolved into a reflex response that every time Zixia thinks he might have disappointed Zilu, an irreparable hunger strikes him. He gathers that the same kind of sensation might be provoked by both of them: the fear of dying from starvation and the dread of being perpetually inadequate.

In fact, in the most testing moments of his life, Zixia is often ravenous. Even on the day he finally became a Confucian disciple, while lining up with other new enlistees at the admission ceremony, the only thing Zixia felt was his bile, like a mass of vipers, gnawing at his stomach.

It was year six of Duke Sorrow of Lu. Jin invaded Xianyü.

The army of Chu was heading to Chen to save the county from the invasion by Wu. Zixia had been with the House of Confucius for more than a year and they—the Master and his followers—were in the mire, besieged by the armies of Cai and Chen in the middle of a wasteland. Having exhausted their supplies, the malnourished followers and disciples had begun to collapse one after another, like ripened fruits falling from a tree.

While the others wept, scavenging the field for scraps of anything edible, the Master himself continued his lectures, reciting books and playing the zither. It perturbed Zixia when he heard that Zilu had flounced over to the Master and raised questions about the integrity of the latter's character.

"Ah no, do you think things will go south for Master Zilu?" Zixia asked Yanyan, putting down the bark he was peeling.

Yanyan chuckled. "I always love this expression of yours, northerner," he said. "And I assure you that things are going right where Zilu wants them to go—in the *Analects*. He will get a dressing-down from the Master, but as payback, this little incident will be recorded and read by generations after us. And this should bring him infinite ecstasy. So now, stop worrying. Scrape off that rough skin quickly and let me have the tender bit."

Zixia carried on removing the brown outer layer of the bark and eventually held in his hand a beautiful slice of wheaten-colored flesh. His stomach rumbled at its luscious fragrance. Biting his lip, Zixia offered Yanyan the delicacy.

"Cheer up," Yanyan said, chewing. "It's a privilege to have me in your debt. I promise good things will befall you in no time."

———

Two days later, the general of County Chu and his soldiers came to Confucius's rescue. After the carnage ceased and the corpses were disposed of in a ditch, the Master announced that it was time to move on and that new disciples would be admitted to fill the vacancies left by the dead.

This should have been the moment of glory, when Zixia waited in the enormous black tent during the admission ceremony, for his name to be called. In spite of the flaring stomachache, he composed himself. He understood he was about to step forward, to kowtow in front of the Master, and, officially, to see his name—Zixia—be documented in the *Analects* as one of the seventy-two disciples.

Nonetheless, in the next instant, he passed out from hunger.

When he woke, everyone else was gone. Zilu was sitting in front of him, his face somber. Terrified, Zixia's stomach cried out a long croak.

"I, I'm sorry, Master Zilu," he said. "Please forgive me."

Impassively, Zilu looked at him. "There's nothing for me to forgive. What happened has happened."

"What happened? Was I admitted?" Zixia said. "I didn't mean to faint at the ceremony. It's just, for the last couple of days, Master Yanyan has been pressuring me into offering him all of my victuals. And I had hoped I would be able to endure the lack of food. I'm really sorry for overestimating my capacity and demeaning you in front of the others . . ."

Zilu stood up and, without saying a word, walked out of the tent, the hem of his cardinal gown vanishing behind the dark drape like the sun being eclipsed by the moon. Zixia felt his abdomen stiffen. He remembered his father telling him that if you ate the wrong kind of bark, the kind that could not be digested, you would be stuffed to death.

He sat on the hard ground in angst until Zilu returned with a clay bowl. He put it down in front of Zixia. "Here, this is for you."

It was a bowl of pearl-white rice, topped with a thick brown paste. Zixia had never seen anything like it before. "What is this goo?"

Zilu chuckled. "It's not goo. It's hai, the Master's favorite dish, in fact." Zilu dipped his index finger in the sauce and wrote the character down on the ground—醢. "Now, this character, *hai*, means 'minced meat.' Originally, it referred to a barbaric method of execution, invented by the last emperor of Shang, King Ferocity. He murdered the crown prince of King Wisdom of Zhou by mincing him alive, and then he forced King Wisdom to eat the meat balls made from his son's flesh."

Zixia gaped at the brown paste. He felt he could still see in it the red strings of mucus. "I don't want it," he said. "I mean, I can't have meat. I'm a commoner. If the others catch me, I'll be in trouble."

Laughing again, Zilu said: "Did I not mention that this one has no association with human flesh? Also, you have been enlisted as a disciple. You're not a commoner anymore, Zixia, you're now a noble scholar who is allowed by law to eat meat. And you must remember, from now on, you shouldn't let anybody pressure you into doing anything against your own intentions."

Zixia listened to his mentor, and he thought of his parents and siblings, of all the millet porridge and buns they had eaten, all the leaves, bamboo shoots, and lotus roots.

He eyed the greasy sludge, its savage stench revolting.

Zixia picked up the spoon. Overcoming his nausea, he smiled. "I'll be honored to taste this hai, Master Zilu," he said. "In fact, now that it is in front of me, I can't imagine how I could ever live without it."

●

The familiar foul smell drifts across the great hall, stirring Zixia's gut. As always, Ziwo has opened the food hamper on his rosewood daybed and is munching a meat pie. Ranyong has secluded himself in a far corner. Immersed in a scroll of what is most likely the script of a new play, he hums tuneless verses, head bobbing.

Zixia turns to Yanyan in the chair next to him, who, like the others, has sunk into his own world and is untangling his long hair with an ivory comb.

Keep acting, you haughty bastards, Zixia thinks.

The room is unusually silent. There is only the sound of the clanking of bronze, as Zigong counts up the ticket money at the top end of the hall. Taking his time, he sorts the coins of various shapes into different piles while murmuring: ". . . nine hundred sixty-two, nine hundred sixty-three, nine hundred sixty-four . . ."

Zixia used to find it insufferably agonizing, when, after the symposium, all the seniors had to retreat to the great hall in the Confucian Estate, waiting for Zigong to settle today's accounts— a procedure that always dragged on for hours.

Back then, Zixia reckoned, had more disciples been assigned to this mission, they could all return home with their wages much earlier. However, the ordinances had been established long before his time. And Zixia, while exasperated, had little power to amend them.

It was Zilu who apprised Zixia of the incongruity of his viewpoint. "The system is no prison," he said. "If you position yourself within it appropriately, you'll find its rules enabling. Zixia, be patient and understand that you're not only in the great hall to get paid, that the most crucial exchanges—the talks—take place there and then."

Zixia waits. The stench of meat writhes around him, irking his skin. He watches Ziwo gorge on his snack, his lips smacking, licking tawny juice off his thick fingers, before finally he looks up and stares directly into Zixia's eyes.

Here we go, Zixia thinks.

"Oi!" calls Ziwo. "You must be starving, Zixia, having shouted yourself hoarse making that racket. Would you like to have some venison pie? And rest assured"—he titters—"this meat is from a pretty fawn I killed last month, no fishy smell at all."

With a crisp clink, Yanyan puts his comb down on the table. "What are you on about? Can you at least try to make yourself perceptible, Ziwo."

"Isn't it clear to us all?" Ziwo wipes the grease off his hands, looking around the hall. "What Zixia told us at the symposium was a very large pile of crap."

"I wouldn't put it that way," says Ranyong, rolling up the script he was reading. "Now, we all know that I don't take sides, so if you'll allow me, I'd like to offer a few words from an impartial perspective." He gives a cough. "First, I'd advise Ziwo to show some basic sympathy here. After all, Zilu had been our fellow senior disciple for many years and, more important, the successor we'd elected, so let us all acknowledge that his death is a tremendous loss to the House . . ."

"Ah, shut your hole, please, you bag of hot air!" says Ziwo. "Save the fancy lines for the stage and the audience next time around. Just be real here and admit that you, too, find Zilu's death suspicious. Why on earth would that hypocrite be concerned with a coup in the royal palace of Wey? And even if he *was* captured by Kuaikui, why would Kuaikui kill him, a disciple of Confucius?"

Nobody utters a word. Zigong's whispers travel down the hall: "one thousand two hundred three, one thousand two hundred four . . ."

Throughout his journey back from Wey, Zixia has been picturing this very scene, and he has rehearsed his response hundreds of times in his head. Still, he swallows hard as he senses Yanyan's cold gaze on his face, his heart hammering.

He says: "I appreciate that you're not the brightest person, Ziwo, but surely even somebody as dumb as you should not have missed a whole session in the symposium, during which, let me remind you, the Master himself deemed Zilu's aiding of Duke Exile of Wey an act of yì. So there's no need for any further discussions on Zilu's motives. On the other hand, I have to say that I share your doubt over Kuaikui's motivation. In fact, I've been asking myself this question repeatedly: Why, when simple imprisonment would suffice in the circumstances, would Kuaikui kill Zilu, and in such an unusual and excruciating way? Unless . . ." Zixia pauses and glances at Zigong, who has his back to the rest of the seniors, still shifting through the coins. "Unless Kuaikui was asked to do so by somebody else. Someone who has been holding a deep grudge against Zilu, possibly since he was beaten by Zilu in the election of successor. And now, with Zilu's death, the position of successor will become vacant to this person, who, as we are all aware, knows Kuaikui very well from his years of serving at the royal palace of Wey as prime minister. What do you think, Zigong?"

The clattering stops. Zigong throws the coins back into the case before turning around. Having been tinged by the grime from the money, his face is veiled by a sallow sheen, giving him the look of a resurrected corpse. He sighs.

"This is why we should have banished the *Book of Poetry*," Zigong says. "Too much literature makes people unhinged. Yes, everyone knows that I didn't exactly see eye to eye with Zilu, but the same could be said for many of us in the House. Plus, isn't it true that the deepest and most heinous loathing is often concealed? If you were arguing that I must have murdered Zilu because I covet his position as the successor—well, since any senior could potentially be the next successor, shouldn't all of us here be equally suspicious?"

"Hear, hear," Ziwo bawls. "That's some forthright insight!"

His palms slap sluggishly against each other, making Zixia think of a loach floundering in the sludge, at the end of a rope. He shoots up from his chair. "What kind of despicable man would slander the dead like this?" He points at Zigong. "Zilu was the most upright and kind person we know. And no matter how much you try to muddy the waters now—"

"Quite the opposite," Zigong says, interrupting Zixia. "I'm only trying to elucidate the situation for us all. Just because Zilu's dead doesn't mean we have to treat him like a saint. In fact, Zixia, didn't you and Yanyan quarrel with your mentor not long ago? And, most important, weren't you the one who accompanied Zilu to Wey and yet brought back only his remains? Then again, speaking of Kuaikui, I'm sure you know him as well as I do, as you are the eighth son of Viscount Ji of Wey."

How the hell? Zixai shudders, blood gushing up to his head. "Stop lying out of your hole," he retorts. "What Viscount Ji? My father grows . . ."

"That's enough." Yanyan reaches over his hand, sinking his delicate fingers into Zixia's wrist. "It is ill-suited for us to carry on this discussion here and now, without the presence of the Master. If there are any unresolved issues regarding Zilu's death, they're for debate in the next symposium."

"I agree," Ranyong says. "Let's not waste our fervor prematurely. We should all get our payment and go home. Then we can take time to work on the best possible ways to mold our fervor into arguments—because our audience, who pay such good money, deserve the best performance."

The audience. Zixia slumps back into the chair. That's right, he thinks, this rat has to be slayed on the stage, so everybody, every prig and scum and fuckup from all over the warring kingdom, will see, with their own eyes, the hellish filth inside.

It has been ten years since Zixia joined the House of Confucius. He has transformed, through the years, from a guileless outcast into one of the six seniors who stand in the center of the hegemony. His fame—his erudition, his grit and literary talent, and even his unrestrained candor and occasional gloom—has traveled far and attracted a steady number of devotees, who would sell their wives or livestock to get a ticket to see him at the symposium. Yet, having familiarized himself with the doctrines and intricacies of the House, Zixia still feels as powerless as he was a decade ago, or even more so, for now he knows that he is disposable no matter how much he strives, that his insignificance is engraved in him, like a birthmark. It was there the moment he was born, and it will remain part of him when he dies.

Zixia can see clearly that he began to feel this way when, a few years after being admitted as a junior disciple, he finally made out the truth of Confucius, when he learned who the Master really was.

It was the spring of year thirteen of Duke Sorrow of Lu. The eastern wind arrived late. The Master's only son, Li, had died the previous winter and the Master had missed the next three symposiums, leaving Ziyüan, then the most reverent senior, in charge of the debates. There had been rumors going around among the juniors, claiming that the Master himself had become extremely sick and might not live to see the early lotuses that summer.

Zixia cannot recall the day without a pit growing in his stomach. He can still smell the musty scent permeating the east wing of the Confucian Estate and he can still see the flowering quince tree budding outside the study. The swollen red burgeons perched on the leafless branches like pus-filled boils.

In the study, there was only him and Zilu, who bent in front of the table, transcribing an ode from the *Book of Poetry*. Holding a fine-trimmed ink brush, Zilu's arm undulated, and the lines emerged on the silk scroll:

十月之交,朔月辛卯,日有食之,亦孔之醜.
彼月而微,此日而微,今此下民,亦孔之哀.

Usually, Zixia would rejoice in the splendid flow of these brushstrokes, but that day the black characters only made him think of crushed insects, their viscera spattering out, mixed with their oozy bodily liquids.

"*The moon and the sun will darken, and doom will befall us in inconsolable despair.*" The words gushed out from Zixia's mouth. "Is it true that the Master won't be breathing for long and that we'll all be left in an unthinkable calamity?"

Resting the brush, Zilu smiled. "You're certainly susceptible to the verse," he said. "But no, you don't need to worry, nothing disastrous will happen to us. Remember that saying: *Good fortune follows upon disaster.*"

"It also says that disaster lurks within good fortune."

"That's right." Zilu chuckled, patting Zixia's shoulder. "You are thorough as always. But the words are merely the immediate appearance of the phenomena. In this case, if we examine the text closely, we'll understand that the essence of disaster and fortune is the same, namely the change of order. The ones who are lost in such change experience it as disaster, while those who employ the change thrive with good fortune."

Zixia was still grappling with Zilu's words when a herald darted into the study.

"Thank goodness, Master Zilu! At least you're in the estate," the herald called out. "The Master sent for all the seniors to go to his chamber immediately."

Zixia's ears whirred; his mouth dried up. He heard his mentor's order, inflected with a tone of urgency, like a drum beating. "I'll get the other five from their mansions," said Zilu. "You must go to the Master's residence now, Zixia, and guard the door to his chamber. Until we arrive, allow nobody to enter."

———

Bowing deeply, Zixia sprinted out of the study and raced towards the northernmost end of the estate, where the Master's residence was. By the time he got there, a large group of junior disciples had already gathered in the courtyard.

The courtyard was paved with white jade pebbles, impressively large. At the back sat a golden building whose ornamental cornices rose into the air, gleaming like celestial ladders. Zixia had never been to this part of the estate. He was still enchanted when he heard: "Let go of my sleeve, you dumb southerner!"

It was a junior disciple trying to pass Yanyan and reach the steps to the golden building. "We need to know what's going on in there," the junior bawled, hauling back his sleeve from Yanyan. "The Master can't wait forever. If the seniors couldn't make it in time in their palanquins, we are going in!"

"You might want to think twice," Yanyan said, his pale face full of scorn. "Are you sure the Master will recognize you? Have you actually been by the Master's side?"

"You mouthy piece of work! You think you're better than us, huh?" Another junior tramped over and shoved Yanyan sideways.

"Let us see the Master! We've all kowtowed to him to be admitted as disciples and that makes us his legitimate heirs!" More juniors joined in.

"Cut it out, morons!" Zixia roared. With a few strides, he bounded to the top of the steps and crouched, arms widespread, blocking the door to the chamber. Below him, the juniors were in riot, their brown robes stirring frantically like muddy torrents, swallowing Yanyan's slim figure. Zixia thought of Yu the Great, the first emperor of the Xia dynasty, who had defeated the monstrous flood in antiquity and saved tens of thousands of lives.

"All of you," he cried. "Just calm the fuck down, otherwise I'm gonna rip off your dicks and shove them up your holes."

When the seniors arrived, the courtyard was eerily quiet. The juniors gave way to them as Zilu guarded Ziyüan, followed by Zigong, Ranyong, Ziwo, Ziyou, and walked through the courtyard to the golden building. At the foot of the staircase were a couple of juniors on the ground, squirming and wailing. On the veranda stood Zixia, who was panting; sweat streamed down his face. Blue veins bulged around his temples and his eyes were bloodshot, like the ox-headed door god from hell.

"Well done, Zixia," Zilu said. But Zixia couldn't respond or move. All he heard was the sound of his own heart thumping. All he saw was a red mist. He didn't know when the seniors filed into the chamber or when the crying began to blare from behind the door.

Only when the door finally opened could Zixia turn his head. Stepping out of the chamber was a man in a sable robe and a tall black hat. The man stood at the top of the stairs, and behind him were the seniors in their cardinal gowns. Zixia blinked, once, twice, three times until he could finally make out these men in a clear light: Zilu, Zigong, Ranyong, Ziwo, Ziyou, and, as the hair at the back of his neck stood up, Zixia recognized, beneath the brim of the black hat, Ziyüan's lined face, his hair white as lead.

Why the hell is Ziyüan wearing the Master's clothes? Zixia was just thinking when the senior raised his ebony sleeves and announced:

"My disciples, I am sad to tell you that my most long-serving disciple, most virtuous of all the seniors, Ziyüan, has just passed away." He paused and expelled a long sigh. "Alas, the grief I'm in is great, as if heaven has resolved to deprive me of my own life! However, we must move on. We are expected to prepare for the funeral and mourn for seven days. Afterwards, when the symposium reopens, we will select, from among you all, a suitable junior to inherit Ziyüan's legacy, to be the practitioner of the *Book of Poetry* and, more crucially, to step up as the new senior disciple."

The juniors in the courtyard stood in dead silence as the old man, whose face was shaded by his hat, made the declaration. Then they all erupted with applause.

"Praise you, Master, I'll follow you forever!"

"Heaven bless you, the great sage Confucius!"

It was at this moment Zixia understood everything. Fucking baloney, he thought. So what, Ziyüan is now the Master and the real Confucius just died? Or was that one even the real one—perhaps he had only inherited the title from some other fellow? He tried to recall the Master's face, which he would have been able to behold had he not passed out on the day of his admission and missed the chance to kowtow in front of the sage. Then he remembered that bowl of hai he had forced himself to swallow.

His stomach spasmed and, with formidable force, a gush of sour and bitter liquid shot out of his mouth.

Shrieks rose as Zixia collapsed to his knees. Desperately, he tried to cover his mouth, but his gut seemed to have turned into a seething abyss from which endless vomit surged, fetid, vile, and rust-colored, jolting through his fingers, splashing on the marble stone and cascading down the steps.

Zixia had no idea that good fortune was about to befall him. His spectacular suffering had moved his mentor so much that Zilu had finally made up his mind to let the new Confucius know that, as part of their agreed quid pro quo, he would like to pick Zixia instead of Yanyan as the next senior, to be in charge of drafting the *Great Preface of Poetry*, the very essay that would be celebrated by thousands of scholars and poets in posterity as the genesis of literary criticism—he had no idea.

For the time being, he continued to retch on the veranda.

稷

When Zixia returns home from the Confucian Estate, the cottage is filled with the aroma of millet.

He gently pushes open the front door. There is no one in the sitting room, the space bare, containing only minimal furniture: an old tea table, two wicker chairs, and a calligraphy scroll hanging on the rammed earth wall. Against the white silk looms one colossal black character: 稷.

Ji.

Usually, he wouldn't have been drawn to the figure on the wall, nor did he appreciate his wife's decision to put the scroll up here. Zixia reckons that his wife cherished the calligraphy simply because it was a wedding gift from Zilu. But he was troubled by it, always suspecting the hulking character was a spur from his mentor, to remind him constantly of his humble origin: millet.

Now, for the first time, he sees it in a different light. The eighth son of Viscount Ji of Wey, he thinks, smiling bitterly.

Would I not have been admitted had you not lied about my background, Zilu?

He removes the old cardinal gown, leaves it on the chair, and walks into the bedroom. The children are asleep in their cot, his daughter cuddling her infant brother, their faces the color of fresh radish. Farther down, a door leads to the kitchen where his wife, Woman Bu, is cooking by the stove.

In the flickering flame of the firewood, Zixia can see that his wife is wearing a waist skirt over her tunic, which brings out the delicate curves of her midriff. Her straight hair hangs loosely above her shoulders, quivering like a silk brocade as she rhythmically stirs the shimmering clay pot.

Zixia inhales deeply. How could I possibly break the news to her? Reluctantly, he knocks on the doorjamb. "I'm home."

Woman Bu halts for a short moment. She picks up bronze tongs and bends to prod the wood in the firebox. "Good," she says finally. "I hope you've got some money."

Her voice is quiet. Nonetheless, it betrays her grievance and brings up a lump in Zixia's throat. "Yes," he answers, walking to the table, and empties the coins out of his chest pocket. "Here's forty."

Woman Bu fetches two bowls from the shelf and begins to ladle the millet porridge from the pot. "Shouldn't it be fifty?"

"Um," Zixia says. "I was late for the symposium today. So had to pay the penalty."

His wife drops two bowls of porridge on the table and hands Zixia a spoon. "That's unfortunate," she says, sitting down across the table. "We could really use the extra ten. The north-facing wall needs to be fixed now that it's getting colder."

"I'll take a look tomorrow," Zixia says. In the shadowy light, the mush in the bowl seems to be covered by a layer of gray tissue. He digs through it with the spoon and takes the first slurp.

Woman Bu gathers the coins into the pocket of her waist skirt before picking up her own spoon. She eats soundlessly, like a cat. Her hair, the ends jagged, falls from behind her ears and curtains her face.

Zixia coughs. "What happened to your hair?"

"I cut it to sell it," says Woman Bu. "Plum needs a new quilted jacket, and we were out of millet. The wigmaker was very nice, though." She blends the gruel in a scrupulous manner as if she is making a potion. "He was impressed when I told him who my father was and offered five more coins in the name of the prominent Marquis Zhao of Jin."

Zixia swallows, the porridge bland, faintly fusty. Somehow, he hears Zilu's voice in his head, resounding to and fro as if coming through a long line of heralds: *I've written to my brother-in-law, Marquis Zhao of Jin. His and my sister's second daughter has just turned fourteen. She is a gentle and sweet lady who's been brought up to be an obedient and pleasant wife. I have confidence that you will make an excellent couple.*

I mustn't let her find out what happened, Zixia tells himself. "You understand that you shouldn't have brought up your maiden name," he says. "You're a woman who belongs to the family of Bu now and ought to refer only to your husband's name when being asked."

The words have fled, despite his immediate regret at what he's said. His wife remains silent and scrapes the bottom of her bowl for the last spoonful of porridge.

"I'll find ways to get more food," Zixia adds. "I can go hunting on the mountain."

"A hunt?" says Woman Bu. "You do know that according to etiquette, hunting is legal only for nobles with titles." She tilts her head. "Would it be good for you to ask Yanyan to accompany you? Isn't he an earl?"

"What are you on about?" Zixia says, suddenly vexed, hearing that name coming out of his wife's mouth. "Why would I ask him?"

"I thought you two get along." His wife glimpses him, the light in her eyes wavering.

"There's no need to trouble him," Zixia says. "I'm sure I'll manage. I know some hidden paths in the mountain where no one would see me."

"And you think instead of asking for some help, it's better to feed your family with illicit game." Woman Bu stands up, returning her empty bowl to the stove before disappearing into the bedroom.

Zixia eats alone. A honey hue is diffused from the waning firewood and cradles him. From the room next door the baby's cry breaks. Before long the wailing settles, replaced by Woman Bu's whispering, her voice indistinct and soft.

Zixia cannot remember the last time his wife spoke to him in such a voice. Perhaps it was on their wedding night, when she told him how grateful she was to her uncle for marrying her to the youngest senior disciple of Confucius and how covetous her sisters, her mother, and her grandmother felt, and the way they were all boiling with envy, tearing their dresses and wringing their sleeves when she left the Zhao estate in a red palanquin.

He was struck by her vitality. There had never been anyone in his life like this. The next morning, when she called for her chambermaid to dress her and received no answer, he told her that he had sent back her dowry because it would be impossible to accommodate the servants in the cottage.

It took his bride a while to comprehend what Zixia meant. Then she went quiet. For some reason, the silence in the room had attained a strange horror that stifled Zixia. He couldn't breathe, as if he were being buried alive.

"This arrived yesterday." Jolted out of his memories by his wife's voice, Zixia turns around. Woman Bu is coming over with a thin scroll in her hand. "I think it's from my father."

Zixia takes the scroll. It's sealed by wax stamped with an illustration of the Vermilion Bird.

"Right." Zixia breaks the seal. His wife cannot read, but she knows well the symbol of the family Zhao. He unfurls the scroll, as if peeling the skin off a snake, the characters contorted and stretched, revealing their meanings inch by inch. Zixia's heart pounds. He prays that Marquis Zhao of Jin hasn't heard of Zilu's death and is not writing to annul their marriage.

"What did my father say?" Woman Bu asks, sitting down beside Zixia, her voice tinged by a fresh zeal.

I could lie to her, Zixia thinks. She is not going to know what the letter says anyway.

He coughs again to get rid of the sting in his throat. "Your father writes that the duke of Jin is well, both he and your mother are well, your brothers are well too, and he, he . . ." His fingers tremble as he reads on.

Woman Bu takes hold of his hand. "Why are you so nervous?"

she says. "It dispirits me to see that you're so agitated, trying to hide my uncle's death from me. I shall let you know that I've already heard the news. Everybody in the marketplace was talking about it, that Zilu was killed by Kuaikui, chopped down into a heap of mince."

A shiver runs through Zixia, yet his hand is locked by the long fingers of Woman Bu, her oval nails the color of rose balsam.

"I was meaning to tell you, but I didn't want to upset you," he says.

"I'm not upset," she replies. "It seems like a fitting death for an old hypocrite like my uncle. And don't worry"—she smiles at Zixia—"just because the tie to our union is gone doesn't mean I'll ask you to divorce me or get my father to nullify our marriage. Rest assured that I'm well-disciplined, with all the noble women's virtues. And once a Zhao woman is married, she must serve her husband well and never utter a word of complaint. She shall not be discharged from the alliance and seek a new suitor"—she pauses, retrieving her hand—"as long as her husband lives."

Zixia wasn't afraid of death before his first child was born, and until he had a family to provide for, he'd never been worried by his lack of wealth. He cannot be sure that, back then, he genuinely never doubted, for instance, the disparity between the earnings of the House and his own personal wages, or that he simply refused to ask himself such a question because, for someone like him, discontent would only yield distraction and was therefore unaffordable.

He appreciates acutely that he is different from the others, who'd go to the theater or hunting together, squandering the fortune they inherited while mingling with one another. Zixia sets himself apart from his colleagues, because, truthfully, he does not belong to their world and no one would come near him—no one except for Yanyan.

One might say that it is not unfathomable that Zixia and Yanyan are close. After all, they've studied under the same mentor over a decade and are both in their twenties, only one year apart. However, Zixia has always been perplexed by Yanyan's affability. Because, unlike Zixia, who joined the house with lice in his hair and thick calluses on his feet, Yanyan arrived in a red sandalwood carriage, well adorned and hailed by spectators. And unlike Zixia, forever humbled for being taken in by Zilu, Yanyan was bestowed with the privilege to choose, among all the seniors, whichever mentor he preferred.

In fact, for so long, Yanyan had been the most prominent disciple among the younger generation, and everyone was astounded that, after Ziyüan's senior position was vacated, it was Zixia, instead of Yanyan, who was named by Zilu as a candidate and won the debate on poetry, along with the new senior position. This was followed by Zixia's marriage to a princess from the high-powered Zhao of Jin, a privilege any disciple would have dreamed of having.

It was the summer of year thirteen of Duke Sorrow of Lu. The soldiers of County Zhen slaughtered the whole army of Song before pillaging six cities, while the troops of Yue, led by their patient and vengeful King Goujian, were marching towards Wu. Zixia should have been walking on air. He had expected himself to rejoice in his triumph, rightfully earned by his years of unrivaled diligence and loyalty. However, with his bride slumbering on their wedding bed, Zixia found himself unable to sleep. Instead, he'd stay awake all night, studying in the kitchen and wondering, with despondency, how Yanyan was.

He had received no messages from him since his promotion. It seemed that his peer had become elusive. Some said he had fallen out with his mentor and been seen storming from Zilu's mansion. Some even went so far as to suggest that he had gone back to the south to inherit his father's title and lucrative businesses.

Is that spoiled fop really this fragile, unable to digest even the tiniest adversity? Zixia thought as he perused another page in the flickering light.

He would not admit how relieved he was when, on a warm, breezy late summer evening, Yanyan knocked on the cottage door.

"How on earth did you find out where I live?" Zixia said as Yanyan smiled at him in his myrtle-green robe, dapper as usual.

"Qufu is not exactly a big city." Yanyan walked straight into the sitting room, carrying a long ebony case under his arm. He took a glimpse at the calligraphy scroll before sitting down in a wicker chair and putting the case on the tea table. "What a quaint place."

Before Zixia could reply, Woman Bu scurried out from the back room. "Is it my uncle . . . ?" she gasped, covering her face as soon as she caught sight of the visitor, and bowed. "Forgive me for my indiscretion, my husband and our precious guest."

"This is Yanyan, a disciple of the Master," Zixia said. "And this is my humble wife."

Folding his hands together, Yanyan saluted Woman Bu. "It's

an honor to finally meet you, Lady Bu. Back when you were under the care of your father, the prestigious Marquis Zhao of Jin, I heard much about your beauty and virtue."

Woman Bu bowed again, deeply. Continuing to veil her face behind her sleeves, she stepped backwards out of the room. "I'll go prepare some tea."

As the rustling of her dress drifted away, Yanyan turned to Zixia and pressed his hands together in another salute. "What a blessing to have a fine wife like this. Forgive me for my belated congratulations, my friend. These gifts are insubstantial, just to express my good wishes for you and the lady." He opened the case on the table, revealing a jade paperweight and a golden ladle inside.

Both were splendidly polished, the emerald and the gold seeming to reflect light off each other, piercing Zixia's eyes. Yanyan had always been generous towards him, but this was the first time for such a lavish offering. He stepped forward and pressed the case closed.

"Your largesse is to be praised," he said, sitting down on the other chair across the table. "And I appreciate your enduring friendship. But if you could indulge my impudence for a moment and allow me to say that my life has already reached such unmitigated fulfilment, it would be unforgivable and rapacious of me to accept gifts like these from you." He forced himself to look directly at his peer while asserting his refusal. He's a subordinate now, from whom you shouldn't be taking donations, Zixia reminded himself.

"Heavens," said Yanyan, chuckling softly. "Haven't you turned into a man of terrific eloquence. You should be pleased to know that, ever since you debuted at the Rostrum, I've received numerous letters from my brothers, cousins, and uncles at home, expressing their admiration towards you, the newly minted senior disciple of Confucius, all enchanted by your profound scholarship and oratorical skills."

"Oh." Zixia gave a cough. "That's kind of them. I didn't realize many in the audience were from Wu—a long way to travel, after all."

"It's all word of mouth. Plus, the transcriptions of the symposiums are extremely sought after in the south. No nobleman could get around without carrying the latest copy."

"Transcription? I've never heard of it."

Yanyan smiled. "Because nobody here knows about it." He winked at Zixia. "It's just me running the project as a sideline."

Zixia's heart raced. "I'm touched that you trust me with this confidential information," he managed to say. "In return, I shall advise you to stop your dealings immediately. If the Master found out about it, the consequences would be unthinkable."

Leaning against the back of the chair, Yanyan shrugged. "I suppose I'll have to take that risk. Just because my county is a bit out of the way doesn't mean the people in the south should be deprived of their chance to learn, nor be seen by the northerners as benighted mobs."

Somewhat touched by Yanyan's words, Zixia sighed. "I completely agree with you. No one should be defined by his origins, and people on the other side of the Yangtze River have as much right to be educated as people here do."

"Thank you." Yanyan clapped. "I knew you wouldn't disappoint me. And I knew from the beginning that you were a free-thinking man of unbiased judgment. Which is why I come to you today with my most sincere proposal. You see, after much consideration, I have decided that it's time for me to leave Qufu and return to the south. My father has set up a brand-new academy in Changshu and my people are studious, thirsty for knowledge. They're all waiting for me to be home and"—he looked at Zixia earnestly—"to bring back a well-renowned scholar like you to enlighten them."

"Sorry for interrupting." Woman Bu reemerged with a tray. Fumbling, Zixia stashed the case under the table before his wife put down two cups of ocher-colored soup. "Is everything all right?" she asked, surveying Zixia's face.

"Just dismiss yourself," Zixia sputtered, his chest tight. He poised himself until Woman Bu left before turning to Yanyan. "Pardon me for failing to follow you. What in the world are you talking about?"

Yanyan fetched a teacup and took a sip. "I am saying that a man of your talent and knowledge should savor only the best tea brewed by spring water, should live in a fine mansion attended by maids and servants. Your wife should be clothed in silk, concerned with nothing but bearing your children. And your children should grow up in abundance, never knowing even the faintest feeling of hunger—if you come to County Wu with me, Zixia, and help start our own institution there, I'll make sure you and your family have the life you deserve."

Zixia felt his hands quivering as the four rammed earth walls, bare and rusty, seemed to close in on him like a casket. He shot up from his chair. "I can't believe it," he roared, "that you actually think so little of me, counting me as some weak-minded man who'd be lured by material comfort—even though when we first met, I already told you, it was not money I was after. Let me reiterate: I strive only to learn, and I devote myself only to the House of Confucius, the Master, and our mentor, Zilu."

He paused, pointing at the calligraphy hanging on the wall. "See? This is what Zilu gifted me: *ji*. He granted me this character because he trusts me to be a man who needs nothing more than millet in his pursuit of knowledge. Because, Yanyan, I don't appraise my life on the wealth I amass, and you, you are a sore loser, acting fatuously for not being chosen by Zilu. But in truth, you have no one to blame but yourself for failing to earn the trust and respect of the others. How dare you propose such a traitorous, illicit plan to me, in an attempt to avenge our institution, our master, and our mentor?"

Yanyan stared at the scroll for a while before swiveling back. "Is that really what you believe, looking at this scrap Zilu gave you?" he said, rising from his seat as well. "Zixia, I cannot talk to you if you insist on acting like a character on a stage. Or, can you only carry on this charade by denying your own agenda? I thought you'd be the one, among all of them, who sees what corrupt, greedy hypocrites these people are, the institution, the Master, and even Zilu. You really think he's given much thought to which of us should be the next senior? And that I should be tormented for not being picked?" He shook his head. "It's all a game, nobody cares."

Yanyan's voice was quiet, but the sneer on his face was unmistakable. Zixia clenched his fists. "You're only calling it a game because you lost."

Yanyan chuckled. "I see little point in continuing this war of words. I should have known that you would only yield at the sight of gallows." Then, looking directly into Zixia's eyes, he parted his thin lips and spewed out his prophecy:

"I'll show you just how insignificant your so-called winning is. Mark my words, in three months' time, I will be made senior. And I'll be expecting you to come to me then and resume our discussion."

Zixia would never forget the thrust in his guts the moment he heard Yanyan's statement, and the way the world around him distorted. He felt the floor was spinning, the hanging on the wall expanded, the character turning into a beast's gaping jaws.

稷.

Horror-struck, Zixia recognized the dismembered radicals of the colossal figure: 禾, 田, 人, 夊—the seedling, the field, and a peasant trudging in the mud.

A savage squeal blares, almost knocking the trowel from Zixia's hand. He shoves the flat blade into the sludge of red mud and clay he's been mixing and looks up. His daughter, who was just playing beside the pile of pebbles and straw, is nowhere in sight.

"Ah shit," he mumbles as the second cry cuts through the cottage.

Zixia dashes into the house. In the bedroom, chopped straw is scattered over the floor. Plum is standing beside the cot, throwing dried grass onto Celery, despite the fact that the infant is bawling at the top of his lungs.

"Stop! Plum!" Zixia shouts. "What are you doing to your brother?"

The girl shakes at her father's interjection and, before Zixia can react, bursts out into a wretched scream of her own.

In astonishment, Zixia watches tears stream from his daughter's eyes like blood surging from a pair of fresh wounds. Plum's wailing outperforms that of her brother for a brief moment before the younger sibling begins to thrust his limbs, screeching in the cot bed as if being murdered.

Zilu. Zixia freezes, queasy as the stench is conjured out of nowhere, mixed with a hint of copper, the red muck on his hands turning into the ground flesh. Zilu. A stifling darkness cloaks him.

"Wow, easy, steady now." He hears a man's voice, someone's hand propped against his back. The next moment, he is guided to the bed and flumps on the solid surface. The nausea subsides.

Before him stands Yanyan, tall and lithe, his sage silk robe pristine. "Are you all right?" he says, carefully removing his hands from Zixia's shoulders.

"Great," says Zixia. "You finally care to show up."

"Of course I showed up." Yanyan smiles and picks up the crying infant from the crib. "Had to come to meet the little master and give him a welcome gift." He produces a necklace from his sleeve and deftly clips it around Celery's neck.

It is a fine golden chain attached to a longevity lock made of jade. The jade is the size of a duck egg, white and flawless, incised with elegant curves.

The boy giggles, clutching the shining object and sending it to his mouth for a taste.

"Me! Me!" Also taken by the novelty, Plum reaches up her hands, tears still on her face.

"Don't you worry, miss," says Yanyan. "How could I forget

about you?" He holds out a golden rattle drum like a trickster and hands it to Plum.

With annoyance, Zixia watches his children, now placid and content, beam at their new toys. "We're not taking these," he says. "And don't you try to buy yourself out of trouble—it might work with other people, but not with me."

"What are you talking about?" Yanyan says, lifting Celery in the air and watching the boy laughing in frenzy. "What kind of trouble am I in?"

This frivolous fox. "Quit skirting around," Zixia says. "We both know you're here because of Zilu's death." He pushes himself up. "Now look me in the eyes and tell me that you had nothing to do with it."

Yanyan lowers Celery into the crib. The silence in the room deepens as he brushes off the shredded straw on the bed, the jingling of the pellet drum ringing sporadically. When he finally turns to Zixia, his face, usually fixed with a cynical smirk, bears now a despondent expression, his eyes flickering with the luster of amber.

"I don't want to lie to you, Zixia." He sighs. "I've been in great distress since the symposium. I feel horrible for lashing out at you on the stage and for failing to defend you later when Zigong accused you of being behind the murder of our mentor. I appreciate that my behavior might have grieved you, but how could you turn on me like this and say Zilu's death was my fault?" Voice breaking, he dabs the corners of his eyes with his sleeve.

Zixia watches his peer. "So you expect me to believe that it is just a coincidence that Zilu was killed after the feud we had with him, after you called him power-crazed and he slapped you? Isn't it too convenient that his death happened in the wake of him declaring his change of heart on carrying out the plan?"

The words have simmered in his guts for days and are now gushing out. At the back of his mind, Zixia can almost hear the heralds reciting: "Carrying out . . . the plan . . . the plan . . . the plan . . ."

Yanyan shakes his head. "I shouldn't feel confounded at all that you'd point your finger at me. Because you never really trusted me—you never trust anybody, Zixia. And equally, I could say that you wouldn't feel too pleased about Zilu renouncing the plan—*your* plan, you're the one who refused to do it my way—the easy way—and insisted we had to do it *your* way, remember? And at the end of the day, like Zigong said, you were the one who went to Wey—your home county—with Zilu and came back with his remains. As for me, I've been in Qufu this whole time, and how could I, a southerner, forge connections with the Palace of Wey, let alone Kuaikui?"

As if stirred by the disquiet, Celery bursts out crying again. Zixia rushes over to pick up his son and rocks him gently. The handsome jade rests on the baby's chest like a steelyard weight, on which Zixia recognizes the converging lines form 芹, Celery. The delicate strokes, like little hands, tug his heart.

"I was frustrated by Zilu's reversal." Zixia turns to Yanyan, his voice softened. "But I would never have done anything to harm him."

"Neither would I," Yanyan says. "You have to believe me, Zixia, the same way I believe you. Whoever schemed Zilu's murder was throwing one stone to kill two birds, to remove Zilu from the position of successor, and to provoke mistrust between us. But shouldn't we be more united than ever, now that Zilu's gone?"

Zilu is gone. Once again, a hazy scent of copper seeps into Zixia's nose, his face tingling. And his only ally left is this man in front of him. Inhaling deeply, he asks: "What shall we do for the next symposium?"

Yanyan smiles. "I must say your performance at the great hall was ingenious, naming Zigong the suspect. If we follow this direction and get him convicted at the next symposium, we'll be very close to reseizing the initiative and setting everything back on track."

"As much as I agree with you," says Zixia, "I have to admit that I don't actually have any evidence to prove Zigong was involved in Zilu's death."

"Come on!" Yanyan chuckled. "You weren't born yesterday. Don't you remember what Zilu taught us about dialectic and evidence?"

Celery grunts in Zixia's arms. In the corner, Plum is playing, tucking in the rattle drum with straw, humming a lullaby Woman Bu often sings. And Zixia hears in his head his mentor's voice: *Evidence is for those who fail on dialectic. When we claim a man is sinful and he starts to argue for his innocence, his sin is proven.*

"You're right," he says slowly, as if in a trance. "I shall begin to work on the strategies of the debate right away. We need a cracking argument, especially now. Without Zilu we are outnumbered. First I need to delineate the potential contentions Zigong and Ziwo might assert . . ."

"My goodness." Yanyan frowns. "What you should do is to stop brooding over the symposium and get some rest." He retrieves a scroll from his chest pocket and sends it into Zixia's hand. "Here's a treat for you, my friend, an invitation to this new play which will be on at the Emerald House in two days. I'll see you there. Until then, no more racking your brain, please. I assure you things will work out." He raises his hands in salute, then turns and walks out of the room.

Zixia puffs out a slow sigh. The light flows in through the window, casting a long and rattan yellow smudge onto the floor. Zixia knows Woman Bu will be returning from the market soon and he is expected to finish mending the wall. However, at present he has a more crucial matter to attend to.

Swiftly, he picks the necklace off Celery before putting him back in the crib. And he claims the rattle drum from his daughter by offering her a millet bun. Then he rushes to the kitchen, moves his books piled on the bottom shelf aside, and hauls out the ebony case.

In the case lie an array of items, all gifts from Yanyan throughout the years: the emerald-inlaid belt, the golden ladle carved with lilies, a carnelian inkstone, a jade paperweight, and a pair of crystal spindles.

Zixia sighs. "I'll give them back to you when this all ends."

Adding the rattler and the necklace to the collection, he locks the box, and, before Woman Bu comes home, pushes it back into the dark.

Zixia hasn't told anyone about the presents because he doesn't want people to misunderstand that he has, in a way, been bought by Yanyan. Confidently, Zixia considers himself someone who'd never be swayed by immediate fortune, because instead of pursuing wealth that might not be permissible, he'd rather strive for a greater purpose, something instrumental and momentous.

Needless to say, back to the summer of year thirteen, Yanyan's visit that evening, along with the madcap proposal, had shaken Zixia. In fact, if he was being honest with himself, he would have admitted that he was envious of Yanyan, who was not only candid enough to voice his discontent but was also ready to take action, to strike back at the ludicrous institution and its avaricious elders. Although Zixia would never bring himself to betray his mentor— he'd never flee with Yanyan to Changshu like fugitives and tutor in a private academy behind the Master's back—he was nonetheless unsettled by Yanyan's rebellious proposition.

If only, Zixia said to himself, if only teaching in private academies were permissible, if only I could find a way to persuade the House to change its ordinances.

The summer passed. The war in the south intensified. The army of Yue defeated the soldiers of Wu, capturing their crown prince. Seven scouts escaped the enemy's slaughter to report the news back to the duke of Wu, only to be executed on the spot by their disturbed commander. A couple of weeks later, while the god of the Vermilion Bird was rising to the meridian transit, Ziyou— the most versatile senior disciple and the practitioner of the *Book of Changes*—was indicted for embezzling ticket money and sentenced to death by decapitation. Straightaway, without even requesting nominees, the Master appointed Yanyan to take over Ziyou's position, entrusting the young man with editing the most incomprehensible book of his oeuvre.

The wind swept from the west, puffing up the city with a chill befitting a bloodletting. Beside the city gate hung Ziyou's head, along with those of other criminals, swinging and knocking against the rammed earth wall like hollowed chimes.

Tormented by the discordant noises, Zixia hurried to his mentor's residence to make an inquiry and was received in the side hall.

"Thank you for this homely present," Zilu said, opening the jar for a sniff. "It seems my niece has mastered her mother's recipe. This smells exactly like the pickled plums my sister made."

"I shall pass your kind words to my wife. She'll be delighted," said Zixia, trying not to recall the rage of Woman Bu as she swept all the jars of pickled plums off the shelves this morning.

Zilu smiled. "I hope you're not disappointed with this union."

"I could not be more content, my master," Zixia said. "As a matter of fact, I wanted to let you know that we're expecting a child already."

"Marvelous!" Zilu directed the servant to bring the sorghum wine. Then the two men held up their cups and bottomed up the crimson liquor.

"I'll pray for you that it'll be an heir," Zilu said, picking up the silver flagon to refill Zixia's cup. "Now that our bond is becoming more indestructible, Zixia, I hope you'll see me as your family and share with me all your concerns."

Zixia received his drink. "If I could be candid with you, my master," he said. "I am quite confused by a recent incident. I couldn't understand the reason for Yanyan's promotion. Shouldn't all candidates debate at the symposium before a decision is reached, the same way I was promoted?"

Zilu sighed. "I'm afraid I have no satisfactory answer. I was not consulted on this matter, either by Yanyan or by the Master. All I know is that carts of jade, pearl, and gold were reported to have arrived in Qufu from Changshu. And somebody saw the entrance of the Master's residence being blocked by those gifts, and the heralds had to work all night to move them into his chamber."

Zixia couldn't believe what he was hearing. He downed the liquor in his cup, guts burning. "Pardon me for being presumptuous," he said. "But how are we supposed to stand such an infringement to the rules of the House?"

"I don't blame you for thinking this way," Zilu said, pouring more wine for his mentee. "One would indeed wonder if the tragic and consecutive deaths of disciples have grieved the Master too much and have impaired his judgment."

"Ah, no," blurted Zixia. "I would never dare to comment upon the Master's judgment. It's Yanyan's transgression that troubles me. How could he buy his way up the ladder while others had to work so hard to earn their places?"

Zilu nodded. "I very much relate to you. In fact, when I was your age, I used to scrutinize and criticize people who were my equals, simply because they were well within my sight. As for my superiors, who were too high up for me to see, I revered them ingenuously." He chuckled, shaking his head. "But you should know, Zixia, that competing against your peers is but a small feat that won't transform who you are. To accomplish the Great Feat you must be able to recognize and ameliorate the flaws of those who hold power over you."

Realizing what Zilu was insinuating, Zixia felt sweat beads seeping out from behind his ears. He stared at the jar of pickles on the table before downing the next cup of spirit in one gulp, in the hopes of drumming up his courage. "Your wise words have made the scales fall from my eyes," he said. "Isn't it conveyed in the *Analects* 12:17: *To govern is to be correct. If one leads by exemplifying the correctness, who would dare to remain incorrect?* In this case, had the Master epitomized the rectitude of being uncorrupted, how could Yanyan even think of offering an inducement of gold and jade?"

Zilu didn't respond. Knitting his brows, he brought the cup to his mouth and moistened his lips.

Perhaps I was wrong, Zixia prayed to himself in the throttling silence. How on earth could Zilu go against the Master? I must be wrong.

"I was hoping that you wouldn't draw such a conclusion," Zilu said heedfully. "Then I could persuade myself that my concerns about the Master's recent demeanor was tainted by my personal agenda, and therefore untrue." He gave another sigh. "But now, since my solicitude has been confirmed by my brightest mentee, I must, as a servant to this house, address this misconduct. Zixia, can I trust you to lend me your support?"

Zixia's heart sank. "By all means," he mumbled, reaching for the flagon and emptying the last drop into his own cup. As the wine pervaded his guts, he heard Yanyan's soft voice: *And I thought you'd be the one, among all of them, who sees what corrupted, greedy hypocrites these people are . . .*

"You must be disappointed in me," Zilu said, a resigned smile on his face. "You must think I'm despicable and power-hungry and that I cannot wait to remove the Master."

Remembering that his mentor never failed to see through him, a shiver ran down Zixia's spin. "Ah no, no . . ."

"You know you can always speak freely with me. I'd feel the same were I in your position. Truthfully, many years ago, I was exactly like you, distancing myself from politics, devoted only to scholarship. But I was wrong." Zilu sighed. "No one can be virtuous alone when the notion of morality is at stake. Once, Confucius was someone who considered wealth and rank like passing clouds, feeding with delight on coarse rice and resting on no pillows but only his own elbow; he'd pay tribute at the commoners' funerals and sing with strangers. But now we have a Master who hides in his golden chamber, misappropriating the institution's funds for personal luxury. Meanwhile, as he grows progressively paranoid, he is abolishing the free discourse of the symposium, dictating every debate with his monotonous voice. Recently, he's begun to rescind the delegation of power to the seniors." He took a breath, glancing at Zixia. "It also pains me to see that you younger generation, with all your talents, are denied a fair share of rewards and recognition, your devotion and diligence underappreciated. So I asked myself, should I remain silent, looking after only my own interests, or should I step up, challenge those above me, and, when I have the power, bring reformation to this corrupted institution?"

The air tremored at Zilu's question. For a while, Zixia couldn't move, feeling only the blood pumping through his veins, filling him with reassuring indignation. So it's not just me and Yanyan, then, he thought, if Zilu also felt this way.

"I am sorry for ever doubting you, my master," Zixia said, composing himself. "Now that I've discerned the causes of your endeavor, I'll fight until my last breath to make you our leader."

"It won't be an easy fight," Zilu said. "Clearly, we cannot press the Master to abdicate—this would be too controversial, bringing us only the opposite effect. But I can, on the other hand, invite Zigong to join me and move a motion to elect a successor in case the Master is found unable to execute the powers and duties of his position. I'm confident this proposal will come through since Zigong would want such a position for himself more than anyone else. In this sense, the risk lies in the likelihood of Zigong being elected. And if the throne is taken by that merchant who stinks of money, the House will lose the last of its integrity, reduced to a mouthpiece for Zigong's clique and patrons. So we must allow no defeat and beat Zigong in the election. Now, are you with me?"

Zixia didn't answer. His mind had drifted away, irresistibly, towards the questions he had been ruminating over since Yanyan's visit: What if the House permits them to teach in private academies, what if they could practice independently instead of being forever enslaved by the House, by the immortal Confucius, what if there is no . . . A vague scheme, whose magnitude had been too great for Zixia to grasp, finally began to reveal itself, the way a constellation appeared on a clear night.

If Zilu also felt this way, then could we have him on our side, Zixia thought. If Zilu is on our side.

"Zixia, are you with me?" Zilu repeated.

"Yes, I'll certainly give you my vote," Zixia answered quickly, his heart racing.

Zilu smiled. "I appreciate it, Zixia," he said. "But what I need from you is more than just a vote. You see, Ziwo will vote for Zigong, and Ranyong will probably wait until the last minute before voting with the majority. So this leaves us in a precarious position, where we'll have no choice but to secure a vote from Yanyan.

In the past, I would have felt much more confident in getting Yan-yan on my side. After all, he has been a dutiful mentee for many years. However, as it happens, since your appointment to the senior position and your espousal with my niece, Yanyan has grown increasingly estranged from me . . ."

Yanyan. That name vibrated in Zixia's ears and his peer's voice returned: *I cannot talk to you if you insist on acting like a character onstage. I cannot talk to you if . . .*

Also ringing in his head was the shriek of his wife, who, after throwing out all the picked plums, flailed her arms like a madwoman, slapping her chest and her abdomen, which had just began to show. *I'm doomed!* Woman Bu's wails joined, echoing in Zixia's head, drowning out Yanyan's accusation and Zilu's persuasion. *The sour pickles are making me sick, so it must be a girl I'm carrying! And what's the use of such a thing? She'll grow up dumb, illiterate, and brainless. All she'll learn is how to serve a husband, and as soon as her period arrives, she'll be married to some wimp and be damned for the rest of her life. I'm doomed! We are both doomed!*

Across the table, Zilu was still talking. The cacophony surrounded Zixia. The three voices, resonating, magnifying, crushed him like a waterfall thundering down on his crown, its force so unbearable that Zixia had to shoot up from his seat.

"I have to go talk to Yanyan," he blurted and, followed by Zilu's baffled gaze, dashed out of the residence.

Zixia ran fast, down the avenue and through the town square, heading to Willow Lane, the Emerald House, a place he knew Yanyan would be at this time of a day.

His ears drummed, his heart thrashing in his chest as if something were trying to escape him. Soon he saw the red lanterns fluttering, the cerise light coloring the faces of the men he had been scanning. Women followed behind them: the concubines, the maids, the courtesans, and the prostitutes.

Zixia looked for Yanyan in the throng of people. Finally, he was rid of self-doubt and hesitancy and knew what *he* wanted to do—he was done with being that peasant boy, following behind the masters obediently. Instead, he would have both Yanyan and Zilu conjoined, for the triumph of *his* plan.

For the first time ever, Zixia was certain, clear as crystal, that he would succeed. He would find Yanyan and tell him that Zilu, having set his eyes on becoming the next Confucius, was in need of their support. It would provide the perfect opportunity for the two of them to abandon the impermissible scheme of retreating to the south, and instead to aim for something greater. They would go to their mentor, all honest and aboveboard, and let Zilu know that they'd give him their votes only if he concurred with their plan—*his plan*—that Zilu must, once enthroned as the Master, put an end to the whole scam: announce the death of Confucius and dismantle this archaic and corrupted institution.

When that happened, the other disciples would accept and surrender to Zixia's personal agenda. Each one of them would set off to a place of their choosing in order to pursue their own aspirations, to counsel the dukes, to engage in trade, to author their works individually, and to establish their own academies.

When that happened, he would return to his hometown, where the fat ears of millet would glimmer in the autumn field and the larks would sing all day when the earth began to unfreeze in the spring sun. And he would set up a school and teach the people there: peasants and carpenters, masons and seamstresses, men and women, sons and daughters, *irrespective of their backgrounds.*

睢

One after another, the guests file into the Emerald House, dressed in their finery. Their hair is combed up, adorned by wigs and hefty jewelry, resplendent as jellyfishes. Their faces, on the other hand, bear the marks of tedium. They whisper, only occasionally.

Zixia watches these people from the end of the queue and suddenly he has a feeling that he is not going to a play, rather, the whole lot of them are waiting to cross the Naihe Bridge—the overpass named Despair that leads the deceased to the underworld.

Getting a chill at the thought, he averts his eyes from the crowd and looks up at the long mahogany plaque hanging horizontally above the gate, on which four large characters are painted in gold.

素以為絢, the plainness grounds the splendor.

Motherfuckers, Zixia thinks. How could they put my words in front of a whorehouse without even asking my permission?

Even after a pimp ushers him to an elevated box beside the stage where Yanyan, in an impressive viridian gown, rises from his seat and smiles at him warmly, he is still fuming.

"I'm glad you made it in time," Yanyan says. "You don't want to miss even a second of this splendid play."

"Splendid, my foot." Slumping in an armchair, Zixia grabs a

mandarin from the fruit plate on the table and sends it straight to his mouth.

"Easy." Yanyan snatches the citrus. "You don't want to eat the skin, unless you like it bitter." He peels it. "Did I not tell you to get some rest? We can't have you at the next symposium being this preoccupied. Remember, there's no room for errors or mishaps." The mandarin is dropped back into Zixia's hand, stripped clean and broken into segments.

Zixia's ears burn. "Allow me to remind you," he says. "Just in the last symposium, who was praised as the master of rén and got the most fervent ovation from the audience? Was that you, or me?"

"Ah now, if you're taking the erratic passion of those brainless fans so seriously."

The curtains on the stage remain drawn while the stalls fill up.

"I don't agree." Zixia sticks the split mandarin back on the table. "At the symposium, the spectators are as important as the Master. You need to have the audience in your alliance to succeed in your intentions."

Yanyan snorts. The viewers downstairs burst out in thundering applause. The two of them look up at the stage, where a tall and slender man in a purple robe appears. He is vertical like a crane, face painted white.

Gracefully, the man bows and in a resounding voice he narrates:

"In the beginning, Duke Derangement of Wey had a concubine, Nanzi, whom he adored. The crown prince of the duke, Kuaikui, offended Lady Nanzi by attempting to assassinate her. Fearful of Nanzi's revenge, Kuaikui escaped Wey . . ."

"You are kidding me." Zixia turns to Yanyan.

Yanyan shrugs. "It is the talk of the town. Didn't you read the invitation I gave you? The play is called *The Legend of Lady Nanzi*."

Zixia's eyes widen. "Are you saying that there will be a scene where the Master . . ."

"I don't suppose it's entirely unforeseeable, the dramatization of that affair." Yanyan shrugs again. "After all, it's recorded in the *Analects*."

Shaking his head, Zixia picks up a segment of the mandarin and sets it in his mouth. "Which genius wrote this?"

"You are truly flattering me." It's another man's voice. Zixia lifts his head and sees Ranyong has stepped into their box, dressed in an auburn gown, holding his hands together in salute. "I'm so honored to have you in the house viewing my show," Ranyong says. "Zigong and Ziwo came yesterday, both very generous with their compliments. But I do want to hear your opinions later, Zixia, especially on the dialogues." His grizzly goatee dangles down his chin, swinging as he speaks.

Of course. Zixia realizes in a flash. Why should he be surprised that Yanyan, rather than toiling away and composing a credible argument, would choose instead to cut corners by beguiling this fence-sitter to take their side.

"Come join us, Ranyong," Yanyan says, beaming. "You must be exhausted shaping up this magnificent production. Zixia and I were amazed by the immediate relevance of the play."

"Oh, drop it," says Ranyong, sinking into an armchair and helping himself to a cup of wine. "Actually, I finished this script a couple of years ago. But no theater wanted to produce the play because they thought it was absurd to have a woman as the hero."

He takes a sip. "With which I respectfully disagree. So you can imagine how pleased I was when, after Kuaikui launched the coup and we learned the spectacular news of Zilu's death, the illustrious Emerald House got in touch and expressed their enthusiasm to put the show on the stage as soon as possible. And with a couple of quick touch-ups to the script, here we are." He drinks up the dregs.

Already waiting with the flagon in his hand, Yanyan fills the empty cup. "A hero is always made by the circumstances."

"Or by good patrons," Ranyong says, knocking back the cup again.

Onstage, a group of actors in ragged clothes are dancing and singing in a circle, surrounding the leading lady in her stunning red dress. Covering her face with her sleeves, Nanzi shudders, weeping while the commoners continue to chant:

"Slaked now you rutting sow, send back our fetching boar."

"This is rather thought-provoking," Yanyan says. "We all tend to believe that power is held by the center and whoever occupies the position is to be revered; however, it's equally true that the center is also surrounded, thus its occupant could risk being besieged and overthrown."

"I hear you, son," Ranyong replied. "The center is indeed full of perils. That's why I'd rather be a bystander. At least I get to live long."

"You're being too modest, calling yourself a bystander," Zixia says. "The *Book of Music* is the most eclectic among the Confucian oeuvre and you yourself, having served the House enduringly, are admired by many of us for your steadiness and magnanimity. Truthfully, a saint cannot conceal his wisdom. Even when he *builds his hut by the stream in the valley*, the pilgrims would still come searching for him."

Ranyong bursts out laughing. "No wonder Zilu regarded the two of you as his star pupils. You certainly inherited his round-about way of speaking and his uncurbed passion for literary allusions. But, come on, even your mentor was not like this when he was your age—in fact, he was quite a hothead."

On the stage, stepping out from a beaded curtain is Confucius, followed by Lady Nanzi, the jade pendants on her dress tinkling. She bows goodbye to the scholar as a rangy man in a cardinal gown storms up to them.

"Heavens," the actor, playing Zilu, roars. "What kind of a saint meets with a wicked harlot in her chamber?"

Ranyong chuckles, swiveling back to the pair. "See? What a dashing character Zilu used to be. Who could have foreseen such a grim ending for him?" He chops the air with his hand.

"It greatly unsettles me," says Zixia, "thinking about the brutal way my mentor was murdered by that hideous Zigong. And if I can be straightforward with you, Master Ranyong, I can't see why you won't help us to convict Zigong at the next symposium and bring justice against this ruthless crime."

"Well well well," says Ranyong. "I'm not entirely convinced that it was Zigong who did the thing. God knows who was behind Zilu's death."

Lifting his chin slightly, he directs his colleagues to look at the stage, where Confucius is in a fury. Reaching his hands upright, the Master bawls at Zilu: "Had I done anything sinful, may Heaven's curse be on me! May Heaven's curse be on me!"

Zixia has read this line from the *Analects* many times, but still he recoils at the crying of the sage. Yanyan speaks up: "Forgive me if this sounds crude and vulgar. But isn't it true that, in this case, who killed Zilu is in fact irrelevant. The more crucial question is: Whom do we want to convict and remove from the stage? And who will you, Ranyong, support to be the next in power? If you don't have enough faith in Zixia and me, can you at least give us a chance to rid you of your reluctance?"

The audience cheers as Confucius, assisted by his disciple, falters off the stage.

"Ha." Ranyong claps. "Finally, a wee spirit of candor. And fascinating questions. In return, I'll ask the two of you one thing: You said you wanted my support, but to which of you in particular shall I give my support, when the next election for the successor comes?"

A clamor rises from the stage, clanking of swords and screeching. Zixia cannot turn his head. He cannot even look up at Yanyan, who also sits in silence. The segmented mandarin is splayed out on the table, like a withered chrysanthemum.

Ranyong laughs. "If it's any consolation," he says, "I shall let you know that whatever your answer is, I'll not be persuaded. You see, I'm perfectly unconcerned with the outcome of this whole drama. I've been in the House for too long and I have seen too many masters rise and fall, championed and betrayed. And the thing is, I'll share with you now, no matter who they thought they were and what ambitions and plans they had for the institution, once enthroned, they all ended up becoming the same person: the autocratic, paranoid Confucius. So whatever you are going to promise me in exchange for my support, you can forget about it—I say this to you, the same as I said to the other two yesterday.

Because once you climb to the top, you won't even remember your initial pledges. The truth is, no one can take power; instead, power seizes and devours you, my naïve and hubristic boys."

Zixia's stomach wrings, a strange yet familiar hunger takes over him, and he bites his lip. On the stage, the commotion has reached a crescendo. A servant scrambles towards Lady Nanzi, sitting behind the beaded curtain, crying: "Madam, we've lost! We are done! Kuaikui is right outside the palace now, with that army of Marquis Zhao of Jin!"

"But, Master Ranyong," Zixia mutters. "Didn't you vote for Zilu? What did he . . ."

Yanyan leans over and grips Zixia's hands, sending him an assuring smile before turning to Ranyong. "I can only imagine how fed up you've been all these years, with all the scheming and empty promises from each of the horrendous politicians of the House," he says. "But I am no politician. Frankly, I'm only a merchant who believes in payment upon delivery. Now, you may or may not know this, but the owner of the Emerald House happens to be my father, who has authorized me to invite you, Ranyong, to be our resident dramatist. Once you sign the contract, we'll devote ourselves to produce, in the years to come, all the exciting new plays you write and to split the profit with you down the middle. What do you say?"

Ranyong freezes and his face turns bright red.

In the stalls, the spectators are shrieking, some weeping, while on the stage Kuaikui, in a suit of iron armor, plunges his sword into Lady Nanzi's chest, slitting the bag of pig's blood hidden in between the actress's breasts, an abhorrent pong wafting around the auditorium.

Motherfucker, Zixia thinks. So this swindler actually owns this dump and he decided to hang *my* word at the freaking entrance, without paying me a dime?

If Zixia allows himself to dwell longer on Ranyong's comments, he has to admit that the possession of power does seem to bring fundamental changes to a man. Another interpretation it is that although the man has remained the same, with the ever-unchallenged position he is in, the necessity for further pretension is negated and his true colors are shown.

Now that his mentor has passed away, Zixia will never find out which category Zilu's case falls into. Although he would prefer to believe that at least in the beginning, when he and Yanyan explained their proposal to Zilu, he genuinely shared their vision. However, later, when his mentor surmounted the higher place, becoming the heir of the House, his view inevitably changed.

Zilu was elected as the successor in the spring of year fourteen of Duke Sorrow of Lu, a time when the Duke went hunting in the western field, followed by his retainers. They captured a kirin, the legendary beast of mercy, and killed it recklessly. The Master was incensed by the news. Thousands had witnessed Confucius ascend the Rostrum, thumping his chest, roaring: "*The kirin appears only during the reign of a great ruler, and for whom is it coming? My practice has come to its end! My practice has come to its end!*"

Only a few knew the truth. The Master's rage was in fact stirred by the plotted rebellion of Zilu. He was lamenting his doom: that he would be reduced to a figurehead by this ambitious successor who, shortly after winning the election, turned his back on his duty of editing the *Annual of Spring of Autumn*, and instead mingled busily with the nobles at the royal court of Lu.

Zixia laughed it off when others hinted at Zilu's dealings with various politicians of Lu and other adjacent counties and didn't bother to look into the rumors. At the time, he was occupied with the most significant mission he'd taken on since joining the House: the writing of the *Great Preface of Poetry*.

For months, Zixia barely left the Confucian Estate. He worked day and night in the study, skipping his sleep and his meals, forgetting even to go home. He perused volumes of books, composed countless lines and scraped them off, wearing out his brushes one after another. He failed to notice that the blooms on the flowering quince tree had long withered and that the bush cherries had blossomed and fruited. When he inscribed the last character on the silk and sent for Zilu and Yanyan to come and view the final draft, the foliage of the pistachio trees in the courtyard had turned scarlet red, fluttering under the autumn sun as if thousands of butterflies were on fire.

After reading the essay, Zilu and Yanyan sat in silence. "So, what do you make of it?" Zixia asked tentatively.

Neither of the disciples responded, nor did they appear to have heard his question. "What do you think?" Zixia tried again. "Please be candid with me. It's only an early draft."

With that, Yanyan finally raised his head. "What are you talking about?" he said. "It's finished, reaching the utmost magnificence possible. I'd personally fight you if you dare to change even one word."

A fierce relief flushed up Zixia's head, making him almost queasy. "Really?"

"I swear on the spirits of all my ancestors," said Yanyan, grinning. He stood up and fetched the silk sheet from the table. "Try this: *the affections are stirred within and take on form in words; if words alone are inadequate, we speak them out in sighs; if sighing is inadequate, we sing them; if singing them is inadequate, without realizing it our hands dance them and our feet tap them.*" Yanyan clapped and spun around in circles, his soles shuffling on the floor like a skipping fawn.

Zixia laughed. "I'm glad you liked it."

"Congratulations," Yanyan said. "You've accomplished something truly extraordinary. Wouldn't you agree, Zilu?"

Zilu, who had remained in his chair the whole time, smiled at Yanyan's inquiry. "It is impressive, Zixia," he said. "I'm pleased that you didn't forget to center this piece with the notion of states, delineating the crucial connection between poems and the political and social circumstance that evokes them." Closing his eyes, he recited from what he had just read: "*the tones of a well-managed age are at rest and joyful; the tones of an age of turmoil are bitter and full of anger; the tones of a ruined state are filled with lament and brooding.*" He paused, looking at Zixia. "These are brilliant triadic correlations that also speak urgently to the time we're in."

"Well," Zixia said, blinking as he sensed a warmth surging towards his eyes. "I can't tell you how important it is for me to receive your—"

"However," his mentor added, "I am quite confounded by your choice of the key poem: 'Cry the Ospreys.' Since the essay is meant to be the *great* preface, why open it with such a lowbrow verse, giving prominence to some commoners' love affair? Yes, the exegesis you managed to derive from it is refined, but why corrupt the argument by presenting, in the first place, such crude work selected from no others but the *Airs*?"

Zixia couldn't speak. As if being hooded in a thick bag, he gulped.

"I thought it was entirely appropriate to bring about the argument using a poem from the *Airs*," said Yanyan. "Didn't Zixia accentuate his intention dextrously? *Airs are the influence.* When the air flows, it turns into the wind, and the wind sways and bends the grass and the trees: the way poetry moves and teaches us. As for 'Cry the Ospreys,' wasn't it recorded during the great late Zhou dynasty and, as Zixia put it upfront: *'Cry the Ospreys' is the virtue of the Queen Consort* of King Wisdom of Zhou."

Outside the window, the florid leaves waved in a gust of wind. Zilu puffed out a heavy sigh, his face ashen. "Good of you to mention King Wisdom." He turned to Zixia. "There are three hundred poems in the *Book of Poetry*, yet you decided to praise the late king with something from the *Airs*, driveled out by a peasant in the countryside. Why can't you select from the *Odes* or the *Hymns*, whose themes are much grander and styles more elegant? In fact, anything in the *Odes* would easily parade the glory of Zhou, like: *right up the bubbles of the spring, we gather the water celery; all coming to court are the lords, the emperor of Zhou sees rippling, their dragon flags*—such a riveting image of our once undivided nation, wouldn't it be a better fit for the *Great Preface*?"

"What's wrong with poems from peasants?" blurted Zixia. "The best lyrics I've ever recorded were sung to me by a girl who grows lotus—" He paused to collect himself. "My master, I know how much you revere the Zhou dynasty and its etiquette. But where do morals and customs lie if not in well-cultivated people, and what stirs people most compellingly if not literature from the like-minded? I believe that poetry comes from people and serves to enlighten them. In this sense, although I appreciate your mention of 'Harvesting Beans,' as the practitioner of the *Book of Poetry* I have to stand by my decision to choose 'Cry the Ospreys' as the first poem of the book and the subject matter of the Preface."

Having never contradicted his mentor, Zixia didn't realize he was trembling until the room quieted and he saw the look on Zilu's face. "Uh, I didn't mean . . ." he said.

Zilu laughed. "What a practitioner of the *Book of Poetry*. Haven't you been wholly enlightened, not at all the beggar I picked up from the street. But trust me, Zixia, there is still a lot for you to learn. Even now, you've thoroughly misapprehended the purpose of the book you're editing. Indeed, the *Book of Poetry* is most widely read among the Confucian oeuvre and therefore rooted in people. But it's not there to enlighten them. The effect of poetry is teaching and discipline." He struck the table with his knuckles. "We don't want to get any radical ideas into the commoners' heads, so they turn into self-righteous rebels, abandoning their farmwork and instead criticizing their lords all day. Using literature, we inculcate them with morals and order so they normalize their thinking and behavior and become compliant and cooperative citizens— only by doing so can we have a strong and well-managed state and accomplish, in the end, the Great Feat." Pausing, Zilu inhaled deeply and stared at Zixia and Yanyan, a disconcerting frenzy in his eyes. "That is," he continued, "we must ally with other powerful counties, end the warring states, and reinstate a glorious renaissance of Zhou, returning to one united China."

"Wait a minute," Yanyan said, sitting down in the chair and

sipping his tea. "Do you mind specifying what this united China is? By uniting, do you mean the bunch of warlords here would join forces to invade and take over Wu and Yue in the south?" He put down the teacup. "Nay, I must respectfully reject this tall tale and remind you of what we have settled: you are to announce the end of Confucius as soon as the one up there dies and the rest of us, the last direct disciples of the sage, should set up institutions nationwide and begin to admit students. Now, this is not only more pragmatic but incredibly remunerative—"

"It's not about money," Zixia interrupted his peer, his heart bashing his chest. "We all agreed, Zilu, that everybody, nobles or commoners, men or women, deserves an education. A fair opportunity for anyone to be literate as long as they wish to, so a maid can interpret the *Analects* and a peasant can make sense of *Rites—A Cultural Prosperity*. Don't you recall? These were your own words."

He looked at his mentor, whose face was crisscrossed with lines, many more than the first time they met a decade ago. How old is he now? The thought occurred to Zixia as Zilu let out a loud sigh. "They say *failing to educate a student is the teacher's fault*. So, for the situation we are in, I have no one to blame but myself. I must have done so much wrong that the two of you have turned out to be such conceited, parochial, and self-seeking youngsters. Yanyan, you are eager to dismantle the institution and start your own lucrative business, but have you considered all the other junior and nameless disciples? Without the House, who's going to take care of their livelihoods? And, Zixia, I know you think you're serving a higher calling and may even consider yourself the savior of the people." He sniggered. "Have you truly seen it from those commoners' perspective? Do you genuinely think that if they know a few characters or some poems, they will be saved from their misery, from the wars, the starvation, the vagrancy, and the destitution? If anything, developing an intellectual mind would only torment them more deeply. The people out there"—he directed his hand outside the window, where the pistachio trees rattled frantically in the wind—"they need food, they need clothes, they need a roof to live underneath. They don't want your teaching, Zixia, what they want is a great ruler, a strong government, a rich, powerful nation that begets a new peaceful era, so they can be *at rest*."

The storm raged, blowing into the study, shaking the windows and the bookshelves. As if coming alive, the silk sheets rolled up from the table, swirling in the air. Somehow, Zixia thought of his children, his one-and-a-half-year-old daughter and his son, born only two weeks ago, whom he had not yet had a chance to see. Now their cries were rising with the wind, shrill in his ears, splitting his skull.

Was I blinded by my ego? he asked himself. Am I truly wrong?

Then he heard Yanyan's voice, unruffled and clean. "Give it a rest, you power-crazed old man," he said. "Quit your lengthy sermon and just say it plainly: What you want is more than to become Confucius; you want to be the emperor."

Zixia feels a gentle tap on his shoulder. From a distant place, someone is calling his name. The voice belongs to a woman, the hand stroking him soft and cool, a dizzy smell of fresh snow and wintersweet.

"Ma?" He calls. Still half-asleep, he turns to the woman standing beside him. "Ma?"

"You should have come to bed," Woman Bu says, frowning. "You can't really rest sleeping by the table. You were shouting a lot there."

Realizing where he is, Zixia sits up and stretches his arms, the small of his back stiff. A nauseating rage, inflamed by the dream he had, still lingers in his guts. For weeks, the feud with Zilu has been coming to him day and night, as if the memory has become a parasite in his body.

"What's the time now?"

"Almost the Hour of Hare. The kids will be up soon." Woman Bu adds more wood to the firebox. "What do you want for breakfast?"

"Nothing for me," Zixia says, sorting the ruffled silk sheets on the table. "I'll eat after the symposium." He needs that hunger to keep himself sharp.

"Right, it's on today," Woman Bu says. "Did you finish the letter to my father?"

Zixia picks up a scripted sheet from the pile. "I did."

Wiping her hands on her waist skirt, Woman Bu skitters over. "What did you write?" She holds the silk carefully.

"Everything you asked me to tell him: the kids are thriving, the wall's fixed, the last symposium was well received, all good." Zixia watches his wife marvel at the black signs, a rosy smile on her face, her newly cut hair brushing the silk. "You know I can teach you to read and write. Just as Plum is reaching the right age, I can teach both of you."

Woman Bu's head jolts up. "What are you talking about? We

can't do that, it's against the law! You think you're helping your daughter by teaching her to read? You are sending her to hell!"

Taken aback by his wife's outburst, Zixia doesn't know what to say, while Woman Bu turns and leaves the kitchen. "I'll get the letter sealed," she mutters.

Zixia puts away the pens and the inkstone and sets aside the stack of notes for today's debate. He washes his face by the vat and ties up his hair.

Woman Bu returns with the sealed scroll in one hand, the cardinal gown in the other. "Here, all done," she says, in her usual quiet voice again.

Zixia puts on the gown, which has been cleaned, its torn hem sewed back by red threads, the fine stitches nearly invisible. The scroll is sealed by clay, the stamp deep, depicting vividly a millet ear.

"Thank you, this is perfect," Zixia says, sliding the letter into his chest pocket. "I'll bring it to the post house as soon as the symposium finishes."

"Also, I've written something for you." Before his wife goes away again, Zixia points at the table, where a piece of fuchsia-colored silk presents columns of thin swirling ink lines, woven into delicate characters that look like flowers:

關關雎鳩, 在河之洲, 窈窕淑女, 君子好逑.
參差荇菜, 左右流之, 窈窕淑女, 寤寐求之.
求之不得, 寤寐思服, 悠哉悠哉, 輾轉反側.
參差荇菜, 左右採之, 窈窕淑女, 琴瑟友之.
參差荇菜, 左右芼之, 窈窕淑女, 鍾鼓樂之.

"What are they?" Woman Bu asks, a strange tremor in her voice.

"It's a poem," Zixia says, suddenly abashed. "You will probably find this senseless. But I thought I'd give it to you because your birthday is near and because"—he clears his throat—"because actually, this poem always makes me think of you. 'Cry the Ospreys,' it's called, and it goes like: *Guan-guan, cry the ospreys, on the islet in the river, the modest, retiring, virtuous lady, for a man like me a fine match.*"

Pausing, he glances at Woman Bu, relieved that there is no sign of annoyance on her face. Instead, she smiles, tucking her hair behind her ear. "It sounds beautiful."

Before Zixia replies, the howling of Celery blasts from next door. Woman Bu runs to the baby. Zixia packs up his notes and steps into the bedroom, where Plum is up and weeping as well.

Holding Celery to her chest, Woman Bu spares a hand to pat the little girl's back. "Shush, shush," she says gently, her breast bare, the infant clutching on, sucking savagely.

"If you want to," Zixia says, "I could read you the rest of the poem when I come back later today."

"Sure," his wife says, her neck craning, her gaze on their daughter and son. "You'd better go now. It's a big day for you."

When Zixia arrives at the Gate of Great Feat, flocks of spectators have already congested the entrance.

"Is that Zixia?"

"Zixia, who do you think should be held responsible for Zilu's death?"

"Zixia, we came to see you from Qin!"

"What's your strategy for today's debate?"

They are buzzing at the sight of his bright cardinal gown while a group of heralds dashes over and surrounds him in a circle. Shoving the fans away, they escort Zixia through.

"Folks, if you want to know what's going to happen, get a ticket!" the heralds bellow.

"Have the others arrived?" Zixia asks one of them.

"They are all in the great hall now, Master."

Damn, just can't beat those early birds, Zixia thinks, passing the unoccupied Rostrum.

The great hall is more packed than usual. Teams of servants and maids shuttle back and forth, like trout in the rapids. It takes Zixia a moment before he finds Yanyan in a corner, accompanied by his servant, who is standing behind him, massaging his shoulders.

"You're late again," Yanyan says, waving the boy to stop.

"What's this circus about?" Zixia sits down.

"I heard the audience will be double the size today," Yanyan says. "Apparently, the House has been promoting this one fairly aggressively. So everybody is hyped."

Zixia sighs, scanning his colleagues. A pair of servants hold up a huge bronze mirror before Zigong, who is trying out a variety of expressions and gestures. His retinue knocks around, remarking on his performance. Ziwo lies on his chest on the daybed, face buried between his arms. He moans loudly as a well-knit servant kneads his back. Beside them, two maids bustle, cooking a gamey stew on an iron stove. Ranyong is assisted by the largest squad. Half of its members chant pacifying verses while the other half play chime bells that hang thickly on a three-tiered wooden frame. Almost obscured by the spectacle, their master settles in his chair, his cardinal gown draping down, rippling with the cadences.

"Tell me, have you given much thought to Ranyong's question the other day?" Yanyan asks.

Zixia is baffled. He was just thinking about the same thing, an interrogation that's been haunting him for the last few days: But which one of you in particular shall I give my support to, when the next election for the successor comes?

Can I trust him? Zixia asks himself. Yanyan would surely be a better candidate due to his wide connections. But will his peer not be corrupted or would he back out of their plan, as Zilu did? Will he be the same person when he resides in the estate, in that golden chamber, dictating the Rostrum, the heralds, all seventy-two disciples, tens of thousands of followers, and the great House of Confucius?

"Nah," he says. "I was busy preparing for the symposium. Let's worry about one thing at a time."

Yanyan smiles. "You're right. And I trust you to have composed the winning argument."

"I wouldn't say that." Zixia gestures around the room. "Everyone is determined to win. But someone has to lose."

Chuckling, Yanyan reaches over his hand and pats Zixia's shoulder, his fingers slender but firm. "No worries, my friend. I assure you that the loser has been determined."

A team of heralds enters the hall and lines up in a row. And the disciples quickly silence their entourages and all rise from their seats.

"Masters," the heralds chorus, bowing. "It's the Hour of the Serpent. Please move to the Rostrum."

———

Zixia has been wearing cardinal for nearly three years now. Throughout the cycle of weeks, months, and seasons, he has debated at the symposium hundreds of times. Nevertheless, all this practice has failed to improve him. Like every other time, when he steps out of the estate, following the other seniors and guarded by the heralds, the hailing from the audience hits him once again like a tidal wave, and he instantaneously loses his hearing.

For an enduring moment, Zixia feels that he has been ejected from his body and is watching himself walk like a puppet, in the terrifying silence, through the grounds, up the Rostrum, before sinking onto his designated mat as the fervor of the audience reaches a climax.

From where he is, Zixia sees clearly the enthusiasts off the stage. However, being deprived of the sound, the image only makes him think of the hungry ghosts, demons, according to his father, who were once people who had starved to death, their faces distorted, arms ravening, mouths wide open.

The ghosts are coming for him.

Zixia almost breaks out screaming when the bronze gong finally rings and the hubbub floods back into his ears.

"Silence!" the herald next to the stage calls, his white robe fluttering in the morning breeze. He puts down the mallet and announces:

"Year fifteen of Duke Sorrow of Lu, twenty-sixth of the leap December, the day of wood traps earth, the Hour of the Serpent. The symposium of Confucius and his disciples commences now!"

"Confucius and his disciples," other heralds pass his words on. "Disciples, disciples, disciples . . ."

The disciples, on and off the stage, all kowtow to the Master, who sits under the black hat of prestige in the center of the Rostrum. The juniors bash their foreheads in unison against the sand and soil; the seniors do the same to their bamboo mats. In a collective voice they chant: "We thank you for guiding us with your endless wisdom. And we pray that you enjoy boundless longevity."

"You may rise, my students." The Master gestures, and after everyone settles back he begins: "A leap December is the rarest among all the leap months and is considered an ominous sign. This year, we did witness turpitude being in the ascendent. Gongsun Cheng—the magistrate of Cheng Town—broke faith with Lu to join Qi and then denounced Qi by returning to our county. Once again, Chu charged its army into Wu, whose people lay slaughtered and destitute. On the other hand, Wu's prime minister Bo Pi refused to receive the body of the ambassador of Chen, even though the latter had lost his life on the way to pass on Chen's support. And the most demoralizing among all . . ."

He pauses. The heralds repeat his words one after another, and the audience, cramming together shoulder to shoulder, ripples like millet seedlings in the field.

". . . denounced . . . refused . . . demoralizing . . . demoralizing . . . among all . . ."

"And the most demoralizing among all," the Master says, "is the concubine of the late minister of Wey, Woman Kong, who not only committed adultery after her husband passed away but also colluded with Kuaikui and opened the city gate for Kuaikui and his accomplices, precipitating the coup in the royal palace, which also led to the end of my cherished disciple Zilu."

Zixia jitters at the name. He glances at Yanyan, who sits quietly with his eyes half-closed, as if in meditation.

The Master continues: "I find myself rather unsettled reflecting on Zilu's death, particularly the method used to kill him: hai, a savage execution contrived five hundred years ago by King Ferocious of Shang. Is the reappearance of hai a sign, warning us of our impending degeneration into another dark era? Now, my disciples, I'd like to enjoin all of you to contemplate this: What has caused this obliquitous moral turpitude and the decline of humanity?"

His question reverberates amid the seniors and, before the last echo dies down, it is reignited by the herald next to the stage, and then the one who stands a hundred steps away from him, and the one after that.

"What caused . . . moral turpitude and decline of . . . humanity . . . decline . . . humanity . . ."

The audience stirs, whispering to one another.

On the stage, Zigong holds his hands together and raises them high above his head, the red corals dangling along the flared openings of his wide sleeves.

"You may speak, Zigong," the Master says.

Zigong puts down his hands and says: "They say a saint is always concerned with the world, never himself, therefore, I appreciate your distress and discouragement, my master. However, we must note that the vileness of King Ferocious was likely hyperbolized by the literary people. And what we should give more attention to, when comparing our time with the Shang dynasty, is our unprecedented prosperity and advances in crafts and mechanics. The ancients had to carve on bones to record their remarks, while we can, thanks to the innovation of inks and brushes, write smoothly on silk sheets and bamboo slips; the ancients survived on two, three kinds of grain while we relish victuals of abundant variety. Not to mention that we can now travel by horse, speeding from town to town in merely days. Moreover, with what do we wage war? Iron, the toughest substance, one our ancestors could never have dreamed of."

Ravingly, the audience calls out after the heralds have projected Zigong's argument.

"Sure as hell! They could never dream of!"

"Iron breaks bronze," Zigong continues, loud and clear. "The vigorous defeat the decrepit—these are eternal verities. the *Analects* teaches us that *one cannot be a wise man unless he perceives the Mandate of Heaven*. And I see Heaven calling on us, amid the contention of the warring states, to be in tune with the progressing trend of history, to banish the weak and to follow the powerful. In this sense, Gongsun Cheng of Cheng, Bo Pi of Wu, and Woman Kong of Wey are all blameless, while those who fail to discern the will from above are destined to be abandoned and crushed."

He slaps his hands together, his sleeves flapping like the roc's wings, whipping up a gust across the stage. "I would propose that Zilu's sacrifice, albeit dispiriting to all of us, was self-inflicted, for he didn't recognize that the victory of Kuaikui was inexorable and lent his counsel to the weakened bloc of Duke Exile and his right hand, Kong Kui."

The heralds echo what Zigong says. The names are repeated. At first they are strange; however, after recurring myriad times, they have become familiar and significant.

"... Woman Kong ... Kuaikui ... Kong Kui ... Kuaikui ... Kong ..."

Zixia's heart beats rapidly. He looks up at the Master, who seems to be staring into the blankness under his hat, his shadowed face inscrutable. Zixia puts up his hands.

"You may speak, Zixia," the Master says.

Zixia salutes Zigong. "Your elaboration on the *Analects* 20:3 is fascinating," he says, "which reminded me how the Master praised your talent for seeing beyond what you've been told. However, the exegesis should never totally depart from the text itself, or be misinterpreted for the interest of the argument at hand. In this case, I am not certain if the word *mìng* ought to be understood as the Mandate of Heaven. What about one's own endeavor that could also shape his destiny? More important, however intrigued I am by it, I cannot overlook the fact that your reasoning was completely evasive as to the question we were asked. Prosperity does not bury the moral turpitude that concerns the Master. In fact, one could even argue that advanced knowledge and material richness have little to do with the peace and harmony of our society."

Zixia pauses. His thoughts, previously dubious in the fog of his mind, now concretized by language, become assuring, even potent. Clenching his fists, he watches the ire on Zigong's face while the heralds broadcast:

"... endeavor ... endeavor ... prosperity ... knowledge ... harmony ..."

Zixia carrys on: "In the *Analects* 6:1, where the Master famously dissuaded Lu from attacking Zhuangyu, he taught us that we should *not worry about poverty but about inequality, not about underpopulation but about troubled minds*—and this precept has been ringing increasingly true to me in recent months. Poverty and hardship cannot corrupt us; rather, it is unequal and unjust circumstances that overturn one's faith. Cheng Town betrayed Lu because one of our high ministers wronged its people; Bo Pi fled Chu to Wu when his whole clan was massacred by his father's political opponent, and unsurprisingly he turned out callous; as for Woman Kong, isn't it most intelligible that she decided to help her brother Kuaikui, not to mention she was led to believe, by an old acquaintance, that her son Kong Kui, whose expanding influence was begrudged by Duke Exile, was in danger. Now, would you correct me if I have been inaccurate in my summation of this matter, Zigong?" He pronounces the name emphatically. "After all, you know Woman Kong better than any of us."

Zigong's face grows gray, his lips trembling. In fact, Zixia's implication has astounded everyone on the stage: Ziwo's mouth is agape, Ranyong fans his face with his hand. Even Yanyan has turned his head. The only ones unaffected are the heralds, who speak to the audience in a monotonous tone:

". . . an old acquaintance . . . acquaintance . . . Zigong . . . Woman Kong . . ."

Zigong points at Zixia, the gems on his sleeves jangling like raindrops in a downpour. "I only knew the late minister Kong when I served alongside him at the royal palace of Wey," he mutters. "But I had no affiliation with, with . . ."

Zixia sighs. "My apologies for raking up old affairs. But, Zigong, to comprehend your bond with Woman Kong truly made me see how bitter the situation must have been to you, when Kong Kui invited Zilu, instead of you, to Wey to provide him with counsel. Your indignation would only have been greater when the

Master disregarded your appeal and assigned Zilu to edit the *Annual of Spring of Autumn*, and when you had to hand over the largest payment to Zilu every fortnight, even though you were the one who did the squalid job of bookkeeping." He gazes at Zigong, smiling. "*Do not worry about poverty but about inequality*—this line came to me again and again when I pondered the reasons for Zilu's brutal death. Wasn't it this cumulative sense of injustice that finally led you to commit the irredeemable deed? Didn't you scheme, via Woman Kong, with Kuaikui, and lay down the trap for your fellow disciple Zilu, your peer who worked and studied beside you for three decades and was, in the end, cut up into pieces alive, slash after slash? And shouldn't I judge you for your crime and crucify you in public to console my mentor's spirit in Heaven?"

He stops, nearly out of breath, his ears humming as the heralds howl:

". . . irredeemable . . . cut up into pieces alive . . . alive . . . in the end . . . judge you for your crime . . . crucify . . . crucify . . ."

The audience screeches. Some of them, softhearted and impressionable, are already weeping.

"How despicable!"

"How could that woman still be alive after all the upheaval she brought about?"

"I never liked Zigong, those creepy eyes of his!"

"Hang him!"

Once again, Zixia feels the stage trembling at the commotion. He glances to his right, where Yanyan stretches the corners of his mouth upwards and nods at him.

Zixia sighs. It's not that I don't trust you, but I have to do what I have to do, he thinks. Then he turns to the Master, who is watching him from the center of the Rostrum, still, his face neither joyful nor despairing.

"My answer is no—no, I shall not crucify Zigong," he exclaims, under the sage's impervious gaze, the vowel rushing to his upper palate, quivering. "I shall not judge him. And I will not. To truly bring solace to Zilu's spirit, I realize, I ought to halt my speculation on Zilu's conniving with Kuaikui and instead examine a much more crucial matter. As I reread the *Analects* 6:1, I became conscious of this." He takes a breath. "What caused Zilu's death was nothing but the inequality of *this* House, the injustice that troubles and torments every one of us. If we are all scholars following Confucius for knowledge, and if knowledge is universal and indifferent, why rank us into hierarchical groups, provoking cutthroat competition among us? Why confine our study within the six books of the Confucian oeuvre and prohibit us from looking outside the walls of the institution to peruse the Hundred Schools of Thought? And with the preposterous wealth we are amassing from the symposiums, why shouldn't all disciples have the right to vote on the pecuniary scheme and to be informed transparently of the House's spending?"

He exhales deeply and looks around at his colleagues: Zigong, Ziwo, Ranyong, and Yanyan.

"What rights?" Ziwo bellows. "Have you completely lost your mind?"

Shaking his head, Zixia stands up from his mat, walks to the edge of the Rostrum, and, with his arms raised, calls directly to the audience: "And when I probed deeper into this matter, I asked myself, as an institution whose purpose is teaching, why should we charge you *ten* coins for attending the symposium? How is it just to demand you spend such a fortune when you only wish to learn? If the Master is concerned with the decline of humanity, and the sage claims that he *takes benevolence as his burden, and only with death does his road come to an end*, shouldn't the symposium be free, open to all under Heaven?"

His declamation rings out, fizzing through his flesh and bones like elixir. Come on, you lot, he thinks, looking at the flocks beneath him. Help me to succeed in my intentions.

Right beside the stage even the herald is transfixed. He stares at Zixia momentarily before recalling his duty and clears his throat.

"Zixia said . . ."

"Silence." From behind them a voice comes, measured and gentle. "Silence," the voice utters again, from the center of the Rostrum.

Hesitating, the herald cries out loud: "Silence!"

The others echo: "Silence . . . Silence . . . Silence . . ."

Zixia has never heard a sound so horrid, throttling him like a shroud soaked with icy water, closing tighter and tighter as the word is repeated.

The audience hisses in bafflement.

"Why are they asking us to be quiet?"

"What did Zixia say? He went on for quite a while there."

"What the heck? Oi, herald, what did he say?"

"Did he say something about money? That's a bit vulgar."

Zixia cannot breathe. A queasiness rises to his head and he feels the stage spinning underneath him. The space around him begins to warp, opening up as if a giant mouth is about to devour him.

"Zixia." He hears a call coming from behind and turns around woodenly.

Glaring at him is the Master, whose eyes are bloodshot, filled with fury. "You unworthy student of mine," he says. "And *you* were implicating Zigong for misinterpreting the *Analects*? You've perfectly misread the line from 6:1 and suggested this most absurd palaver about the so-called inequality of the House. Is it because of the penalty you got last time for being late? In any respect, before you spouted your drivel, you should have learned that *bù jūn* in the text does not mean 'unequal'; rather, it means 'unbalanced,' indicating when, in a regime, the governing bodies are not in their designated positions. And the *bù ān* says nothing about people's minds; it warns us that society will be thrown into chaos when the subordinate wants to overturn his superior, when the incompetent, inflated by ridiculous delusion, attempts to steal power from the capable—that's what this line means: *not worry about poverty but about political imbalance, not about underpopulation but about societal disorder.*"

Zixia cannot believe his ears. The words the Master has uttered penetrate his mind with pronounced force, drilling down further as the heralds echo.

". . . the subordinate . . . the superior . . . the incompetent . . . the capable . . . overturn . . . steal power . . . steal . . . power . . . power . . . disorder . . . disorder . . ."

All of a sudden, Zixia sees the answer—the horrifying revelation. Zilu. Was it the Master who . . . He looks at the saint, whose face has aged profoundly since he put on the black gown, his hair lead white.

Zixia exerts himself to try and make a sound when he sees Yanyan raise his hands, his cardinal gown swaying with his movement, a golden sheen glimmering against the red brocade under the sun.

"Forgive me, my master," Yanyan says. "I have to make a confession."

Ah, for fuck's sake, Zixia thinks, looking at his peer. Don't bother saving me now. Are you trying to get yourself ruined as well?

"You may speak," the Master says.

Yanyan bows. "Thank you, my master. And I beg for your punishment. I'm afraid I have failed you and my fellow disciples. I have certain pivotal knowledge, yet I've kept quiet because of my sentimentality and misjudgment." He sighs. "Throughout my years of studying under the guidance of Zilu, alongside Zixia, I have observed a great deal of conflict between Zixia and our mentor. Zixia is distrusting, always paranoid that Zilu would disfavor him due to his humble upbringing. In private, he often vents his discontent, not just towards our mentor but also the House. Most recently, before Zilu went to Wey, he had read the *Great Preface* Zixia drafted and then provided some criticism, which, to my understanding, had wounded Zixia's pride and as such he had with Zilu the fiercest feud."

What was he talking about? Zixia cannot believe his ears. Is he saying what I think he's saying?

"I deserve all the blame for concealing the truth," Yanyan continues, looking firmly at the Master. "I had been perturbed since Zixia followed Zilu to Wey, fearing something disastrous would happen. And when he returned with Zilu's remains, I knew he must have been involved in the misdeed. However, I failed to report it to you because I was blinded and corrupted by the companionship he and I have shared for more than a decade." He pauses and sighs. "But now I must come forward because our institution cannot stand any more slander. I must disregard my personal sentiment and, for the greater good, divulge to you all: Zixia was the one who orchestrated Zilu's death and I have evidence to prove it."

He turns to Zixia and Zixia sees his face. Pale as always, the blue veins are gleaming beneath Yanyan's skin, like the epiphyllum flower blooming for just a second before dying.

"He is carrying a scroll." Yanyan points at Zixia's chest. "A letter to his father-in-law, Marquis Zhao of Jin, who, as we all know, took Kuaikui in when he was in exile and backed Kuaikui's takeover of Wey."

Zixia bursts out laughing, finally breaking his silence. He retrieves the scroll from his chest pocket and thrusts it up in the air. "Is this what you were talking about? Yes, this is indeed a letter to my father-in-law, but it's about domestic matters, which I wrote on behalf of my wife!"

"Very well," the Master says. "In this case, just open it and read it out loud to all of us."

The placid tone of the command gives Zixia a chill. Only by lifting his hands does he realize that they are trembling rapidly. He inhales to steady himself and breaks the clay seal.

The silk unfurls and Zixia sees, in astonishment, strange characters appearing in columns. The handwriting is florid and graceful, yet unfamiliar. It doesn't belong to him, or any of the men he knows.

Dear Father, it says. *As your humble half-son, I thank you for your help in unplugging a thorn from my heart. I'll be forever in debt with you and Prince Kuaikui for your generous support . . .*

It's her. Zixia slumps down on the Rostrum, a musty odor rising from the corroded wood. He thinks back to Woman Bu's outcry earlier this morning, when he had proposed teaching their daughter to read and write. She cursed him for sending the girl to hell—because this whole time, able to read and write yet having to act like an illiterate, she must have been there herself.

He now sees clearly that Yanyan must have planned this because he distrusted him, just as he doubted Yanyan, that, at the end of the day, they believe only in themselves. What he cannot fathom is why Woman Bu would be persuaded by Yanyan to forge this letter. They have met behind his back. How many times? And what is she going to do after he dies, as a widow with two children? Is she going to get remarried? To whom?

He is still searching for answers when a herald walks up the stage, picks the letter from his hand, and presents it to the Master.

The Master peruses the letter and announces the verdict:

"I now conclude: it is Zixia who murdered Zilu!"

The audience thunders into claps and cheers, some gasping, some swearing.

It is almost the Hour of the Horse. The spectators, along with the disciples, are waiting eagerly for the execution of the convict as the sun ascends to its zenith.

Kneeling down on the stage, Zixia is staring at the hem of his cardinal gown, his ears, once again, filled with an eerie silence. The hem is torn, its color fading. Meticulously, he studies the ruptured stitches and the gradation of the redness until a herald appears with a tray. The Master speaks:

"Although affectingly aggrieved by Zixia's misdemeanor, we must ensure he receives an appropriate punishment, so that the morals of the Confucian House can be rehabilitated, and order restored. Now, historically, the first person who was killed by the method of hai was Bo Yikao, the crown prince of King Wisdom of Zhou. Bo, first held hostage by King Ferocious of Shang, was killed by being cut into pieces alive. Afterwards, Ferocious used Bo's minced meat to make cakes. He sent the meat cakes to Wisdom and ordered him to eat them. From this, we can learn that the completion of hai manifests as the meat of the executed being consumed by a family member."

Zixia lifts his head and he sees a bowl being offered to him by a herald in a white robe.

In the bowl is a sludge of dense brown paste.

"Zixia," the Master calls. "You're not exactly Zilu's family. But having studied under him for ten years, I assume he was like a father to you and you like a son to him. So I ordered this bowl of hai to be made for you, using the remains in the jar that you brought back. I consider it most suitable for you to eat this right here in front of everyone before we send you off the stage to the guillotine. What do you think?"

Zixia looks around the Rostrum, feeling the floor whirling. The faces are all so familiar, circling him like gray pigeons. Ziyüan, Zigong, Ziwo, Ranyong, and Yanyan.

He smiles.

Extending his arm, Zixia picks up the spoon, pushes it in the meat paste, digs out a large dollop, and feeds it into his mouth. The hai is warm and fragrant, viscous and hearty, reminding Zixia that he is in fact starving.

ACKNOWLEDGMENTS

Thank you to Carlos Rojas, Phillip Lopate, Rey Chow, Nicky Harman, Chad Harbach, and Catherine Platt, who have guided and helped me since the earliest days of my journey as an English writer.

Thank you to Hélder Beja and the Script Road Macau Literary Festival, whose commission prompted me to write my first article in English. Thank you to Frances Weightman, Sarah Dodd, and the Leeds Centre for New Chinese Writing for having me in Leeds on so many wonderful occasions and inspiring me to write my first story in English. Thank you to Martin Doyle and the *Irish Times* for publishing that story.

Thank you to Eoin McNamee, Marie Caulfield, Nell Regan, Mike McCormack, Mia Gallagher, Declan Meade, and Thomas Morris for their friendship and support.

Thank you to Madeleine Thien, Jan Carson, Lan Xu, and Lucy Caldwell for the trips we took, the chats we had, and the wine we drank together, and for inspiring and encouraging me to work on *When Travelling in the Summer, Shooting an Elephant,* and *Stockholm.*

Thank you to Lucy Caldwell (again), Alex Preston, Allison

LaSorda, and Danny Denton for their brilliant and insightful editorial notes and for publishing some of the stories in this book.

Thank you to the teachers and writers at the University of East Anglia, especially Andrew Cowan, Jean McNeil, Philip Langeskov, Tessa McWatt, and Naomi Wood. Thank you to Catherine Gaffney, Tasha Ong, Emma Bamford, and Vijay Khurana for reading the early drafts of the stories and giving me invaluable feedback.

Thank you to my agent and sometimes therapist Matthew Turner and all the wonderful people at RCW, especially Peter Straus, Stephen Edwards, Katharina Volckmer, Sam Coates, Tristan Kendrick, Natasia Patel, and Aanya Dave.

Thank you to my editors Angus Cargill, Rebekah Jett, and the phenomenal teams at Faber and Scribner who have helped bring this book to life.

Thank you to Daniel—my husband, best friend, and first reader—who is incredibly patient and kind and puts up with me on a daily basis. Thank you to my father, who is my most fervent critic and the first reader of my Chinese books.

At last, thank you to my mother and my son for being in my life.

ABOUT THE AUTHOR

Yan Ge was born in Sichuan, China, in 1984. She is a fiction writer in both Chinese and English, and is the author of thirteen books in Chinese, including five novels. Her work has received numerous awards and has been translated into eleven languages, including English, French, and German. The English translation of her latest novel, *The Chilli Bean Paste Clan*, was published in 2018. Another translated novel, *Strange Beasts of China*, was published in 2021 and was a *New York Times* Notable Book of 2021. Yan Ge started to write in English in 2016. Since then, her writing has been published in *The New York Times*, *The Stinging Fly*, *The Irish Times*, *TLS*, *Stand Magazine*, *Brick*, and *Being Various: New Irish Short Stories*. She was on the judging panel of the International Dublin Literary Award in 2019. She lives in Norwich with her husband and son.